Until November

Aurora Rose Reynolds

Contents

Chapter 1

WALKING INTO THE lobby of the hotel, the warm air hits me in the face. It's October and I can already tell winter is going to be rough. The lady behind the counter Glances up from her computer with a look of shock on her face. I can't blame her. I look like I feel, which is crappy.

"Oh, honey, are you okay?" she asks. I hate that question.

"I'm fine." I try to smile. "I need a room. Something that's dog friendly if you have it."

"Of course," she says, looking back down at her computer and typing. "How many nights?"

"Just one." I lean on the counter, feeling the exhaustion of the last few days catching up to me.

"Room 312 is dog friendly. You just take the elevator to the third floor and make a right. It will be seventy for the night and fifty dollars deposit for the dog."

I hand over my card. Waiting for her to finish checking us in, I look down at my new companion. I still can't believe he saved my life.

From what I can remember, I was attacked and he came out of nowhere, jumping on the guy attacking me. The cops said that if it wasn't for him, I probably would have been killed or in a coma. Instead, I just had a concussion, two broken ribs, and a sprained wrist.

Beast was the first thing I saw when I woke up in that alley with the smell of garbage and urine all around me. I thought I was dead until I heard whining and felt a warm, wet tongue move across my face. I opened my eyes to see a huge face looking down on me like some kind of doggie angel. He stayed at my side while I gathered my strength to get up. He never left me alone, not even when I stumbled into the apartment to call the police. He was my own personal guardian through every moment.

"Here you go, honey," the receptionist says, handing me the room card and bringing me back to the present. "The elevator is right down that hall." She points to the left.

"Thanks," I mumble, ready to get into bed.

"I know it's none of my business," she says, and I stop to look at her, "but I hope you were able to get in a few licks before you left his ass."

"It's not what it looks like." I smile and shake my head.

"Mmm hmm, honey. If you say so."

I don't have it in me to argue with her so I just let it go and smile. "Come on, boy." I drag Beast along with me toward the elevator while trying to carry my bag. "You can smell everything in the morning when I'm not so tired," I say through a yawn while pulling him behind me.

When we finally reach our room, I'm overwhelmed by the smell of dog urine. I wonder why they take fifty dollars if they were obviously not using it to get the smell out of the carpet. I'm too tired at this point to care and just happy to have a bed. We could sleep in my car, but with all of my stuff in it, there's not a lot of room. I take Beast's leash off and go to the bathroom, carrying my bag with me.

After brushing my teeth and washing my face, I look in the mirror and cringe. I look like a cow. My face is black and blue, my green eyes are red and puffy, my upper lip is cut, and I have so many bruises that even my hair hurts. I pull off my jeans, sweater, and bra but keep on my tank top and panties; then crawl into bed. Leaning over, I turn off the light. Two seconds later, I feel the bed bounce with Beast's huge body as he curls into me. And then, I'm out.

The sun is shining through the crack in the curtain. I moan and roll over. Beast is lying on his back with his legs straight up in the air and he's snoring. He is the strangest dog I've ever met, not that I have a lot of experience with dogs. I've always tried to avoid them. When I was four, we went to visit one of my mom's friends out in the Hamptons. They had a dog that attacked me. I ended up in the hospital with stitches from my eyebrow to the corner of my eye. Ever since then, I've had a deep fear of dogs; including the small ones that everyone thinks are so cute because they look like you could put them in your pocket. My dog, Beast, is not small. I Googled dog photos after I found him and from what I can tell, he's a Great Dane. He comes up to my waist when he is standing on all fours. I'm five four and when he stands on his back paws, his head is a good four inches above mine. Surprisingly, I'm not afraid of him at all. Actually, I don't think I would have made it through the last couple days without him.

"Come on, buddy," I say as I pat his stomach. He rolls his body to the side, looking at me like I'm crazy. "Yeah, it's time to wake up and get back on the road if we want to make it to Dad's by tonight," I say while getting out of bed. He still doesn't move.

"Whatever. I'm going to shower," I tell him like he cares. Stumbling my way into the bathroom, I start the shower. As steam fills up the small room, I take off my tank top and panties and climb in. I peel the paper off the cheap hotel soap and wash my body. After I've scrubbed from head to toe, trying to be careful around the cuts on my legs and arms, I find the shampoo but realize there's no conditioner. I regret not digging through the stuff in the car last night to find all my bathroom supplies. Getting out and drying off, I try to finger comb my hair enough that I won't look totally crazy when we make our way down to check out. Not that it will matter.

One look at my face and no one will care what my hair looks like. I find clean underwear and sweats, then throw on a hoodie and put my hair up in a messy knot at the top of my head. I slide my sunglasses up to rest on my head till we get downstairs. Walking out of the bathroom, Beast is sitting on the bed, looking like he has been waiting for me forever. Typical male.

"Come on, boy. Let's roll." I pat my leg and he jumps down from the bed to walk over to me. Sitting at my feet, he waits for me to attach his leash. "Okay, sweet boy, I'll feed you outside," I say while double-checking the bathroom to make sure I didn't leave anything. Walking to

UNTIL NOVEMBER

the elevator with beast in tow, I slow down so he can smell everything he missed last night.

The elevator opens up and the person stepping out almost stumbles at the sight of Beast. I mean, he is big but he is not that scary looking. His fur is dark gray with black spots, his nose is pink, and his eyes are almost blue. He's actually really beautiful. I give the guy a look and apologize. "Maybe my face is what scared him," I say to Beast when the elevator door closes. He tilts his head in agreement. On the first floor with the elevator door open, there's enough light to put on my sunglasses so I slide them down my face.

Walking to the checkout, I notice there is a new desk clerk. I'm praying we don't have to have another awkward conversation. That's when I spot a key card drop box and make my way to it without a second look at the front desk.

Once I drop my key inside, the smell of coffee hits me. My feet move without my command to the source of my weakness. I love coffee. I drink so much coffee every day that my coffee consumption alone could support a small country. Coffee in hand and a bagel hanging out of my mouth, we make our way out to my car. Outside, the cold air hits my lungs and it feels amazing. I walk to my other baby, my light blue convertible VW bug. I pop the trunk and drop my bag inside, then dig out Beast's food and water bowl and set them down on the ground. Leaning against my car, I watch Beast scarf down his food while I enjoy mine. Once he's done, I put his bowls back in the car and take him to the grassy area near the parking lot to take care of his business. Looking up at the sky, and all I can think is that in just a few hours, my life is going to be so different.

DRIVING IS NOT fun. Okay, let's be clear, driving in *my* car with a giant beast of a dog, going from New York to Tennessee, is not fun. My car is small and with all my stuff packed in the trunk and the back seat, there is no room for Beast. I feel bad for him being stuck up here with no place to lie down. But I have to say, he is pretty inventive. At one point, his butt was on the seat while the upper part of his body was lying on the floorboard. It didn't look comfortable to me, but apparently he didn't mind because within a few minutes of finding that position, he was snoring. Who knew dogs could snore so loud?

We've been stopping every couple hours to use the restroom and stretch our legs, so we still haven't made it out of Virginia. To be honest, I'm just glad the roads are clear. You never know what kind of weather you're going to run into during this time of year. October is one of those tricky months. Some days are beautiful and sunny with fall in the air, and other days are freezing and all you want to do is go hibernate for the winter.

I hate the cold. Maybe after I get settled with my dad, I'll take a trip to a beach somewhere. The only good thing about winter is being able to wear cute sweaters and boots. But I do miss my dresses during the winter. I wear a dress every day during the summer. I've taken sewing classes just so I could make my own summer dresses. There's nothing like getting up in the morning, taking a shower and slipping on a dress and a cute pair of sandals. There's no work involved. You can add a cute jacket or extra jewelry but you don't have to. A dress is simple. During the winter, not only do you have to wear pants and boots but you have to make sure that your shoes go with your top and jacket. Yep, I hate the cold.

My phone is blasting Breathe by Anna Nalick and it startles me out of my daydream about summer and dresses. Looking at the screen, I see its Dad calling.

"Hi, Daddy."

"Hi, baby girl. Just checking to see how far you are."

Looking at my GPS, I say, "We're still in Virginia and have about six hours left. I've been stopping a lot for Beast."

"Oh, yeah. Forgot you're bringing that thing you call a dog with you." He chuckles under his breath. "I hope you know the only reason I'm letting you bring him into my house is because he saved your life."

I sent him a picture of Beast when I told him he was coming with me. Dad was shocked. He told me that girls were supposed to have little cute dogs for pets, not things that looked like they would eat you.

"I know, Dad, but he's a really good dog." As if he knows we're talking about him, Beast lifts his head and barks. "I know, sweet boy," I coo at him.

"Yeah, I guess it's not such a bad thing that he can help me scare off all the guys who start sniffing around."

"Ha ha, Dad!"

"Well, baby girl, I'll call you in a few hours to check on you."

"Okay, Dad. Talk to you then."

Hanging up with my dad, I have a smile on my face. I wonder how different my life would be if my mom had left me with him rather than taking me with her. I also wonder why she took me to begin with.

My mom met my dad at a graduation party when she was eighteen. They had one night of drunken, unprotected sex and I was born nine months later. Two weeks after that, my mom took off with me to live with her cousin in New York. Growing up, my mom wasn't involved at all. I had a nanny from as far back as I can remember. Her name was Miss B. She lived in the apartment next to us. She was the person I always counted on.

If something happened, I would go to her. She would bandage me up or tell me I shouldn't cry over boys because they were all stupid. She is the only parental figure I've ever really known and when she passed away, I felt like my world crumbled around me. My dad found me not long after Miss B's passing.

At first, I was angry and refused to reply to any of the letters he sent. Then one day, I received a huge box stuffed full of cards from every birthday, Christmas, and Halloween that he'd missed. Some looked old and some looked new, but they all said the same thing. "Dreaming of when we will spend this day together." Since then, we talk every day and he has become one of my best friends.

"Okay, boy, were gonna go take a break. What do you say?"

Yes, talking to my dog is now becoming a habit. Most likely, a bad one. I need to make sure no one is around when I do it or I'm going to look like one of the crazy people who think their animal is sending them messages from the other side. That would not be a good thing. I have enough problems without adding insanity into the mix.

I pull off at the next rest stop and park close to the area designated for dogs. I let Beast out and he shakes his coat and stretches his legs in front of him. We walk over to the grass and I hear another vehicle pull in. I turn around to see if the person getting out has a dog as well because I don't want to break up a dog fight and I have no idea how Beast will react to other dogs. I notice the car is still running and no one is getting out.

The car is a silver Ford Edge with New York plates. The windows are tinted so dark that you can't see anything inside. Something buzzes across my skin. Beast must feel it too because he begins to growl. Trying to act casually, we start walking back toward my car. I see the back passenger-side door on the Edge open. That's when I run, with Beast right along beside me. I get my door open and he jumps across my seat.

I'm just able to get the door closed when I see a guy walking in my direction. He's wearing a black hoodie and black jeans. The hoodie is up so I can't make out any details of his face, but I know he's white because his hands are resting on his hips. Without a second look, I put my car in reverse and press the gas pedal. Boxes go sliding as I turn my car to get out of the rest area. I slam the car into drive and start speeding away, hoping I won't see the Ford Edge in my rear view mirror. My heart is going a million miles a minute and I keep checking for any signs of the Edge. Fortunately, it's nowhere in sight.

I start thinking about the whole situation and realize that my imagination is going a little crazy after being attacked. I mean, what are the chances that someone from New York would follow me just to try and hurt me again? A few hours later, there's no sign of the Edge. When I check my GPS, I have less than two hours until we get to my dad's. Looking down at my gas gauge, I see that I have to stop soon to fill up.

With that thought, my calm heart starts to speed up again.

It's after seven at night and the interstate is quiet with just a few cars traveling, but there are lots of semis on the road. The next exit offers every kind of fast food available, so I'm hoping there will be a lot of people there. No, not just people. I'm hoping for the scary trucker type of people. I exit the interstate and pull into the well-lit gas station. There are a few other cars getting gas so I hop out and go inside to pay. There is a Dunkin' Donuts, and like a parched man in a desert, I find myself standing in front of their counter. After getting my coffee, paying for gas, and getting another bottle of water for Beast, I step out into the parking lot. Keeping an eye on the parking lot, I walk quickly to my car.

"That's a beautiful dog you have there."

Screaming and stepping back, I almost fall over the hose that is going from the pump into my car. "Sorry I scared you, honey. I just saw your dog and he's a beauty."

"Oh, thanks," I say while holding my chest. Getting a look at the guy, he looks harmless. He's dressed a lot like Santa Claus, including the suspenders with a red and black plaid shirt tucked into his jeans and black boots. I can't help the smile that comes to my face. He smiles back.

"Russ," he says, sticking out his hand.

"November," I say, shaking it.

"What kind of dog is he?"

"Great Dane, I think. I'm not sure. I only looked up pictures online after I found him. His name is Beast."

"You found him and named him Beast," he laughs.

"Well, actually, it's a long story but I guess he kind of found me."

"That I believe!" he says with a sad look on his face. "You take care of him and he'll take care of you, honey. I used to have a dog like that and he traveled everywhere with me. Even took my back a couple times when I got into a jam. They really are man's best friend." He looks so lost while talking about his dog that I want to say something but don't know what. I reach my hand out and squeeze his. He squeezes mine back, and then I drop mine to my side and give him a small smile.

"Welp, gotta hit the road. Have a load to drop off in Nashville. You drive safe."

"You too," I say as he walks to the cab of a semi and climbs inside. Then, without thinking, I lift my fist up in the air and pull down. At that, he blows his horn and is on his way. I can't help the smile that hits my face.

My GPS announces that we have reached our destination as I'm driving up a long, private road. In the distance, I see a large blue house with a white wraparound porch. Sitting in the dark in a rocking chair is my dad. I slow down to take him in. He has his bare feet stretched out in front of him with a cup in his left hand. He's wearing jeans with a blue V-neck T-shirt. His dark hair barely touches the collar of his shirt and is pushed back from his face. His skin looks tan, like he spends a lot of time out in the sun, but around his eyes is lighter. He probably wears sunglasses when he's out enjoying the sun.

I pull up as he starts down the stairs. I try to open my door but he's already there, pulling it open. Getting out of the car, my hands start to shake and all of the stress and worry from the last few days comes to the surface. Now that I'm here, my dad will take care of everything. He is my biggest supporter and the person I can always count on to have my back. He pulls me into a giant hug, shaking me around. When he finally sets me in front of him, he looks down at me and his hands go to my face.

"You look more beautiful than the last time I saw you, baby girl. Even with all the bruises," he says, holding my face gently in his hands. His face changes and his jaw tightens. "If I ever see the fucking guy who did this to you, he's going to wish he was never born. I hope they catch that fucking coward," he says, letting go of my face and hugging me into his chest while kissing the top of my head. "Welcome home, baby girl."

That was all I needed to hear for my whole body to relax into his.

Welcome home. I actually had a home and it felt beautiful. "It feels good to be home," I say with a smile. Just then, Beast pushes his way between us. Dad bends down to show him some love. He scratches his head, and in return, Beast licks his face.

"Hey, now. None of that," he says while standing. "So, baby girl, are you ready to see your new place and get a lay of the land or do you want to just see your room and pass out?"

Laughing, I say, "I'll just see the room and pass out. It was a long drive."

"I know that you wanted to get here quickly but you should have stayed another night in a hotel."

I didn't tell my dad about the rest stop because I didn't want him to worry. I was probably just being paranoid. But after that, all I wanted was to get to my dad's house and put as many miles as I could between me and New York.

"I know, Dad, but I just wanted to get here."

"I'm glad you made it here safely. Let's go inside so you can get settled and rest." He puts his arm around my shoulder, taking me with him.

In the house, I'm surprised that everything looks like it's straight out of a magazine. By the front door is a long, black table with a bowl filled with keys and coins. The wood floors are so dark; they almost look black.

Walking down the hallway, we enter a room with the tallest ceiling I've ever seen. The beams going across the room are the same color as the wood floors. There is a wall of windows from one side of the room to the other. The kitchen is open to the living room with an island in the center that is as big as a dining table with five stools in front of it. The appliances in the kitchen all look new and unused. The countertops are a light granite with brown and red streaming through them. In the living room, there's a leather couch that looks more like a bed with a low back.

The entertainment center is built into the wall and two leather re-cliners sit on either side of the low couch. The throw pillows and blankets on the back of the couch match the granite in the kitchen. All the colors in the room blend perfectly together. Everywhere I turn, I see caramel, dark brown, and red.

"Wow, Dad, this is beautiful."

"Thanks, baby. Your grandmother decorated it."

"Grandmother?" I ask.

"Yeah. She can't wait to meet you. I know we haven't talked about my family much, but they all know about you and are excited to get to know you."

"Awesome," I whisper, still in shock that my mom took me when I was a baby. She never talked about my dad at all. I never even knew who he was until I turned eighteen and he tracked me down. Every time he has come to New York to visit, he never talked about his family and I never asked. I figured his story was the same as my mom's. Her parents died before I could meet them and she didn't have any brothers or sisters.

My mom has always been a loner unless you have something she wants. Then, she will attach herself to you like a life-sucking parasite.

"Everyone will be here for breakfast. They wanted to come tonight but I thought you might get overwhelmed on your first night home. Also, we need to talk about you doing the books for the club. Your degree will help me get the office straightened out. I don't have a lot of time to manage that part of the business. Lynn moved away with her husband and I haven't had a chance to replace her."

"When do I start?" I say, smiling.

"Well, tonight I want you to rest." He squeezes my shoulder. "And for the rest of the week, I want you to recover. After you're feeling up to it, I'll take you down to the club and show you the office. Hopefully, you can set something up so you can work from home."

"Sounds good to me." Walking through the kitchen, there's a set of stairs going down to the basement. "Wow, Dad, I thought you loved me and now you're taking me to the dungeon."

Laughing, he shakes his head. "No. There's a basement apartment.

Your grandma and everyone else came over and worked on it all day yesterday. They rushed over as soon as they found out you'd be staying with me. It also has its own entrance so you can have some privacy." He flips on the light.

"It's perfect." There's a small living room and kitchen when you first walk in. He leads me down a short hall and opens a door. The bedroom is huge and there's also an en-suite. I'm so overwhelmed that I start crying.

"It's okay," Dad says while dragging me into his body for a hug. "We just want you to be happy here."

"This is so nice. I can't even tell you how happy I am," I say into his shirt, giving him a squeeze. It's the truth. I have never seen a more perfect space. It's amazing that this is someplace to call my own.

"Well, I'm gonna go unpack your car while you get some sleep," he says, kissing my forehead. He turns to leave, then stops and looks at me over his shoulder. "I'm really happy you're here, November. I can't even tell you how happy this makes me." With that, he's gone. Leaving me to think about how different my life could have been.

Waking up in the morning to the smell of coffee and the sound of voices above me, I climb out of bed. After I shower, I put on a pair of my favorite jeans. They are so dark; they're almost black and look good with an off-the-shoulder lavender sweater and dark brown riding boots. I blow out my hair and tie it into a ponytail that hits the middle of my back. I put on some makeup to try to conceal the bruises that are now starting to turn green. With a little mascara, some bronzer, and blush, I make my way upstairs. Beast is sitting at the island next to a woman with the same hair as my dad. When she sees me, she jumps off the stool and runs to me, pulling me into a tight hug.

"Oh, sweet girl, you're finally here," she says, holding me away from her body and putting her hands to my face. "You look so much like your great grandma Ellie. She was a beauty and you have your daddy's eyes and hair." Pulling me back into her chest, I want to cry for the little girl who missed out on this.

"Thank you," I say, trying to control the tears I feel coming.

"Oh, honey, you don't have to thank me. That is a gift given by God and good genes. Lord, I'm just so happy that you're here and I can see for myself how beautiful you are. Your daddy showed us all pictures from his cell phone but that's not the same. He is very proud of you." That does it. I cry like a baby. I don't think I've ever cried so much in my life. The whole situation is surreal. I feel both lucky and scared, wondering if I am going to disappoint them.

"Okay, okay," Dad says, cutting in. "Enough of the sad stuff. Let's introduce you to everyone, kiddo."

Meeting all of my family is a little terrifying. My dad's brother, Uncle Joe, is a little bit taller than my dad, but has the same body type. You can tell he takes care of himself like my dad does. They both have bulky muscles. My uncle's dark hair is starting to gray and he looks like he could model for a cool biker magazine with his goatee and tattoos. He brought my cousins too. His twin sons are the complete opposite of each other.

Chris and Nick are twenty-five years old. Chris looks like a surfer with dirty blond hair and a golden tan. Nick looks like a rock star with dark brown hair and light skin covered with tattoos. My dad's cousin, Maddy, her husband, Mark, and their two-year-old daughter, Alyssa, are also here. They even have a few other family friends over to meet me.

Breakfast is delicious and I am really enjoying getting to know everyone. They all seem genuinely nice. We talk about what I plan on doing after getting settled. I explain about having a degree in business management and that I'm planning on helping my dad at the club. That's when the vibe changes and all hell breaks loose.

"You're what?" Uncle Joe asks, yelling so loud his face turns red.

"Um, I'm going to help my dad?" I say, my answer sounding like a question. I look around, wondering what I missed and why he's so upset.

"Watch it, Joe," my dad growls.

"No niece of mine is going to work at the strip club…that we own together, I might add."

"Strip club?" I ask in complete shock.

"She is not going to be working *in* the club. She's going to be doing the books and managing the office. She won't be there during club hours and will never be in the front of the house."

"I don't care if she's working in the front or in the fucking alley, she's not working there."

"Last time I checked, she is my daughter and I own half that club. You have no say in what she does or doesn't do. I want her to work for me, and like I said before, she will never see the front of the fucking club."

"Do you want to work there?" my uncle asks me. I'm put on the spot and I really don't want to answer him.

"Um…I…ugh." I take a deep breath before trying to respond. "I didn't know that it was that kind of club," I say in a whisper. Not that I had anything against strip clubs. I mean, to each their own, right?

"Okay, Joe," Grandma cuts in. "If November wants to work there, that's her choice. And, Mike, if she doesn't want to work there after finding out what kind of club it is, that's also her choice. You know I don't love that club but I do love you both and I supported you in your decision to open it. But, as for November, it will be her choice and her choice alone if she wants to help you out on the business side of the club. I'm not happy about the look on her face right now and I'm telling you both that you will let her make her own decision."

After Grandma says her peace, everything goes back to normal but I can still feel the tension between my dad and uncle. I want to work with my dad but I also don't want to cause a problem between him and his brother.

I can't wrap my mind around the fact that my dad owns a strip club. When I imagine a strip club owner, I picture an evil, fat, old guy with beady eyes, tacky suits and a bad comb over. Not someone like my dad. He's a kind, handsome, put-together, forty-five-year-old man.

After pondering this for a few minutes, I realize that I am proud. Knowing my dad and the kind of man he is, I can't help but think of the women who work for him and how lucky they are. In the stripper industry, I'm sure respect is hard to come by. But one thing I know for sure, he respects the women who work for him. So with these thoughts floating in my head, I turn and smile at my dad. He smiles back even bigger.

AFTER TWO WEEKS of getting settled in and healing, it is time to start living in the real world again. The world where you need things like a job and money to survive. My dad and I are going to the club to meet some of his employees. To say I'm nervous is an understatement. It takes me longer than normal to get ready. I mean really! What do you wear to the strip club that your dad owns?

After settling on my gray, empire-waist sweater dress with black legging and black boots, I curl my hair in large waves down my back and put on light makeup. Looking at myself in the mirror, I'm happy to see all the bruising is gone and I look like myself again. I go upstairs to give Beast some love, before Dad and I take off. I know Beast is happy here. He has a large backyard and room to run, and I take him on a walk every night.

"Okay, Dad. I'm ready!" I yell into the living room while scratching Beast behind his ears.

"Wow, you look beautiful," he says, kissing my cheek. "Let's get this shit over with."

I smile at him, knowing that he's nervous. I think at this point, he's more nervous than me.

"Dad, it's going to be okay." Going with my dad to his club is completely nerve racking for me. I mean, my dad owns a strip club where naked girls work. I'm freaking out on the inside but trying to act cool. I don't want him to feel any more uncomfortable than I know he already does.

"Just so you know, baby girl, the women who work for me are not your friends. There is nothing wrong with what they do, but you are not going to be hanging with them."

I raise my eyebrows at him and he shakes his head. "I know you won't be there during club hours, but I want to make it perfectly clear— there is no reason for you to ever be in the front of the house when you're in the building. You can come in, sort shit out in the office, but there will be no drinking at the bar and no socializing with the employees. The only reason I'm bringing you here tonight is because I want the people I trust to meet you. That way, you will always have someone to go to in case I'm not around."

"Dad, don't worry so much. You're giving yourself grey hair and soon you're going to look like Uncle Joe."

"Very funny!" he says, smiling.

The club is pretty much how I pictured it. Not that I've been in a strip club, but what do you really think of when you imagine a strip club. There's a long bar on the back wall with stools in front of it. Off to the side, there's a stage with two poles and a girl dancing. Along the stage, there are four tables with guys of every age watching the show. In the back of the room, the lighting is so dim that you can barely make out the couches. Behind them is a wall of mirrors. Looking around, I'm surprised that everything is new and modern.

"Okay, baby girl." My dad snaps me out of my perusal. "This is Rex." He points to the guy behind the bar. "Rex, this is my daughter, November. She's going to be doing the books and helping me out from behind the scenes. You won't see her much, but I wanted you to meet her so if I'm not around, she knows who to talk to."

"Hey, girl," Rex says, wiping his hands on a towel. "Nice to finally meet you."

"You too," I say as my dad pulls me into his side.

"Wow, Mike, with your ugly mug, I didn't think you could make such a pretty girl," Rex says and I feel myself turn red.

My dad looks down at me with so much pride. "Yeah, I did good," he says, smiling.

"Oh, geez, Daddy, stop," I say while squeezing his middle and rolling my eyes. That's when I feel someone's watching me. I look around, but don't see anyone.

"I'm gonna take her to the office and show her my mess," Dad says.

"Okay, man, but when you're done, we need to talk about the shit Skittles pulled the other night."

"Once November leaves, I'll be on the floor," my dad says, pulling me with him.

After meeting a couple other people, we go into his office. He was not joking—the place is a mess. It's going to take me weeks just to get everything organized. There are papers, books, and files everywhere and the computer looks like the first one ever invented. "Well, here you are. You can start tomorrow morning. Just try to be out of here by three. Once you get stuff figured out, you can always move your office to the house if you feel like that works better."

"Okay, I'll start tomorrow. It's gonna take some time just to get things sorted. After that, I should be able to do it from home most of the time."

"Sounds good," Dad says, looking around. Just then, the phone rings on the desk. He moves some papers around. When he finally finds the handset, he puts it to his ear. "Yeah, okay. I'll be out. He hangs up, I have to go, baby girl. There's a problem out front."

"That's fine, Dad," I say to his back as he runs from the office. Looking around for a few minutes, I see that I have my work cut out for me. I decide to go home and get some sleep so I'll have all my brain cells in the morning when I come back to this disaster.

I walk out into the cool November air. I pull out my phone and text Dad that I'll see him tomorrow. The music is now just background noise, but I can still smell the alcohol, perfume, and beer that lingers on my clothes from being inside the club. I'm almost to my car and my mind has drifted to Beast. I want to take him for a walk before it's too late and we have another skunk incident like we did the other night. "Yo!" I hear shouted from behind me. I jump and end up dropping my purse and keys to the ground. I pick them up, and then look around.

All the air is pushed out of my lungs. The most beautiful man I have ever seen is standing a few feet from me. He is more than a foot taller than my five-foot four—inch frame. His dark brown hair is cut so short that I can see his scalp. His jaw is square; it looks like its cut from glass. He has a couple days of stubble on it that makes me want to rub my cheek across it to see how it feels. His nose looks as if it may have been broken, but it does nothing to take away from the beauty of his face.

With only the light from the street lamp above us, I can't tell his exact eye color, but they look blue or light gray. His lips have a perfect cupid's bow at the top and bottom. They're so full, they would make my mom, the queen of lip injections, jealous.

Taking in his face, I'm completely caught off guard by the anger I see in his eyes. He is about three times my size. His arms are so large he could squash me like a bug. I can make out the definition of almost every muscle in his torso. His body is as impressive as his face and the thermal shirt he's wearing does nothing to hide it from me…or anyone with eyes. His legs are planted shoulder-length apart. His jeans hang low on his hips, and with the way he stands, I don't even think a tornado could move him. He crosses his arms over his chest while looking down at me.

I take a step back toward my car and remind myself that I need to breathe. I adjust my keys in the palm of my hand so they become a weapon. He doesn't miss this move, judging by the flash of surprise I see cross his face.

"Hi," I squeak out.

"Yeah, hi," he says back in a mocking tone that surprises me. "You need to have an escort to your car anytime you leave the club." He's practically growling at me.

"Wh–Wha–What?" I ask, stuttering.

"You," he says slowly, like I'm stupid, "need an escort anytime you leave the club to walk to your car. All the girls know this shit."

"Um…okay?" I say, still not understanding.

"It's my boy's job to make sure your ass is safe from the building to your car. So don't piss me off by not doing what you're told. And trust me, sweetheart, I don't give a shit if you're fucking Big Mike. Next time, wait for one of the guys to walk you out here."

"Who's Big Mike?" I ask. I've only been in town a short while, how can rumors of me and some guy already be going around?

"Big Mike, the guy you were hanging on and calling Daddy!" he says with distaste. "I don't give a fuck if you're sleeping with the boss. He should have told you this shit himself or had the decency to walk your ass out here to your car."

Oh my God! Ewww... Now, I get it. He thinks I'm sleeping with my dad. Gross! And he's being totally rude.

"Excuse me?" I ask, narrowing my eyes, hoping he gets the message that he should choose his next words wisely.

"What part don't you understand, sweetheart?" he says, mocking me. I'm sure at this point, my eyes are bugging out of my head and steam is coming out of my ears.

I jerk my hand out angrily in his direction. "I'm not 'sweetheart', I'm November. I'm also Big Mi—"

"Don't give a fuck who you are." He cuts me off.

"Wow, you are so flipping rude, buddy."

"Don't care that you think that shit either."

"Who the hell do you think you are?" I ask him, hands on my hips, my anger bringing my New York attitude out in full force.

"The guy who's waiting for you to get in your car and leave so I can go do my job instead of standing out here with you."

"Ugh, you are such a jerk," I growl, feeling like I should kick him.

"November?" I hear my dad call me. I smile on the inside. This is going to be good.

"Yeah, *Daddy*, over here!" I yell back, exaggerating the daddy part. I look at the guy in front of me, daring him with my eyes to say something. He doesn't, but his eyes narrow.

My dad walks towards us, and then sees big jerk face standing across from me. He pats him on the back while smiling. "Hey, Asher," my dad says.

Oh my God, seriously? Asher. Why did this guy have to have a hot-guy name? Why can't his name be Urkel or Poindexter? I mean really, some things just are not fair.

"I see you already met my daughter." I can't help the small giggle that climbs up my throat from the look of pure shock on the big jerk's face. Okay, it's safe to say that his look makes me feel somewhat better. My dad looks down at me, smiling, not understanding what has gone on for the last few minutes.

"Um, yeah, Dad. He was just telling me that I need an escort when leaving the club," I say through my laugh.

"Oh," my dad says, scratching his head. "Yeah, I didn't think about it because you're not…uh, you don't work here…I mean, you work here, but not really *in* here."

"Dad, it's okay. Asher didn't know and just wanted to make sure I was safe."

"Yeah, okay," he says, looking a little sheepish. "Anyway, Asher, this is my baby girl, November," he says, pulling me into his side. "She just moved here."

I look to Asher and he still looks stunned, but there's also something else working behind his eyes.

"Hi," I say, sticking out my hand with a big smile on my face. When he puts his hand to mine, I feel a jolt go from our connection straight through my body. What the heck is that?

"November," he says softly, looking down at our hands, and it makes me wonder if he feels it too. Then, without another word or look, he turns around and walks back toward the club. Well, alrighty then. He might be hot, but he's definitely strange. I look at my dad and he's watching him go.

"Um… Hey, Dad, I'm gonna go," I say, regaining his attention.

"What?" he says, while looking at me.

"I'm leaving."

"Oh, yeah. Of course, honey. I'll see you tomorrow at home." He bends, kissing my forehead. When I pull out of the parking lot, I can see a tall figure leaning against the door to the club. He appears to be watching my car leave. My pulse starts to race as I wonder if it's Asher. Then, I remind myself that he's a jerk and not to think about him anymore. Sadly, I don't stop thinking about him until my head hits my pillow and I'm dead to the world.

Chapter 2

"I'M COMING, I'M coming. Geez, you have to slow down, boy. My boots are too high for running," I say, following Beast to my car.

The minute I asked him if he wanted to go for a ride, he was running out of the house, dragging me behind him. Today is the day we visit the nursing home, and I swear he knows exactly where we're going. We have been doing this every week since we came to town.

Beast loves the attention and the elderly love Beast. It's been six days—not that I'm counting—since I last saw Asher. I wanted to ask my dad about him, but I chickened out. Really, I just want to see him again. I don't really want to talk to him because, truthfully, he's a jerk. But I do want to look at him. He has made me consider taking an art class. Maybe something like body sculpting or painting. It's not normal for a guy to be that beautiful. Now I sound like a weird stalker. Like that movie where the guy puts the girls in the hole and forces them to eat so he can wear their skin. Okay, I'm not that creepy, thank God. I need to stop. Maybe, he brainwashed me? I need a hobby.

The last few days have been uneventful. Monday, Grandma and me went up to Nashville and got new computers. One is for my dad's home office and one is for the club. Tuesday, I went to the club at seven in the morning so I would have plenty of time to get the computer set up and to start organizing the office.

I don't know what I thought I would find, but there were no lap dance spread sheets or pole dancing tables. It was all normal office paperwork. Spending reports, payroll, and ordering sheets. I finished as much as I could before I had to leave at three. The next few days went the same. I was at the office till three, making dinner with my dad before he went to work, walking Beast in the evening, and then setting up my dad's home office before I went to bed at night.

I'm getting settled. I feel more at home here in Tennessee than I ever felt in New York. Everyone in town is so nice. They always have a smile for you. The thing I had to get used to was everyone waving at you when you pass them on the road. At first, it caught me off guard. Then I asked my dad about it and he said it's just what they do. Now every time I pass someone, I make sure to wave. Okay, okay, my wave may be a little dramatic but I like it and it makes me smile.

"Alright, boy. Let's go inside," I say as I turn off the car. The nursing home we visit is a long brick building. The front sits on a hill of green grass with large pine trees that give shade to sitting areas located all around the building.

"Hi, Beth," I say quietly while giggling. Beth is in charge of greeting people as they come into the building. At least she should be greeting people but she's always asleep in her wheelchair with her chin tucked to her chest and her blue hair is the only thing you can see.

"Damn." I sigh to myself. Now I want some cotton candy. Every time I see her hair, I get a craving for the stuff. I look down at Beast and his head comes up. "Looks like we're gonna be making a stop at the store on our way home, boy." I should have bought more than one pack of cotton candy the last time I was there. He looks at me and tilts his head.

"Okay, boy. First stop is Max, so you better be on your best behavior," I tell him, walking into Max's room. Billie Holiday is playing on an old record player and Max is sitting in his chair with the newspaper in front of him.

"Hi, Max. I brought Beast here to see you," I say loudly, knowing he never remembers to put in his hearing aid.

"Well, hello there, pretty lady. How are you today?" he shouts at me.

"I'm good. How are you?" I ask, bending to give his wrinkled cheek a kiss. I find his hearing aid in a small bowl by his bed and hand it to him. He shakes his head and puts it in.

"Well, gotta say that my day just got better," he smiles. "Hey, Beast. How are you, boy?" he asks as Beast places his head in his lap for a rub.

"Betsy was in here earlier bugging me about going to the dance tonight. I keep telling her that I'm not interested but she won't leave me alone. She's already stopped by four times," he grumbles.

I laugh. Betsy is one of the older ladies here and has more energy than I do. She's always on the hunt for a new man. "Aw, Max, you should go. You might have fun. I hear the band that's coming is really good."

"Nope, I aint going. You couldn't pay me enough to go to a dance."

"Well, you don't have to dance. You could just go listen to music."

"Not happening, darlin', and we're not talking about it again."

I giggle. Max is set in his ways. I know there will be no convincing him. We visit for a while longer until I look at the clock and see how late it is.

"Oh, crud, Max. Beast and I better go. We have a few people to visit before dinner."

"All right, darlin'. See you in a few days," he says while still petting Beast. "And see you too, boy."

Walking down the hall, the smell of cleaning supplies is overwhelming until we reach the assisted living units. Then, it's like walking into a country club. The floors are beautiful printed carpet. There are fresh flowers on all the tables along the wall. The whole place looks warm and inviting with sitting areas and cozy nooks to read. I can't help but feel bad for the people who can't afford to live on this side of the building.

"All right, boy. One more stop. Remember, be good," I say, looking down. He just looks at me, and then back toward the direction we are walking. I was just dismissed by my dog.

Walking into Miss Alice's room always makes me happy. She has photos and things from all over the world on shelves and bookcases. Her husband was in the military and they traveled a lot. When he retired, they moved to town and opened a hardware store. They were married for sixty-two years and when her husband passed away, she refused to move in with her family. She moved here when she could no longer be on her own. But still, the room feels like a home.

"Hi, Miss Alice. How are you?" I ask, leaning down and kissing her cheek.

"Oh, November. I'm wonderful. I was just talking to my grandson. He's on his way to visit too."

"That's nice. We won't stay long then. I just wanted to bring Beast by and say hi," I tell her, sitting down.

"Hey, you handsome boy. Come here and give me some sugar," she says, patting her leg. Beast walks to her and puts his head in her lap. "You are such a sweet thing, just like your mama," she says, making me smile.

Beast is like my child. I feed him, love him, and make sure he is cared for. But I hope one day I find someone to have a real family with. I don't want to be single for the rest of my life and become known as the crazy dog lady. Since I'm allergic to cats, I can't even be the norm and have a million cats. Well, I could but then I'd just walk around with puffy eyes and a runny nose.

"I hope my grandson gets here soon. I would love you to meet him. He's very handsome," she tells me with a big smile on her face. I can see her mind racing with ways to hook us up. "I keep telling him he needs to settle down. He has never brought a girl home, and he's getting too old for all that playing around business that men these days do. I want great grandbabies before I leave this earth. Back in my day, it was normal to get married young. I was eighteen when I got married and I stayed married until I lost my James. I miss him every day and still love him. I want that for my grandsons."

"Well, I hope they all find the kind of love you had, Miss Alice. It sounds beautiful," I tell her truthfully. I can see the love she still carries for her husband whenever she talks about him.

"What the fuck are you doing here?" I jump and Beast barks at the sound of the voice. I slowly turn around, praying I'm wrong.

"Asher James Mayson, you watch your mouth. Don't talk to my guest like that," Miss Alice scolds him. I can feel all the color drain out of my face and my stomach drops to my toes. Oh my God, he's more beautiful than I remember in his dark green thermal with the sleeves pushed up to his elbows and the colorful tattoos on his arms. They are so bright that even his tan does nothing to take away from their beauty. His jeans are light blue, over washed, and hug him perfectly. Great! Just flipping great. He's Miss Alice's grandson. Can my life get any worse?

"Hi," I say, trying to smile but I know I probably look like I'm in pain. I stand up ready to bolt. "Come on, Beast. Miss Alice has a guest and we need to go to the store." Yes, now I'm talking to my dog out loud in front of hot jerk-face. Ugh, I'm such a loser. "Well, Miss Alice, I'll see you in a few days," I say, leaning down to kiss her cheek.

"Okay, sweet girl," she says quietly. She looks like she wants to say something but she closes her mouth, and then glares at her grandson. I'm sure if she could make him catch fire, she would. If I could make him catch fire, I know I would. I turn and walk down the short hall toward the exit when I feel pressure on my elbow.

"I'm gonna walk November out. I'll be right back, Gran," Asher says from behind me.

Crap, crap, crap. "Umm…no–no, that's okay," I say, trying to pull my arm free from his touch. I can already feel his fingers burning into me.

"No, I'll walk you," he whispers near my ear, causing goose bumps to breakout across my skin.

"Fine," I mutter because I don't want to cause a scene in front of Miss Alice. I'm sure she likes me, but I'm not so sure she would like me to ruin the chances of her having great grandchildren when I 'accidently' kick him in the nuts. She doesn't say anything as we leave. She just waves goodbye with a face-splitting smile. Oh, if she only knew.

"Come on, Beast. Asher is walking us out," I say, and then bite my tongue. I really need to work on not talking to my dog in front of people. Once out the door, I pull my elbow from his grip. "Look, I'm sorry. I had no idea that she is your grandma. I just bring Beast here to see anyone who wants the company. I watched a show on TV about animals visiting with people in hospitals and nursing homes; it said how much joy it brought them. I figured I'd give it a try. I have a beautiful dog who loves attention, so why not, you know."

Asher's not saying anything and I realize I'm rambling. Crap. "So we're just gonna go." I turn to leave, but he grabs my hand, pulling me back.

"Hey, not so fast. You just surprised me. I didn't expect to see you here."

"Well, I really like your grandma and she likes Beast, so if you just tell me the days you're gonna come, I'll make sure not to show up then."

"That's not gonna work for me."

"Okay," I say, feeling my shoulders slump. "Well, have a good day." *And don't fall off a cliff.* I say under my breath as I turn to walk off again.

"Meet me tonight," he says and I know that I must have heard him wrong. His rough voice and his southern accent are making it hard to concentrate on what he is saying. I swear I heard him wrong. I look over my shoulder.

"What?" I ask, scrunching my nose.

"You, me, tonight, beer, a game of pool?"

"Um…" Nope, didn't hear him wrong. I look around to make sure that it's still just me and him in the parking lot.

"It's just a beer," he says, smiling.

"You're kind of a jerk," I tell him. It's something he probably hears all the time.

"I can be, but it's still just a beer, November." The way he says my name makes me think this is a lot more than just a beer and a game of pool. Plus, when a guy admits that they are a jerk, is that really a good thing? "Just meet me at the Stumble In at seven," he says, taking a step closer to me. All of a sudden, I can feel the heat from his body, smell the scent of his cologne, and I can finally make out the color of his eyes.

"Light blue with gold flecks," I mumble to myself. My lips part and my eyes glaze over. All my senses are on overload.

"Pardon?" he asks and I realize I just said that aloud.

"Nothing," I mumble, still staring at him. I realize that I probably look like an idiot so I take a step back. He smiles, revealing one perfect dimple and I know in that moment that I am so screwed. Crap!

"Meet me at seven," he repeats, taking a step closer to me. His hand comes up, moving my hair to behind my ear, and I'm totally lost. Just floating away in a hot-guy fog.

"Um…" I blink, trying to pull myself together. "Okay, seven," I say, wondering what the heck just happened. The words are out and I need to get away from him and his Jedi mind tricks. I turn to go but am tugged back. I almost fall on my butt when I turn my head and see Asher squat down to pet Beast.

"Alright, babe. Seven. See you then." His smile gets bigger, like he knows something I don't. He stands from his squatting position and winks. I turn around because I need to go; go before I throw myself at him and ask him to help me give Miss Alice great grandbabies.

"Come on, Beast." I tug on his leash, but he wants to stay with Asher. "I know the feeling, boy," I whisper.

WALKING INTO MY dad's house, I'm assaulted by the smell of garlic and butter. I stop in my tracks when I realize he's home. "Crap," I whisper to myself. Dad's home. Of course, he's home. We have dinner together every night. I try to act normal as I walk into the kitchen. My dad is standing in front of the stove, wearing an apron that looks like a girl in a bikini. I start laughing. "Hey, now. What's so funny?" he asks, smiling.

"Nothing, Daddy," I say, giggling.

"I'll have you know that your uncle got this for me."

"I'm sure he did," I say, smirking. Uncle Joe is a funny guy.

"Well, I like it. I look hot," he says, holding his hands out to his sides.

"That you do," I agree, shaking my head. "So what are we having?" I ask, hopping up on the counter.

"Shrimp Alfredo, garlic bread, and salad."

"Yum. Sounds good. I'm leaving at six thirty to head to the Stumble

In," I say, glad that it sounds casual.

"The Stumble In. Why are you going to the bar on a Thursday? I'm not driving you to drink already, am I?"

"Um…no. I'm meeting someone there?" I say, asking rather than telling him. Please don't ask who, I pray.

"Is that a question or are you meeting someone?"

"Well, I um…ran into Asher at the nursing home when I was visiting his grandmother and he asked me to meet him."

"You're meeting Asher at the bar?" he asks with a look on his face that doesn't bode well for me.

"Yeah, it's just a beer, Dad," I say, using Asher's words.

"I don't know how I feel about this. I know you're not a kid, but Asher is not the kind of guy I expected you to date. Don't get me wrong, he's a good man." He shakes his head. "Just promise me you'll be careful. I don't want to see you hurt."

"Promise, Dad," I say quietly. The last thing I need is to get my heart trampled on again. Been there, done that. And Asher's boots look like they would do a lot more damage than my ex's. "Besides, Dad, he knows I'm new in town and probably just feels bad for me or something."

"Or something," he says under his breath and I ignore him.

Dinner was awesome and Dad quickly dropped the uncomfortable conversation about Asher. Thank God. So now, I am standing in front of my closet, trying to pick out something to wear. What do you wear to have a beer with a hot guy who you don't want to like?

I haven't ever really dated random guys. The one serious relationship I had in college went bad after my mom slept with him. I caught them together at his apartment after he sent me a text saying he was going home after class because he wasn't feeling well.

Me, the loving fiancé that I was, showed up out of the blue to check on him. When I let myself in, the place felt strange. I wanted to turn around and run out but I walked straight to his bedroom. When I got there, all I heard was him moaning. It sounded like he was in a lot of pain so I opened the door to find my mom on top of him. I couldn't even speak. I shut the door silently behind me and sent him a text telling him that I stopped by to check on him but saw for myself that he was feeling much better. He called a million times after that and sent flowers, cards, and texts, but I didn't care. I ignored all of it. I cut him out of my life, mailed him back everything that I had of his—including the ring— along with a note telling him to stop calling or I would press charges for stalking. After that, I never heard from him again.

"What do you think, Beast? Red sweater dress or T-shirt and jeans," I ask, holding the items up for Beast to look at. He doesn't even lift his head. His big body is lying across my bed with his head on his paws.

"You're right. The dress is too much." I take off my boots and leggings. I put on my tight, straight-leg, dark-blue jeans with holes all over them.

With my jeans on, I decide to go casual and pull out my converse sneakers that are gold with glitter. I put on a long sleeve, scoop neck, white T-shirt and a black, front zip hoodie.

"Now, hair up or down?" I ask Beast, who still hasn't moved. "Okay, I agree. I'm just going to leave it down," I tell him, putting on some lip gloss. I look at the clock and I'm running late. Once out the door and in my car, my nerves start to get the better of me.

"Calm down, calm down, calm down," I chant aloud. It's not helping so I turn on music and start singing along. Okay, not singing, I'm rapping. I love listening to rap music. Yes, some of the stuff they say is a little, um, questionable, but it makes me happy.

So, with music thumping and me rapping, I pull up in front of Stumble In. There are a lot of cars parked out front. It seems this is the place to be on a Thursday night. I check my face in the rearview mirror and add more lip-gloss, and then get out and walk toward the building. My hands start to sweat and I feel slightly sick.

Once I open the door, all thoughts leave my head. Asher is sitting at a table with three other guys who all look similar to him. The thing that gives me pause is the girl standing next to him. She is so close that her giant boobs are squishing out of her white tank top. I can also see that she's wearing a red bra. I mean, really. Who does that? I want to puke or run away, but all I can do is stare at him. Then, she bends her head to the side and her blonde hair hides what she's whispering into his ear.

"Hi." I jump at the sound and turn my head. "You must be new. I'm Nick," the guy standing next to me says. I take a step toward him so I'm not blocking the door. He's very cute in that 'boy next door' kind of way. He has dirty blond hair and blue eyes. He's wearing a button-up shirt and khakis that are both perfectly pressed. He's also the only guy I've met here that isn't wearing jeans.

"Um, yeah. Hi, I'm November," I say, putting my hand out. That's when I'm pulled by my waist. Startled, I scream, then look to discover Asher is standing behind me, holding me against him.

"Not happening, baby," he whispers in my ear. I can't help the shiver that slides down my spine.

"What?" I ask, completely confused.

"Later, Nick," Asher growls and I realize what he's doing.

Heck no! I walked in and he has a girl practically sitting on his lap, but I can't even introduce myself to Nick. I pull myself away, or try to because his arm just gets tighter. Screw it. I stick out my hand in Nick's direction. "Hi, Nick. I'm November. It was nice to meet you, but I just realized that I forgot to wash my hair and need to go home to do that. So, maybe I'll see you around?" I tell him.

"Uh, yeah sure," he says, looking between me and Asher while running his hand down the back of his neck. With that, I pull myself out of Asher's grasp and walk out the door that I walked through less than three minutes ago.

"Hey, what the fuck? Slow down."

I spin around, almost running into him. I'm so pissed that I can feel my blood heating. "Look here, buddy," I poke his chest. "I don't know what your problem is, but you just embarrassed me. God!" I shout. "Why the hell did I even come?"

"He was going to hit on you and that's not happening, especially right in front of my face."

"Really, you big jerk. I'm shocked that you noticed because you had big-boobed Barbie basically sitting on your lap when I walked in." I poke him in the chest again. "And, for your information, all Nick was going to do was shake my hand."

"Big-boobed Barbie?" He laughs and I want to kick him. "Are you jealous?" he asks, smirking.

"I'm not jealous. I'm embarrassed and pissed off." Even though I am jealous, there is no way I will tell him that. It seems to me that he probably already has trouble walking into buildings with the size of his big, fat head.

"Okay, I'll try not to embarrass you anymore. Now, will you please come inside with me?" he asks, giving me puppy-dog eyes. "My brothers are here, but they have to leave in a couple hours and we want to get a few games of pool in first."

I really must have lost a lot of brain cells when I was attacked, because all I can say is, "Fine." I walk back toward the bar with him when he puts his arm around me. "God, I must be crazy," I say under my breath.

"Just so you know, you look beautiful tonight," he says in my ear. "But if any motherfucker touches you, I will not be happy."

"Can you please try not to be a jerk or piss me off for the next hour?" I ask, looking up at him.

"I'll try," he says, bringing me closer to his body.

I try to pull away, but he just holds me even tighter. So, I do what any woman does when she doesn't get her way. I cross my arms over my chest to let him know that I'm in no way cooperating. I hear him chuckle. I look up and glare at him, but all it does is make him smile bigger. Back inside, we walk up to the table he was sitting at earlier. The girl is gone but the other three guys are still sitting here. And they are all beautiful.

"Guys, this is November, Big Mike's daughter." All the guys are sitting so I can't tell how tall they are, but they look big and gorgeous.

Trevor has dark brown hair that is cut short like Asher's. He has brown eyes with the longest lashes I have ever seen, his jaw is square with a couple days' worth of stubble on it, and he has an amazing smile but no dimple.

Nico has dark blond hair that needs to be cut. He looks like the baby of all of them with darker blue eyes than Asher's and his face is more round than square. He has his left eyebrow pierced and gauges in his ears. If I had to use one word to describe him, it would be 'trouble,' but the good kind that you sneak out of your bedroom window in the middle of the night to go look for.

Cash looks the most like Asher with light blue eyes, dark brown hair, and a square jaw, but his smile is sweet and he's blessed with two dimples rather than one. I feel like I just hit the hot-guy mother lode. If my best friend, Tia, were here, she would be freaking out.

"Shut the fuck up," Nico says, jolting me out of my hot-guy daze.

"I didn't know Big Mike had a daughter, let alone a daughter who looks like you. What did he do, hide you away all this time?" Cash asks and I laugh.

"Um, no," I say, feeling heat hit my cheeks. "I've been living in New York with my mom."

"Why did you move here?" Nico asks.

"I just didn't feel safe staying in the city anymore, so I moved down here. I was already planning to move to Tennessee in a few months, but with what happened, I just came earlier." I could feel Asher's arm around my waist tighten so much that I could make out each of his fingers.

"What happened?"

"Just a wrong place wrong time thing," I say, not wanting to talk about it.

"Well, I'm glad you're okay," Nico says.

"Yeah," they all agree.

"Yo, bro, you may want to loosen your grip before your hand fuses with her waist," Cash says, laughing. The whole situation starts to feel uncomfortable and I need to put some space between Asher and me.

"Well, I came here to have a beer and play a game of pool so that's what I'm gonna do," I say and try to walk away toward the bar, but quickly feel an arm go around my chest.

"Where do you think you're going?" Asher whispers in my ear. I can feel the warmth from his breath against my skin and I have to fight myself to keep from leaning into him.

"To get a beer?" I tell him.

"What kind of beer do you want? I'll get it for you while you sit with my brothers."

"Are you always this bossy?" I ask, trying to tug free.

"Nope, just with you, baby," he chuckles.

"Oh, joy," I say, sarcastically. I can feel his body shake with laughter.

"So what do you want to drink?" he asks.

"Corona with lime," I tell him, debating on whether to take off the minute his back is turned. He must see my intention because he pulls out a stool, picks me up, and sits me on it.

"Sit here. I'll be right back." He looks at his brothers. "Watch her," he says and they all look at him like he's gone crazy. I'm glad to know that I'm not the only one who thinks so.

"So how did you meet our brother?" Trevor asks, looking across the bar at Asher who has turned around and is watching me.

"I started working for my dad and—"

"What?" they all cut me off. "Shit, when do you go on? I'm so gonna be there," Nico says with a goofy smile on his face. Then I realize what I just said.

"What?" I shriek. "No, I mean I work for him doing the books," I say, laughing and shaking my head. "Sorry, no. I'm not a stripper."

"Damn, that's a shame," Cash says, smiling and I laugh harder.

"What's a shame?" Asher asks while walking up to the table with two Coronas. He hands me one.

"That November is not a stripper," Cash says and they all laugh. I can feel my face getting red.

I look at Asher and see his jaw tighten. "Anyway," I say, cutting in, "your brother thought I *was* a stripper. He made a big deal about me going to my car without an escort." Thinking back on it, the whole thing is pretty funny. "He even thought I was sleeping with my dad because I called him 'Daddy'. I mean, ewww," I say, scrunching up my nose. "The look on his face was priceless when my dad came over and introduced me as his daughter." Everyone started laughing, even Asher. "So I work for my dad doing the books for the club. It should take me about a month to get organized and then I won't even need to be there."

"That's cool," Trevor says and they all nod their heads in agreement.

"Do you want to play pool?" Nico asks, looking over at the now empty pool table.

"Sure." I shrug and get off the stool. I take off my hoodie and wrap it around my purse. Trevor grabs it and puts it in the booth, then I start walking towards the pool tables with the boys following behind me. I can feel Asher's hand on my lower back, guiding me through the bar. We're a few steps from the table when big boobed Barbie steps in front of our group. I step around her and leave them to deal with her.

"Where are you going?" I hear her whine. Why women do that, I will never know. Do they not know that it's annoying?

"We're gonna play pool," I hear Asher tell her.

"What? Wait," she says. I turn around and see her grabbing on to his arm. "I've been waiting all night for you to get here and you're going to ditch me?"

"You can't ditch someone you're not with," Cash mumbles from beside me.

I turn around and start setting up the table. I have no interest in watching her throw herself at him. "Okay, guys. Who's gonna break?" They all look confused. "Are we gonna play or what?" I ask, looking at each of them.

"I'll break," Nico says, walking to pick a stick from the wall.

Standing near the table, I feel heat at my back. "You keep walking away from me," Asher says and I almost laugh because he sounds upset.

"Oh, I'm sorry. I didn't realize I was supposed to stand there while you got rid of big-boobed Barbie."

"You could have taken me with you when you went."

"I'll try to remember that next time," I say, shaking my head.

Nico, standing next to us, starts laughing. "Wow. The first one who is immune. I smell a recipe for disaster brewing," he says. Asher smiles down at me like he's happy about something.

"Whatever." I give him my most sarcastic smile. Playing pool with the guys is fun. Asher and I are laughing and having a good time. The guys are telling me funny stories about people in town and Asher introduces me to some people who know my dad.

A ton of people drop by the table, talking to his brothers or just introducing themselves to me. After an hour, I start to notice there are a lot of women gathering around us. Whenever I try to make eye contact with them, they give me a dirty look. It's odd and I have no idea who any of them are. Then, more and more women start coming around the table. There are so many that it's hard to shoot without ramming the stick into one of them.

Asher is standing near me when a very pretty woman with a perfect body, deep red hair, and milky white skin comes up to us. She is wearing an outfit similar to big-boobed Barbie except her bra is black. I'm starting to wonder if this is some kind of dress code because they aren't the only two women wearing something similar.

"Hi, Asher," she purrs, placing herself between me and him while pressing her boobs into his chest.

"Jen," he replies without really looking at her.

She stage whispers in his ear so that we can all hear, "Are you coming to my house tonight?"

"Why would you ask that shit? I haven't been to your house for over a year," he says, crossing his arms over his chest. She is almost as tall as him. I realize they would make a beautiful couple and would give Miss Alice amazing looking grandbabies. That's when I know I need to leave.

Yeah, he's hot but it's clear that he's a player. Not only that, but I would say we don't fit at all. I'm cute but not beautiful. I'm also not skinny. I have a tummy, big boobs, and a bigger butt; on top of all that, I'm short. It will never work. Not when I can see the women he normally goes after. They all are perfectly skinny women who look like models.

I keep telling myself that this isn't a date and I don't want him like that, but honestly, no woman in their right mind would look at a guy like him and not get their hopes up. And, after hanging out with him and getting to know him a little, I find out that he's kind of sweet and really funny. But now I'm done. Date or not, having women come up and rub themselves all over him with looks that say they know exactly what to expect if he takes one of them home is too much. I know I need to bounce as in B-O-U-N-C-E on out of here.

I DON'T WANT to make it obvious that I'm leaving because of the women that are hanging around, so I'm biding my time and talking to Nico. Then some girl named Becky comes over and I've had enough. I can't hold it in any longer and I know if I don't leave, I'm going to ask all the women standing around how the hell they made it into the girl's club. I'm pretty sure there is a rule against acting desperate written on the first page.

"Okay, guys," I say, looking at my watch, or where I would have one if I ever wore a watch. "I gotta go. I need to take my dog for a walk before it gets too late." All the guys turn to look at me.

"You're leaving to walk your dog?" Cash asks in a tone that says he doesn't believe me. But I don't care anymore. I just need to leave quickly.

"Yeah, I walk him every night. So, I guess I'll see you guys around sometime. It was nice meeting you all."

I walk to the booth that has all of our coats and dig mine out from the bottom of the pile, along with my purse. Turning around, I bump into a solid wall.

"Sorry!" I say.

Asher is glaring down at me with a look of disbelief and what appears to be anger on his very handsome face. I want to laugh. What does he really expect? He brought me to a place where every five minutes, he's getting hit on. It was totally rude! He has so many females vying for his attention, I am sure he won't even notice I was gone. Plus, I've lived with a woman who had to be the center of attention and I refuse to date someone who has the same problem. Not that this is a date…I'm just saying; I won't do that to myself.

"Excuse me," I say, trying to walk around him. He grabs my hand and starts pulling me out the door behind him.

"Later, November." I hear from behind me along with a lot of laughter.

"Yeah, later, guys," I yell back, trying to pull my hand free without making a scene.

"Can you slow down, buddy? Your legs are a lot longer than mine," I say to Asher's back. He doesn't say anything but he does slow down. Whatever. I just need to get home and forget this day ever happened. Once I'm at my car, I pull my hand free and start searching for my keys.

"Well, thanks for the beer," I say, looking in my bag. "It was um…fun. Ah…there you are, you sneaky little buggers," I say when I find my keys. I go to unlock my door and my keys are snatched out of my hand.

"Hey, I need those," I yell, trying to reach for the keys that are now in Asher's hand.

"You can have them back after you tell me why the fuck you're leaving."

"What? I already told you I have to walk Beast. He's looking forward to it," I say, and his lips go into a flat line.

"Yeah, you said that about your dog. But I know that's not the real reason, so tell me why the fuck you're really leaving."

I put my hands on my hips, realizing I'm pissed off once again. "Listen, buddy, I have to go walk my dog. I've told you three times now." I show him three fingers just to make sure my point is made.

"What the fuck? We were having a good time then all of a sudden, your face looked like someone stole your ice cream and you had to leave."

"You're so annoying! Can't I just want to go home to my dog?" I ask.

"I know there were a lot of people in there and—"

"A lot of people in there?" I ask, completely shocked. Did he not notice the harem of women gathered around us? Yes, his brothers were there and they are just as hot as him, but they didn't ask me to come here. Asher did.

"I just thought you would like to meet some people. I know you're new to town."

Well, at least now I know for sure that this was in no way a date. He just wants to be nice and introduce me to people. Wow, I'm such a loser. Now, I'm pissed off that I made myself believe that maybe he liked me. And I'm even more pissed off that most of the people he introduced me to, are women that he has slept with. I mean, really. Is he recruiting?

"Well, buddy, I did have a good time. Maybe when we do it again, you can tell *all* the chicks that you're sleeping with, or have slept with, to come by and we'll all hang out. They seemed so excited to meet me. How does that sound to you?" His mouth is hanging open and he looks shocked. "Can I have my keys now?" I ask, holding out my hand. I feel like an idiot for saying it, but I know there is no way to shove the words back down my throat.

"It's been a long time since I slept with any of them."

"I'm sure!" I say, holding out my hand. "Now, my keys?"

"It's the truth," he says and I see a tic in his jaw.

"Okay," I say, not believing for one second the crap that's coming out of his mouth. "Can I have my keys?"

"No. We're taking my jeep."

"What?" I can actually feel my eyes popping out of my head like I'm some crazy cartoon character.

"We're taking my jeep to get your dog and take him for a walk."

"No, *we're* not doing anything. I'm getting in my car and going home to walk my dog," I say, pointing at myself. "By *myself*. You can do whatever it is that you do."

Chapter 3

W**HY THE HELL** am I sitting in his car? Oh yeah, I remember; he picked me up and carried me—kicking and screaming—over his shoulder to his jeep. Then, he dropped me in the driver's side and forced me over to the passenger's seat while holding my hand so I couldn't escape.

"You're a jerk, you. Know that, right?" I say with my arms crossed over my chest.

"You already said that, babe." I swear, I can see a smile on his face. "But if you would have just agreed to get in my jeep, we wouldn't be having this conversation."

"Why do you even want to come?" I ask in a huff.

"I'm not ready to have you out of my sight."

"Why?"

"Because I'm interested."

"I'm sure." I roll my eyes. "So if you're interested, then why not ask me out like a normal guy instead of basically kidnapping me?"

"Why? If I asked you out, you would have blown me off and avoided me. This way, you don't have a choice. I have your keys and your phone."

"You have my phone?" I screech, opening my bag to see if he's telling the truth. "How did you get my phone? Oh my God, you're insane. I'm driving down a dark road with an insane person who's kidnapped me."

I hear him laughing and I look over to make sure I'm not imagining things. He has a really great laugh. Ugh…Why can't he have a crappy laugh? I shake my head in disgust.

"Relax, I just want to spend more time with you. Your dad trusts me, so you're safe. Tell me about your mom," he says, completely ignoring my question about my phone and the fact that he kidnapped me.

Geez…

"We're not talking about my mom. And my dad might like you but he doesn't trust you. He says you're a player. And after the performance I saw tonight, I'm agreeing with him."

"I'm no saint, but I have been honest with every woman who has hit my sheets. They know the score before anything goes down." As much as it makes my stomach knot to think about him with all those women, I have no right to judge him.

"You're right. I'm sorry," I whisper. I hear him let out a breath and I swear I feel his whole body relax from across the cab of his jeep.

"So, tell me about your mom."

"We're not talking about my mom."

"Why not?"

"Because my mom stresses me out. Talking about her gets me upset, even when she's thousands of miles away."

"Well, my mom is awesome. She works for me and my brothers doing office work at our construction company. She bakes us cookies at least a couple times a week and makes sure we eat lunch."

I start giggling, thinking about him and his brothers, who are all built like redwood trees, having their mom bake them cookies and reminding them to eat lunch.

"She sounds sweet," I say, laughing, because it really is nice. I hope one day I can be that kind of mom to my kids. "What does your dad do?" I ask.

"Dad's the sheriff. He's been a cop forever. Mom never worked till we graduated high school."

"You're really lucky. My mom was never really around," I say, leaning my head back against the seat and closing my eyes. I can actually feel the sadness in my own words. He reaches over and squeezes my knee. I can't deal with anyone feeling sorry for me, especially not him, so I change the subject.

"So your brothers work construction with you? And you work for my dad?" I ask, confused.

"We all work together. I started the business after I got out of the Marine Corps. Then, when each of them graduated from college, they bought into the company. I don't work for your dad. My cousin owns a business that supplies security and bodyguards to businesses like your dad's. Every once in a while, he'll call me in and ask me to check on one of his men."

"It's great that you get to work with your family" I say, thinking its' good that he doesn't work at the strip club. I don't know how I would feel about dating a guy in that line of work. Not that we're dating, I remind myself. "Your family seems really nice. Well, your grandma and brothers, do anyway."

"We're all close. It's not always easy working together but at the end of the day, we know that we're family. Do you have any brothers or sisters?"

"No. My mom had bigger dreams than having a family," I say as we pull up in front of my house.

The house is completely dark. The only light around is coming from the headlights of Asher's jeep. "What the hell?" I mumble, starting to feel nervous about going inside. Not because Asher is with me and we're alone and I don't know him no, this is more the feeling, you have when you wake from a bad dream and the fright stays stuck to you for a while after you wake up.

"Why didn't Mike leave a light on for you?" Asher asks, looking over at me.

"Uh…I don't know. I'm always home way before he leaves. Maybe he just forgot," I say, starting to get out of the jeep. I stop when he opens the glove box and pulls out a gun. "What are you doing?" I ask in shock.

"Safety." That's all he says before he opens his door. I follow his lead and open mine. Before I even make it to the front of his jeep, he's next to me, grabbing my hand. The warmth from his touch is soothing, and I swear I can feel him rubbing his thumb back and forth against my skin.

We start to walk up the porch when he stops. "Is there another way to get in the house?" he asks, turning towards me.

"My apartment is in the basement and has its own entrance," I tell him, looking around.

"Stay close," he says softly. I hold on to the back of his shirt, walking so close that I don't think you can slip a piece of paper between us. I can hardly see in the darkness. The only source of light is coming from the moon, which cutting through the clouds. Walking around the side of the house, my heart starts pounding. It feels like it's going to jump out of my chest. My breathing starts to pick up when I think about what happened the last time I went home after dark.

The night that I was attacked, I had been walking to my apartment from the subway. I passed the alley next to my building and a guy grabbed me from behind, covered my mouth then dragged me down into the shadows next to a dumpster. That's where he proceeded to beat me. I fought as much as I could and was feeling dizzy by the time he stood over me, grabbing my head. I knew he was going to bash my head into the concrete so I closed my eyes and started to pray. Then, he was gone and I could vaguely see Beast attacking him.

Asher must notice me shaking because he stops and pulls me into his big, warm body. His arms go around me and I feel his lips touch my hair. He smells like spicy, warm man and it makes me want to crawl into his skin. He pulls my face out of his chest and brings his face towards mine.

"It's okay, baby," he whispers, putting his forehead to mine. "I won't let anything happen to you. I want you to breathe deeply for me, okay?" I am so caught up in how close he is that I can't think about anything but leaning in and touching my mouth to his. I shake my head to clear it and take a deep breath. I wonder if he can read my mind because even in the darkness, I can see the white of his smile.

"You ready?" he asks. I feel his breath against my lips, so I pull my face away and nod, not trusting myself to speak. My apartment door is down a short set of stairs. Asher's in front of me and he opens the door. "Stay here until I come and get you," he says, entering my dark apartment.

"Okay," I say as my hands start to shake. After a few minutes, Beast comes running out. I bend down to pet him but his fur feels wet. What the heck? Holding my hands close to my face, they look really dark. Then the light comes on and I scream. My hands are covered in blood. "Oh my God! What happened?" I say, running my hands over Beast's body. He's also covered in red but I can't feel any kind of cut or hole on him. I'm shaking so badly that I have to sit on the ground. Beast immediately crawls into my lap.

"Fuck," Asher clips, coming outside. He pushes Beast off me and pulls me into his arms. "Baby, it's okay. Calm down."

"I tho…I…I thought Beast was hurt but I can't find anything wrong with him. Why is he covered in blood?" I sob while he rubs my back and pulls me tighter into him.

"Beast is fine but we need to call the police. Someone broke into the house and used something red to write on the walls. Somehow, Beast got it on him before they locked him upstairs." Before he can finish what he's saying, I run into my apartment. The living room is trashed. On the wall, in red letters that look like blood, is a message.

No sun – no moon!
No morn – no noon –
No dawn – no dusk – no proper time of day.
No warmth, no cheerfulness, no healthful ease,
No comfortable feel in any member –
No shade, no shine, no butterflies, no bees,
No fruits, no flowers, no leaves, no birds! –
November!

"What the hell?" I whisper as Asher picks me up and carries me back outside.

"I know that poem. It's *November* by Thomas Hood. Why would someone write that on my wall?" I ask, trying to figure out what the words mean.

"I'm not sure," he says. And I feel him kiss the side of my head.

"I can walk, you know," I grumble. He doesn't answer or put me down until he drops me in the passenger side of his jeep. With my feet out the door, he stands between my legs. His arm wraps around my body and one of his hands reach in his back pocket for his phone.

"Hey, Dad. Gotta problem. I'm at Big Mike's house with his daughter, November. Her apartment was broken into. Yeah, Mike's daughter. We're not gonna talk about that shit right now. Yeah, see ya." Closing the phone, he tosses it behind me on the driver's seat. I'm looking down at my hands. They're covered in red gunk and so are my jeans. All I can wonder is who would do this and why.

"Look at me, baby." I lift my eyes to his and they are warm and concerned. "I will make sure you're safe. I promise."

Looking into his eyes with the jeep's interior light reflecting off them, I can see he's worried. Instinctively I begin to tell him about New York and being attacked before I left. He listens the whole time. His eyes turn darker and his jaw is getting tighter with every word. He shakes his head when I finish, pulling me in for a hug that I think is more for him than for me.

"Thank you for helping me," I say.

"You," he says, kissing my head, "never have to thank me for doing something I want to do."

"Well, I'm glad you were here." And that's not a lie. I can't imagine what would have happened if I had come home by myself.

"Fuck, baby, me too," he says, letting out a long breath.

I look down at Beast, who is sitting at our feet, looking up at us and waiting to see if we're still going for a walk or if I might have a treat. His head tilts when I start talking to him. "Looks like you're gonna get a bath, boy." He tilts his head in the other direction. "And when you're done, I need take one too," I say then realize that I am, once again, talking to my dog. I look up at Asher and he's smiling. I say the first thing that pops into my head.

"Do I look like Carrie?"

He bursts out laughing then kisses my forehead. "Yeah, you're covered from having that damn dog sit on you while you hugged him. When my dad gets here and checks everything out, you can shower."

"Oh my God," I whisper, horrified when I remember that his dad is the sheriff. "Your dad's coming?"

"Yeah, baby. He's the sheriff."

"Oh my God, your dad's coming," I repeat. Without thinking, I stick my hands up the front of his shirt and use it to wipe my face. "Is that better?" I ask.

"I can't believe you just did that," he says, sounding completely shocked.

"Oh, God. Your dad's going to meet me looking like Carrie," I cry out. I still have my hands up his shirt so I repeat the process of wiping my face. Then I use the inside to wipe my hands. I look up because he's not saying anything.

"I can't believe you just did that."

"Okay! So, is most of the red off my face?" I ask.

"You owe me a new shirt," he tells me.

"Fine, whatever. But is the red gone?"

"Yeah, baby. The red is mostly gone but now I don't know if I should kiss you or spank you for that shit."

"Whatever," I whisper and press my forehead against his chest to hide my huge smile. My belly is doing acrobatics at the thought of him kissing me. Two minutes later, red and blue lights flash up the driveway and two police cars pull in next to Asher's jeep. Looking around Asher's big body, I see a very tall man with grey hair mixed with dirty blond walking towards us. This must be his dad.

"Dad, this is November," Asher says, taking a step back. Then, he pulls me from the seat. When my feet hit the ground, he puts his arm around me, dragging me into his body. His dad is smiling when he walks towards us.

"Hi, November. I've heard a lot about you visiting my mama with that dog of yours. She's been bragging about you for a few weeks now. But I didn't know you were Big Mike's daughter. I don't think anyone even knew he had a daughter," he says with a kind smile on his face.

"Your mom is a very nice lady, Mr. Mayson. And, not a lot of people know about me," I tell him as if he doesn't already know it.

"Please call me James. Mr. Mayson makes me feel old."

"Okay," I say laughing.

"So what happened tonight? You said someone broke in?"

Asher tells his dad about the red writing in my living room and Beast being covered in the same liquid that was used on the walls. And how all the lights were off in the house when we got here.

"Okay, darlin', do you know of anyone who would want to hurt you?" he asks, looking at me.

"No, but the reason I moved here is because I was attacked in New York. Then, on the way here, I pulled into a rest stop to let Beast out and a car with New York plates pulled up a couple minutes later. The strange thing was that I was parked in the area for dogs and they never got out with a dog. I got spooked and ran back to my car but didn't see them again. So I don't know if it was just my imagination or if I was really in danger."

"There's no telling," he says, looking more concerned. "Did you ever receive gifts or anything unusual before you were attacked?"

"No, nothing like that. Why? Do you think I have a stalker or some-thing?" I ask, a chill sliding down my spine.

"Don't know. I'm gonna do some checking around and see if we can find anything. Can you stay with someone else for the night? I don't think you should be alone."

"Um...I...uh...have to call my dad. I'm sure I can stay with my grandma or my uncle."

"You're staying with me," Asher says, making my heart pound.

"I don't think that's a good idea," I say, looking up at him.

"Well, I don't give a fuck. You're not leaving my sight and I don't think your grandma or uncle want me staying at either of their houses with you. So you're staying with me."

Rolling my eyes at Asher, I see his dad watching us. He looks smug for some reason.

"Your son is very annoying and bossy," I tell him.

"I'm sure with you he is, darlin'," he laughs. "But he's a Mayson, so I also know that his bossy side is coming from a very safe place," he says, looking at me. His smile is so warm that my stomach does a flip. "What did I tell you, son?" he says, looking at Asher. "When it happens—BOOM!" He makes a motion with his hands of an explosion.

"When what happens?" I ask.

"Nothing," they say at the same time.

"Alrighty, then." I look back at Asher. "I need to call my dad."

After telling him everything that happened, Dad wants to come home. I explain that Asher and his dad are with me and that he doesn't need to worry. I know the club is busy, because every few minutes, someone is asking him a question while we are on the phone. I tell him that Beast and I are going to stay with Asher for the night.

To say my dad doesn't like this idea is an understatement. It takes ten minutes to assure him that I won't do anything stupid but he still makes me put Asher on the phone to reiterate his point to him. The only thing Asher says is, "She's safe with me, Mike," then he hands me back my phone.

So now I, a hosed-off Beast and my overnight bag are on our way to Asher's place. We drive out into the country. All along the roads are open fields. "So you live out here?" I ask, looking at his profile in the lights of the dashboard.

"Yeah, I bought the land I live on when I first started my business. I began building my house not long after."

"Wow, that's impressive. How old were you when you started your company?" I ask, wanting to know his age but trying to be sneaky about it.

"I was twenty-two when I first started."

"Oh. How long ago was that?" I hear him chuckle and I look over at him. "What's so funny?"

"I'm twenty-seven, babe. Nothing is ever easy with you, is it?" he asks and I hear amusement in his voice.

"Cool," I say, feeling like an idiot that he figured me out. We pass a large red barn then turn down a dirt road. I can't see anything ahead of us until we go over a small hill. My breath catches and I'm stunned. I don't know what I expected but I didn't expect to see a large, two story log house with a wraparound porch on the second level. Beams are holding up the space for parking below. I see a car and four wheeler parked under it.

"You built this?" I ask and even to myself I sound breathy.

"Yeah. It took me four years to get it finished because I was working on it between jobs."

"It's beautiful," I say because…wow, it's just amazing.

We get out of the jeep and start walking up to the front porch. Beast is walking behind us and it's so quiet out here that I can hear his tail cutting through the air. He's so excited to see this new place and explore. Asher lets us inside and I am completely stunned by what I see. It's huge. You can see the logs in the walls. It's all warm wood and open. There are giant windows that jut out and make the space almost seem larger. There is a sunken living room with a long, dark blue couch in the center of the room. It looks like it needs to be replaced but it also looks really comfortable.

On the wall, there is a huge entertainment center and off to the side is a floor to ceiling fire place made out of different types of rocks. There are no pictures or throw pillows of any kind. Actually, looking around, I realize that there are no decorations anywhere. We turn a corner and enter a giant kitchen with stainless steel appliances, granite countertops, and a large island in the middle with the stove built into it. It looks like a chef's dream but it also looks unused.

"Do you cook?" I ask. That's the only reason I can think someone would want a kitchen this large.

"Some," he says with a look on his face that I can't read. What the heck? This is a top of the line kitchen. I would love to spend hours in this kitchen baking or just sitting at the island and drinking coffee.

"Oh, well, it's a really nice kitchen." I mean, what else can I say?

"Glad you like it," he says in a way that makes me think he's really glad I like it. I follow him down a hall that runs beside the kitchen. I look for Beast but don't see him so I turn around to search him out. When I walk back through the kitchen, I stop. Beast is lying on the couch on his back with his legs straight up in the air. I feel an arm slide around my waist and Asher speaks close to my ear. "Looks like he made himself at home." A shiver runs across my skin and I know that he can feel it when his arm goes tighter.

"Should I tell him to get down?" I ask.

"No, baby. He's fine," he says in his deep drawl. I love that he calls me baby, and at the same time, it scares me that I love it. "Let me show you the bedroom," he mumbles. At his words, I get another shiver. This one's in a completely different place.

We walk past two rooms with the doors open. One is an office and the other is a workout room. Across the hall from both is a bathroom. At the end of the hall, he opens the door. I follow behind him and realize that this is his bedroom. There is a platform bed that's so big, everyone I know could sleep on it and no one would even touch. The sheets and blankets are a mess and there are clothes scattered all over the floor.

Next to the bed is a wall of windows and the shades are slightly open. I can see a deck off his room as well. Beside the bed are nightstands built into the wall. There is a long, black dresser in the same color of the bed and side tables. There are two doors. One is open and I can tell that it's my dream closet. It's the size of my apartment back in New York. I walk towards it without thinking and turn on the light. I could fit a chair and a table in the space and still have room to add a king-size bed.

There are shelves on both sides that have a few pairs of shoes and boots on them and along the walls there is plenty of space to hang clothes. There are a few pieces of clothing hanging but most of it is in piles on the floor.

"Oh my God, I'm in love." I hear Asher laughing behind me so I turn to look over my shoulder. "You have committed a huge crime," I tell him with a completely straight face. He's still laughing. "No, seriously, this closet should be taken care of and should never have stuff defacing the floor."

He throws his head back, laughing so hard that the tendons in his neck are out. I catch myself wanting to run my tongue along them. I double blink at that thought. When his eyes come back to mine, he's still chuckling.

"I don't even like doing laundry. I'm not a big fan of hanging shit up," he tells me.

"Oh, of course," I whisper. Geez, I'm such a dork. He's a guy. They don't care about dream closets and having the space to show off all their fashion treasures. I step out of the closet and cross my arms under my breasts. His eyes drop to my cleavage so I quickly uncross my arms. Then, I realize I'm standing in his bedroom and I'm sleeping in his house while he's here.

I look at the bed then back at him. He's watching me the whole time. When we make eye contact again, there is something working behind his beautiful blue eyes that makes me hold my breath. He breaks eye contact and runs his hand over his head. I clench my hands into fists. I want to know if his hair will feel prickly against my palms. "Um…" I say, trying to clear my brain now that it seems to have gone into an Asher fog. He looks up and smiles. I see his dimple and that doesn't help. Now I want to lick his cheek and taste his dimple. His smile widens and I swear he can read my mind. Crap, crap, crap.

"Here, let me show you the bathroom and you can change and get ready for bed," he says.

Thank God for small favors, I think to myself until we walk into the bathroom. There is a large walk in shower that's made out of rock with a glass door that makes it look like an open cave. Next to the shower is a bathtub that dreams are made of. Well, at least girl dreams. I can't picture Asher filling it with bubbles and having a soak. Then, I'm bombarded with thoughts of Asher naked and in the bathtub. I'm staring at the tub when I hear him moving behind me so I turn around. He has my bag in his hand and is setting it on the sink.

"Feel free to take a bath and get into bed. I gotta make a few calls." I would love to take a bath in his tub. Well, I would love to take a bath in his tub with him but I push that thought away.

"Uh, thanks," I say, feeling strange. He smiles and leaves, closing the door behind him. I stand there for a few more minutes, trying to figure out what the heck is happening. Then I realize I've been standing here staring at the tub so I jerk out of my Asher tub fog and go to the sink. I took a shower before I left my house so I just dig through my bag and find my pajamas. They're white cotton sleep shorts with a yellow drawstring that matches a yellow tank top. I tie my hair in a knot at the top of my head and wash my face. Then I dig through my bag and find my toothbrush and toothpaste.

After I'm done, I put on some nighttime skin cream. That is one thing my mom taught me. It was good advice to never go to bed without night cream. She would say, 'No man wants a woman with wrinkles.' How she would know this, I don't know. She has been getting Botox since she was twenty and that's probably the last time her face showed an expression that wasn't surprise.

I open the door to the bedroom and the room is dark except for one of the bedside lights. I realize Asher made the bed while I was changing and for some reason that makes me smile. I think about going out and getting Beast but he won't move if he's asleep unless I carry him, and that's not going to happen. I wonder where Asher is sleeping. Then I realize I'm tired and don't care. I look at the clock on the side table and see that it's after two in the morning. Without thinking, I crawl into bed. It smells like him so I pull the covers over me and I'm, once again, dead to the world.

I WAKE UP feeling warm and cozy. It takes me a minute to realize that it is not Beast behind me. Beast doesn't have arms. I keep my eyes closed and hold my breath, trying to figure out what has happened. Then, I hear the door open.

"Oh my," I hear a woman's voice say and my eyes pop open, and I'm looking into the eyes of a beautiful, older woman and she's looking back at me. Asher's arm goes tight around me and I look over my shoulder. "Morning, baby," he rumbles into my ear. I'm so humiliated that I blurt out the first thing that pops into my head when I turn back to look at the woman.

"We didn't have sex!" I basically yell at her.

The lady looks at me again and smiles so big that I can see all of her teeth. "I'll just be in the kitchen," she says and Asher starts laughing as she's closing the door behind her. I swear I hear her giggle. As soon as I know the door is closed, I turn to Asher. I'm really going to kill him.

"What are you doing here?" I ask.

"This is my bed," he says, smiling. Grrrrrr. I want to choke him.

"I thought you were sleeping on the couch or, like, in another room or something," I say and wonder why he thinks this is so funny.

"Why would I do that? My bed is big. Plus, your dog was taking up the whole couch."

"You should have woken me up. I would've slept on the couch with Beast," I tell him, trying to shove his arm off me.

"My bed is big enough for both of us. We didn't even have to touch, but the minute I got into bed, you were all over me," he says, hugging me tighter.

"Oh my God, you're so full of it. I was asleep. I didn't even know you were here. How could I be all over you?" I yell at him knowing full well that my face is turning red.

"When I climbed into bed, you wrapped yourself around me," he says, watching my face. I can feel it getting redder by the second.

"I didn't," I say, even though I most likely did. I have always liked to cuddle.

"You did," he says, smiling.

"Whatever," I mumble, trying to hide my face.

"At least tell me that's not your mother," I say, covering my face with my hands.

He starts laughing and pulls me down in the bed so I'm basically lying under him. Feeling his skin against mine, I uncover my eyes and see that he's not wearing a shirt. How I missed that, I have no idea. His chest is awesome. It's wide and you can see the definition of all the muscles. He doesn't have a lot of chest hair, just enough that you could feel it against your chest as he moves inside of you. His tattoos start under his collar bone and go around his shoulders and down his arms. They look like fire but it's all tribal. Running in and out of the flames are names and a pair of military type boots. Then the same design goes down his other arm but with a gun and a military type hat. It's shaded in black and has bright colors running through. It's truly a piece of art.

"Yes, that's my ma. She probably came to make sure you were okay. I'm sure Dad told her what happened last night," he says, startling me out of my perusal of his body and tattoos. I look up into his smiling face, wondering what he thinks is so funny about his mom finding me in his bed.

"This is so embarrassing. She probably thinks I'm a slut," I say, wondering if this is normal for him.

"She doesn't think anything except that you slept here after your apartment was broken into. Now, we need to get up, but first, you need to kiss me," he tells me with a straight face.

"What?" I whisper.

"You need to kiss me. All night you slept cuddled into me. You can't do that to a man without at least kissing him." His face is close to mine and his eyes are warm. My eyes drop to his mouth. I can't help it; he has a nice mouth.

"Kiss me," he whispers, his mouth brushing mine.

"No," I whisper back, watching his eyes darken.

"Okay, then. I'm going to kiss you," he says against my lips. My brain is screaming, yes, yes, yes. Then I feel his lips touch mine softly. My hand moves to his bicep to hold on. When his mouth moves away from mine, I want to pull him back. Then he licks the seam of my mouth, and the minute his tongue touches me, my lips part.

I kiss him back, first softly then wildly. My other hand reaches for his hair and I run my palm against it, feeling it prickle my skin, happy to know it feels as good as I thought it would. When his hand goes to my hair, I can feel him pull out my hair tie and grab a fist full of hair at the back of my head. The bite of pain feels so good that I moan into his mouth. He bites my lip softly then sucks my tongue into his mouth. I follow him, doing the same.

He growls and his other hand travels along my side until I feel his fingers near my breast. I press myself into his hand and he growls again. My other hand goes from his bicep to his back. It is so smooth and hard at the same time. I'm mesmerized by the sensation of his thumb traveling across my nipple, I whimper, arching into him. He pulls his mouth away from mine, shoving my face into his neck. "Fuck!" I am so turned on that I don't realize what is happening until I hear his mom from the kitchen.

"I'm making coffee, kiddos. Where is the dog food?" she asks through the door.

"Oh my God," I whisper into his neck and I can feel his body start to shake. "This is not funny," I tell him and he laughs harder.

"You're right. This shit is not funny. I'm harder than I've ever been in my life and I know Ma's not gonna leave until she see for herself that you're okay." I don't want to think too much about it, but the thought of me turning him on and making him harder than he's ever been makes me smile and I can't help but giggle.

"Are you laughing at me, baby?" he whispers in my ear. I start laughing louder. Then he starts tickling me. "Don't laugh at me, baby." I'm laughing so hard that I think I might pee my pants so I started begging him to stop. "Please, I won't laugh at you anymore. I promise, I promise," I say through my laughter. He stops and looks down at me and both of his hands cup my face.

"Jesus, you're so fucking beautiful." The way he says it and the way he is looking at me, makes me believe that he really thinks I'm beautiful. I can feel my face go soft at his words. He bends his head and kisses me again. This time, it's soft and sweet. When his mouth leaves mine, we are both breathing heavily.

"You're the one who is beautiful," I tell him softly, running my fingers down his jaw. His face goes soft and his eyes warm. His mouth is coming toward mine again.

"Alright, kids, coffee's on and I still can't find the dog food."

"Ma, Jesus! We'll be out in a minute to feed the dog," Asher yells.

"Asher James Mayson, you watch your tone and don't use the lord's name in vain," his mom says.

I have to bite my lip but when I can't hold it and start laughing, I have to cover my mouth so his mom doesn't hear me.

Without warning, he knifes up and pulls me up with him. We are suddenly standing next to the bed. He bends to kiss my nose then turns and walks towards the bathroom. I'm stuck in place, looking at his back muscles as he moves.

I am still standing in the same place when I hear the toilet flush and he walks out. Then I am in a complete Asher fog because he is still shirtless and the tattoos on his arms and chest are on full display, along with his eight pack abs and the sexy v leading into his loose sweats. Who knew that abs like that were real.

"You gonna feed Beast or do you want to stand there and stare at me some more?" he asks. I look into his face and see a very arrogant smile with his dimple out.

"Whatever," I mutter and hear him chuckle as I walk around the bed with my eyes to my feet.

Once in the bathroom, I shut the door and look at myself in the mirror. My green eyes look brighter, my lips are swollen from kissing, my cheeks are pink, and my hair is wild. I remember how I ended up looking like this and smile, then quickly frown. Asher is hot but I'm not the kind of girl that sleeps with, then makes out with, a guy after one date. Plus, we weren't even on an actual date. Then again, I didn't know that we were going to sleep together.

Shaking my head at my own crazy thoughts, I decide that I'm just going to be honest and tell him that I don't do casual. I'm sure that will scare him off. I brush my teeth and pull out a bra and zip up sweatshirt from my bag. After putting both on, I head out of the room to the kitchen.

When I get there, Asher is sitting on a bar stool, still shirtless, with a cup of coffee in front of him. Once he notices me, he does a full body sweep. I get a smile out of him but it's a small smile. This time, there is no dimple. Hmmm.

"Hi, I'm Susan, Asher's mom." At the sound of her voice, I jump. I'm so caught up in Asher's missing dimple that I forgot his mom is here. She comes around the island and takes my hand in hers.

"I'm November," I say, smiling back at her. She is very pretty. She has short, dark brown hair that is cut into a cute mom bob. Her eyes are the same color as Asher's. She's wearing a white button-up shirt with a large turquoise necklace, dark blue jeans, and brown cowboy boots. She looks very country chic and I'm instantly in love with her. Then she grabs me into a tight hug. The instant her arms wrap around me in a motherly hug, I want to cry.

"It's nice to finally meet you, November," she whispers into my hair. I hug her tighter, closing my eyes against the tears that want to escape. She steps back and holds me at arm's length. "Well, you are as beautiful as everyone said you were."

I am taken off guard by her comment. I mean, my dad calls me beautiful and Asher told me that this morning, but that was in the heat of the moment. I'm not ugly but I've always just been cute. Even my ex-boyfriends have only ever said that I was cute and my mom never once in my life has called me beautiful.

"Thanks," I mutter, feeling awkward. I can feel heat rise up my cheeks. She smiles brighter and turns towards Asher. They both share a smile and I feel like I'm intruding on a private moment.

"Do you like coffee?" she asks, walking back into the kitchen.

"Like is not the word I would use for how I feel about coffee," I say. She tilts her head to the side, giving me a questioning look.

"Um…I love coffee," I say, feeling like a dork. "I'm pretty sure that my coffee consumption alone is helping to get the United States out of debt." I'm rambling and both she and Asher laugh. I hear scratching and look to the side. Beast has his big paw on the glass door, wanting in. I walk to the door and when I open it, Beast comes in with such force that he knocks me on my butt and starts licking me like he hasn't seen me in weeks. I'm laughing when I look up and see Asher and his mom watching me with the same smile on their faces.

"Alright, let her up," Asher says, pushing Beast away. He stands over me with his legs on either side of my body, looking down. "You're too much," he mumbles. His hands take mine to lift me off the ground.

His words hit me hard for some reason. My mom used to tell me that I was too much, but every time she said it, she would get a look on her face that said she didn't know why she even bothered with me. I don't want to look at Asher and see the same disgust on his face so I let go of his hands, avoiding his eyes. I walk to the island where his mom has a cup of coffee waiting for me. I pour in some milk and add two scoops of sugar. She and Asher are both watching me. I need to get away so I can pull myself together.

"Thank you for the coffee," I say, looking at Asher's mom with tears clogging my throat. "I'll be right back. I just need to get Beast's food out of my bag." Walking out of the kitchen and down the hall, I feel like an idiot. My mom isn't even here and she is making me feel like crap. I'm at the door of Asher's room when I feel an arm around my waist and I'm flying through the air. I let out a girly scream then land in the bed with Asher on top of me.

"Wh… Wha… What are you doing?" I ask, stuttering and trying to shove him off me.

"What happened back there?" he asks, holding me down. I can't tell him that my mom has made me a total nut case so I just press my lips together, trying harder to shove him off. I don't want his mom to hear me scream at him that it is none of his business. "You were laughing one second and then you closed up. What happened?"

"Nothing. I just need to get Beast's food. Now get off me," I say, shoving at him.

"Tell me what happened. Did I hurt you?" He really looks worried.

"What?"

"When I pulled you up, did I hurt you?" he asks again, making me feel even worse.

"No, you didn't hurt me. I'm fine now. Can you please move so I can feed my dog?" I ask, shoving him again.

"So what was it then? One minute you were rolling around on the floor with your dog, laughing. Then you looked like someone smacked you. I'm not letting you up until you tell me what happened." I feel tears and I don't want to cry in front of him. How can you tell someone that has an amazing mom that yours totally messed up your head?

"You wouldn't understand," I say because he really wouldn't. No one could understand how it feels to have the person who is supposed to protect and guide you through life make you feel completely worthless.

"Try me," he whispers. His hand moves from where he was holding me down to glide through the hair at my temple. I feel tears start to fall and I try to look away but he's holding my face in his hands and bends over to kiss each eye. "Please tell me, baby," he whisper.

I can't help it. His voice is so soft and his warmth is all around me and I feel safe in that moment. Maybe safer than I've ever felt.

"My mom's not like yours. She's not sweet, she doesn't hug, she doesn't tell people that they're beautiful, she would never make anyone coffee." Tears are falling harder and I feel like I have sand in my throat. "I know it's stupid, but my whole life she has made me feel bad about myself. My mom is abusive; physically, verbally, and emotionally. She has cut me down my whole life. It took me a long time to realize that what she has drilled into my head isn't true, but those wounds are still there and they run so deep that there are times I can still feel them inside me. Even when someone makes a passing comment that anyone else would laugh at; to me, it feels like a cut."

I realize that I have my eyes closed so I open them and see that Asher looks pissed. His whole body is tight and his teeth are clenched. I start to get scared and he must have read my face. He looks into my eyes and I feel his whole body relax. His jaw unclenches and his thumb travels over my bottom lip.

"It was what I said about you being 'too much.'" He doesn't ask, it's just a statement. I nod my head because I can't talk. "You're beautiful when you laugh. Not too many women would get tackled to the ground by a dog, even their own, and laugh about it, definitely not in front of a man. That's why I said you were too much. I love that you don't care what people think and that you act like yourself around me. I'm sorry your mom is a bitch. I bet she's jealous of you so she cut you down, hoping you would always feel inferior to her. Hopefully, we can work on filling all the marks she left," he says softly.

His fingers wipe away my tears. I feel it down to my soul. The words he said feel true but then I remember that I can't trust it or believe him.

"I can't do casual," I blurt out. I want to cover my face or go hide in the bathroom. Instead, I close my eyes. His body is shaking, so I open my eyes and he's laughing. "What's funny?" I ask, irritated.

"Do you think I would try that with you, knowing that your dad, uncle, and cousins would come to kick my ass if I wanted something casual?" he asks, searching my face.

"Uh…" That never crossed my mind.

"This isn't casual. Christ!" He growls. "You've met my brothers, mom, dad, and grandma. No woman I've ever dated has met my whole family. I've wanted you from the moment I saw you in the club, hanging on your dad. That's why I was pissed when I caught you outside. Then when I saw you with my grandmother, I knew I was fucked. She'd been talking about you for weeks, telling me that I need to meet this girl that's so beautiful and sweet. She told me that she just moved into town and I should ask her out before someone else did. She was right. I realized yesterday that I needed to stake my claim before some stupid fuck got to you. That's why I did what you called 'kidnapping.' I like to call that 'securing my future.' We're going to see where this goes, November, and while we're doing that, it's not going to be casual."

"Okay," I say, feeling excited and a little scared from the tone of his voice and the look in his eyes. I can tell he's dead serious.

"Okay." He kisses me softly. "And just so you know, if your mother ever comes to visit, I won't be nice."

"I don't think my mother will ever come to town." I'm looking over his shoulder at the same time as I'm praying that I'm right. I truly hope my mother never shows her face in this town. My dad would flip and my grandmother would probably shoot her.

"Alright, now we need to get up before Ma comes in here. She's worried about you after what happened last night and the look on your face when you walked out of the kitchen. Let's go have breakfast then go meet your dad at your house." As if Asher summoned it from thin air, my phone starts playing Highway to Hell, my dad's ring tone. Asher stands, bringing me with him, then walks to his jeans on the floor and pulls my cell out of his pocket and hands it to me. I turn around and put my phone to my ear.

"Hi, Dad."

"Hey, baby girl. How are you feeling?"

"Um, I'm good. I'm getting ready to feed Beast and then I'm going to eat breakfast with Asher and his mom."

"His mom is there?" he says, sounding surprised.

"Yeah, she came by this morning. Mr. Mayson told her about what happened last night and I guess she wanted to make sure I was alright."

"Hmm," I hear my dad say then he's quiet.

"Dad, you still there?"

"Yeah, I'm here, baby girl. So what time are you going to be home?"

I turn and see Asher leaning against the door, watching me. "What time do you think we'll be at my dad's?" I ask him.

"In about an hour and a half, baby," he says softly. I feel a small smile touch my mouth at the word baby.

"Asher says about an hour and a half."

"I heard him, baby girl. Can you put him on the phone for me?"

"Um, sure. Hold on. Dad wants to talk to you," I say to Asher, holding out my phone. He slides it from my hand and kisses me on my nose then takes a step back, putting the phone to his ear.

"Mike," I hear him say. "Yeah, we'll talk when I get there."

Then he hands the phone back to me. "Dad," I say, hoping that with the tone I'm using, he understands that I'm not being stupid.

"See you when you get here, baby girl. Love you." He hangs up before I can tell him I love him too. Asher is watching me.

"Is everything okay?" I ask, looking at the phone.

"It's all good, baby. Let's eat."

"Okay," I say, feeling dread creep up my spine. I know Dad is going to say something to Asher when we get to the house and I am suddenly nervous about going home. We walk back into the kitchen and Mrs. Mayson is standing at the stove.

"Do you like grits?" she asks with a smile. I have no idea what grits are and she must have read the look on my face.

"Okay, how about some eggs and toast?"

"That's fine. Thank you, Mrs. Mayson."

"Call me Susan, beautiful."

"Okay. Do you have a bowl I can use to put Beast's food in?" I ask Asher. He gets up and walks around the island to pull out a huge bowl. The kind that you would use to make cookies or bread in. He fills the bowl to the top. I watched this in horror, too stunned to stop him. I always measure his food so he doesn't eat too much. I read online that you have to be careful with big dogs and their diets.

"What are you doing?" I ask as Asher sets the bowl down on the ground.

"Feeding the dog," he says with an eyebrow raised.

"You can't feed him that much."

"Why not?" he asks.

"Because I Googled it and they say to measure it."

"Babe, he's a dog. He knows when to stop eating." He's looking at me like he thinks something is funny.

"How do you know that?" I ask, tilting my head.

"I've had dogs my whole life."

"Oh…" That's all I can say. Beast is my first dog and all the information I have is from Google. He chuckles and I kind of want to punch him in the arm for laughing at me.

"Whatever," I say, shaking my head. His arm goes to the back of my head and he kisses me. I can hear his mom laughing. Oh my God, how embarrassing.

"You can't kiss me in front of your mom," I whisper when he pulls away.

"Just did and it won't be the last time." I hear his mom laugh again and I look at her, smiling down at the stove. Her head comes up and she looks happy for some reason.

"I love this, honey. Asher and his women, well, all my sons and their women, none of them ever came around. At first, I thought maybe they were embarrassed of me and their dad. Then, James and I were out one night and we saw Cash with this girl. Let me tell you…after that, I was glad they never brought anyone around if that was what they would bring home."

"I was lucky enough to meet some of those women first hand last night when Asher took me to the bar."

"He didn't?" His mom looks over at Asher with narrow eyes.

"He totally did." I smile and look over at Asher who looks like he's ready to strangle me.

"Asher James Mayson, I thought I taught you better than that?"

"Ma, we met the boys there to play pool. I don't have any control over who goes to the bar."

"I can't believe you took her to play pool for a first date." She looks at me. "I swear I raised him better than that."

"It wasn't a date," I reassure her.

"Jesus, Ma," Asher grumbles. He looks at me and his eyes narrow. "It was a date." All I can do is shake my head and smile.

"You know, even when Asher was married, we never met the girl. All we knew was that they met when he was stationed in Texas and got married at a court house. We weren't even invited." I feel my heart drop into my stomach at the thought of him married. Stupid, I know. I mean, I was engaged and thought I would spend the rest of my life with the douche bag.

"Ma, Jesus! What the fuck!"

"Watch your mouth, Asher James." She glares at him then looks at me. "Sorry, I thought you knew."

"Um, no. That's okay. I mean, we just met and we all have a past. Some of it beautiful and some ugly," I tell her. There are some things in my past that are ugly too. Like the guy I was going to marry before he slept with my mother. How much uglier can you get? Her eyes are soft and she gives me a sad smile.

"So what are you kids planning for the day?" she asks, thankfully changing the subject.

"Going home then I need to have my dad take me to get my car." I am standing at the corner of the island. Asher pulls my hand, dragging me in between his legs. He has a hand on my hip and I look him in the eye and give him a death glare. He runs his fingers down the side of my face and smiles.

"I'm gonna give Ma the key to your car. She can have Nico or Cash bring your car home for you. Then you need to pack up some stuff and bring it over. I'll be out for a while, I gotta go up to Nashville to check on the job site and make sure the fire inspector doesn't shut us down. I'll give you a key so just come in and make yourself at home."

I know I have an 'are you crazy' look on my face, but he is telling me to stay the night again.

"I'm not staying here," I tell him.

"You are staying here. Your dad works the club at night and doesn't get home till after four in the morning."

"I'm not! I'll just stay with my grandma," I tell him, even though I don't want to stay with her. She has three cats and every time I walk into her house, my eyes get so swollen that I can't blink.

"If you try to go to your grandma's, I will go there and drag you back here so I suggest that you just come here and save us both the trouble."

"Are you crazy?" I ask, thinking that I know the answer is yes. "I'm not going to stay here."

"We'll talk about it later." I have a feeling that we are not going to talk about it later and that he is going to try to boss me into doing what he wants me to do. I glare at him again and he has the nerve to laugh. Then his mom slides some eggs and toast in front of us and then comes around the island and sits down. I move out from between Asher's legs and sit on the stool between him and his mom. I turn towards her, completely dismissing him and he knows what I'm doing because he's still chuckling. He grabs my neck and kisses me again.

"Stop doing that," I tell him, glaring.

"Nope." It's all he says before letting me go and starting to eat.

"So, November, have you been to Nashville shopping?" his mom asks.

"Yeah, but only once. My grandma and I went up there to go shopping for a new computer."

"Oh, no, honey. I mean real shopping?" she says and I start laughing.

"My grandma's not a big shopper. We only went to Nashville once and before we left the house, she made me call the store we were going to and make sure that the stuff I needed was there and then had me put it on hold so all we had to do was walk in and pick it up."

"That sounds like her." She laughs. "You and I need to do a girl's day. We'll leave early and hit the shops then go get a mani-pedi."

"Really?" I breathe. I went all the time with my best friend, Tia, to get mani-pedi. I would always get jealous of the girls who were there with their moms. I always wanted to do that.

"Really," she says, touching my face. "How about Sunday?" she asks.

"Yeah, that would be great."

"It's a date." She is smiling again. "I never had a daughter. I kept trying for a girl and ended up with four boys. After that, I gave up. So this is going to be a lot of fun."

I had a mom, but my mom never asked me to go shopping with her let alone go shopping and get our nails done. Suddenly, tears start to sting my nose and she pulls me in for a hug. "I'm really looking forward to it."

"Yeah," I say, hugging her back.

We finish breakfast, then I let Beast outside as Asher walks his mom to her car. When he comes back in, he just looks at me and says, "Gotta make a call."

I go to his bathroom to get ready. I put on black leggings and an oversized off-the-shoulder sweatshirt in a soft peach color. It matches my ballet flats perfectly. Then I braid my hair to the side and it falls over my breast. I put on some blush, mascara, and lip gloss, then I finish with peach body spray.

I shove everything back into my bag and carry it with me to the living room. When I get there, Asher isn't there, or in the kitchen, so I look out the sliding glass door. He is standing in the yard in a pair of worn out blue jeans, his light brown work boots, and a dark gray thermal that fits like a second skin. Just looking at him makes my mouth go dry. I watch as Beast comes running at him with a stick in his mouth. Asher wrestles it away from him and throws it as Beast takes off. He looks so beautiful, playing with my dog. Then I remember what he said earlier. If I'm not mistaken, he is kind of my boyfriend. With that thought, I want to do some kind of acrobatics…or maybe a cheer. He kissed me and introduced me to his mom. Well, technically she just showed up, but that had to count, right?

Plus, he said this wasn't casual even though deep down, I don't completely trust what he was saying. But, I've decided that I'm going to give him the benefit of the doubt until he proves that he doesn't deserve it. He must feel me watching him because he turns around and smiles at me and my breath is stuck in my lungs. He calls Beast and they both come up the stairs at the same time and walk into the house. Without stopping to close the sliding door, he comes right to me, picks me up and kisses me. When he breaks away, I'm in another Asher kiss fog.

"You ready?" he asks and all I can do is nod. He slides me down his body and kisses my nose. My legs are jelly so I hold onto his T-shirt to keep me from falling on my face. He smiles like he knows what he's doing to me. I glare at him because no girl wants a guy to think that he's got it going on even if he does. "Okay, babe, get your ass to the jeep." He steps away and closes the door.

I watch him move then realize I'm just standing here watching him. I'm finally able to break out of the fog and grab my purse and overnight bag. I walk to the door with Beast at my side, saying over my shoulder, "Don't tell me to get my ass in your car. It's rude!" Then, I open the door and walk out to his jeep. His laughter follows me.

Chapter 4

W E PULL UP to my dad's house and he is standing outside. I start to open my door when Asher stops me. "Wait till I come around and open your door." This confuses me.

"Why?"

"Do you always have to ask questions?" I think about it for a minute then realize that I do always have to ask questions. Sometimes I ask questions that make no sense or questions that I know the answers to, but I still like to ask them. Asher is watching me and then he starts laughing.

"What's funny?"

"Nothing, baby. Just wait till I come around to open your door. Will you do that for me?" Because he asks nicely and isn't being bossy, plus he called me baby and I'm really starting to love that. I nod my head in agreement.

"Good," he says then kisses me softly and runs his nose across mine. I'm in such a fog that I don't even realize that he's gotten out of the car until my door opens and he's holding a hand out to me. His jeep is one of the cool ones with giant tires that were made for taking into the hills to go mudding.

"Do you go mudding?" I ask. Looking up at him, and not for the first time, I realize how tall he is compared to me. I come up to the middle of his chest and my head has to go way back to make eye contact. The good thing is I never have to worry that my heels will be too high. My ex never liked me wearing heels because he didn't want me to be taller than him.

"Mudding?" he asks, bringing me back to topic.

"Yeah, you know, where you drive a truck through mud and… I

don't know what else you do when you go mudding." He starts laughing again and I have no idea what is so funny, so I just wait till he gets control of himself.

"I haven't gone mudding since I was seventeen."

"Oh," I say with disappointment. I kind of wanted to go. Not that I know much about it, but I saw a video once and it looked like fun.

"If you want, we can take my four wheeler out and drive through some puddles during the next storm."

"Really?" I ask. That sounds like fun.

"This is why you're too much. Not too many women go from talking about getting manicures and shopping to wanting to get muddy."

"I'm versatile."

"Yeah." He kisses me, and just when it starts getting good, my dad yells at me.

"November!" Crap, I forgot where we are. I put my face in Asher's chest and giggle. My dad is mad. I've never made my dad mad before.

"November!" my dad calls again.

"Oh, Lord," I say, looking up at Asher. He is smiling down at me. I turn my head and my dad and Uncle Joe are standing on the porch. Both of them have their arms crossed and feet planted apart. I don't think this is going to go well. Asher grabs my hand and starts walking. I am dragging my feet behind him, trying to avoid the confrontation that is coming.

"Hi, Daddy. Hi, Uncle Joe," I say in my sweetest voice. My dad knows my game because he's glaring at me and Uncle Joe is shaking his head but his lips are twitching. Then I hear Asher chuckle and both Uncle Joe and my dad look at him like he has a death sentence.

"Oh, geez," I say, leaning my head back in exasperation. "I'm going to be twenty-five soon, so I'm way past the stage of my life where my dad tries to run men off," I say, pinning my dad with a glare of my own.

"You're never too old for me to look out for you and to make sure that every guy knows that if he tries to screw you over, I will shoot him."

"Okay," I say, looking up at Asher. "If you screw me over, my dad will shoot you." Asher looks down at me and I can see that he wants to smile but he's fighting it.

"Go inside and pack, baby," he says, running his knuckles down my jaw. I glare at him.

"I'm not staying with you." Geez, what is so hard to understand? We had one semi date. It's way too soon to start nightly sleepovers.

"You are," he says in a tone that I'm sure would work on someone, but that someone is not me.

"I'm not," I say, my voice getting louder. I look at my dad for support but I see that he is now fighting a smile. Then, I look to Uncle Joe and he's straight out smiling. What the heck?

"Baby girl," my dad calls and I look at him. "I think it would be best if you stayed somewhere at night until I can get a security system put in. But I agree that maybe Asher's place isn't the best bet. What if you went to stay with your uncle tonight?" Now I know I'm going to end up at Asher's. My uncle is a hardcore biker and always has some biker babe staying at his place. My grandma and I stopped by his house one day and there were two random women, both basically naked, wandering around his house.

Besides, he doesn't really have room for me. His sons are both older so he turned one of their rooms into a work out space and the other room into an office. He has a couch but I would rather not sleep on it knowing that some woman could come out of his room at any point.

Uncle Joe was married for eighteen years. From the time he found out that the woman was pregnant till his boys graduated high school. I never met the lady but from the stories I was told, she was a major bitch to him and his sons.

At the time, he felt he was doing the right thing by keeping his family together. But as soon as my cousins went to college, he no longer felt the need to pretend who he was. I guess under the suits that he used to wear to work he was secretly a bad ass biker.

"I'm staying with Asher. No offense, Uncle Joe," I say, looking at him with a smile and hoping he won't be mad. He smiles back at me and I know he doesn't mind.

"What about your grandmother?" my dad asks.

"I would stay with her but I'm afraid I might die from allergies." My dad looks like he is trying to come up with somewhere—anywhere—for me to stay. The moon, a convent, prison, perhaps? I don't think he cares as long as Asher is not there.

"Baby," Asher says, getting my attention. "I need to talk with your dad and uncle for a minute but I'll be in to say goodbye before I leave." He is looking down at me and then his eyes go to my dad.

"Alrighty, then," I say. I look at my dad and give him the look that says *be nice*. Then I start to walk away but I'm pulled back by my sweatshirt. I look over my shoulder at Asher and see he's holding on to me.

"You forget something?" he asks.

"Uh…no," I say, turning around to look at him and wondering what I could have forgotten.

"Kiss me," he says, with a completely serious expression. I can't believe he just said that in front of my dad.

"I'm not kissing you in front of my dad and uncle," I hiss at him and he has the nerve to smile.

"You kiss me or I'll kiss you. Make up your mind, and make it quick. I need to talk to your dad then I've got shit to do." I cross my arms over my chest and glare at him. He *cannot* be serious.

"Don't tell me to kiss you in fro—" I'm cut off when Asher pulls me to him and kisses me. It's closed mouthed and ends before it really starts, but I'm speechless that he just did that in front of my dad. I try to pull myself together but I'm completely stunned by what just happened. Then, I hear my dad laughing and I look at him just to make sure I'm not imagining things.

"Shouldn't you be getting your gun or something?" I say, looking at my dad while throwing my hand out in Asher's direction.

"Nope," he says, smiling. "Now I see what James was talking about when he called me this morning." My dad re-crosses his arms over his chest and leans back on the heels of his boots.

"Great! Just frickin' great," I mutter to the ground, rubbing my temples. I look up and glare at Asher. "Seriously, stop kissing me in front of our parents," I say, pointing at him. Then I turn around and stomp all the way up the stairs and into the house. I slam the door for good measure before I realize that I left Beast outside. I open the door and call Beast but all three heads turn to watch me. I glare at all of them then slam the door again.

This time, I can hear laughter from the other side. "Whatever," I mumble as I make my way down to my apartment.

SITTING ON ASHER'S back deck with my Kindle in my hand, my feet up on the railing, my head tilted back and enjoying the sun on my face, is practically paradise. I can hear Beast running back and forth in the yard, chasing something. I let my mind wander to thoughts about my day.

After my tantrum, I went down to my apartment and looked around. It was obvious that my uncle and Dad had been busy. The red was gone and there were three full garbage bags. I walked around to see if anything was missing but couldn't find anything out of place. The chair and couch were now garbage because the cushions had been slashed. I walked into my bedroom to make sure everything was in its place and it looked perfect. There were even yellow roses sitting on my side table. I walked to them and noticed the card.

You deserve beauty. Why are you forcing me to become ugly?

"What the heck?" I whispered. These were from the person who broke into my apartment. My hand started to shake and I wanted to cry. I knew my family had worked hard to make that space special for me and now I didn't even want to be down there. I sat on the ripped couch and had my face in my hands, thinking about how I was going to fix this. I smelled Asher and he pulled my hands away from my face. He was crouched in front of me and looked worried.

"Is everything okay?" I asked, thinking he and my dad got into it.

"I think I should ask you that," he said, pulling me up then sitting on the couch with me in his lap.

"Whoever did this left me flowers." I felt Asher freeze underneath me as I handed him the card.

"What the fuck," he whispered.

"How am I going to fix this?" I asked. "Everyone worked so hard for me to feel welcome and now this is happening and I don't even know why." He started rubbing my back so I cuddled into his chest with my head under his chin.

"I'm going to give this to my dad. The rest is just stuff, baby. Your family is just glad that nothing happened to you." He ran his fingers along my jaw then kissed the top of my head, I couldn't help but to sigh. I wanted to close everything off and pretend that this wasn't happening.

"I'm glad I wasn't here when it happened," I said, cuddling closer.

"November," my dad called from the top of the stairs. "Nick Stevenson is on the phone. He says he needs to talk to you." I felt Asher's body go tight under me again. I lifted my head to look at him and he was pissed.

"Nick who?" I called up the stairs.

"Nick Stevenson. His dad is a lawyer in town."

"What the fuck?" Asher clipped then he stood, taking me with him. He dragged me up to the kitchen where my dad left the phone on the counter. I watched in horror as Asher answered the phone. Well, if you understand caveman talk, he answered the phone.

"I know I made myself clear yesterday so why the fuck are you calling?" Asher growled into the phone.

"Oh my God, Asher. Give me the phone," I yelled as I reached around him, trying to grab the phone from his hand but he's so damn tall that it was useless.

"Hold on," Asher said, handing me the phone. I wanted to kick him but he wrapped his arms around me, holding me close. I was counting in my head, trying to keep calm and it wasn't working.

"Nick, I'm sorry," I said, apologizing for Asher's rudeness while shoving Asher but he didn't even move.

"Um, its okay, November. I'm calling to set up a time for you to meet with my father. He represented John and Ellen Armsted before they passed away and he needs to go over a few things with you regarding their will. Can you come into the office on Monday at around eleven?"

"I'm sorry, Nick, but I have no idea who John or Ellen are." I was completely confused. Armsted is my last name but John or Ellen didn't ring any bells.

"John and Ellen Armsted were your grandparents on your mother's side."

"Oh… Why do I need to see your dad?"

"It seems that your grandparents had you in their will before they passed away and my father needs to meet with you to talk about it. I don't know what it says but if you can meet here on Monday, he will discuss it with you."

"Um…sure. Monday at eleven," I said into the phone.

"Okay, November, see you then."

"Yeah, see you then," I said, confused about the conversation. I heard the phone cut off and felt Asher's arms give me a squeeze.

"Is everything okay?" I remembered what he did and I'm pissed at him. I turned in his arms and stood on my tiptoes so I could get in his face.

"I can't believe you answered the phone and worse, you were rude to Nick. He didn't do anything to you."

"Babe, he wants to get in your pants." I could feel my head getting ready to explode and I knew my eyes were bugging out.

"He does not."

"He does and that shit's not happening."

"Oh my God, you're insane. He just introduced himself to me at a bar because he noticed I was new. That's all it was. Then he calls to tell me that I need to meet with his dad because my grandparents put me in their will and you go all caveman on him for no reason." I pushed at his chest.

"Am I a man?" he asked.

"Yes," I snapped, not knowing why the heck he asked that stupid question.

"Then I think I know what the fuck I'm talking about."

"Whatever," I said with clenched teeth. "I don't have time to argue with you. I have stuff to do and you need to go to work."

"Don't be pissed, babe. It's done. Now he knows that I was serious yesterday. Hopefully he spreads that shit wide so I don't have to deal with anyone else."

"You do realize it's 2013, right?" I glared at him.

"Are you mine?" He nuzzled my neck then I felt his tongue and I forgot I was mad and he was rude and that, once again, he embarrassed me.

"Yes," I say, even though I was questioning my sanity. I just couldn't help it when his mouth was on my neck. Then, without warning, he picked me up. I squealed and my legs automatically went around his waist so I wouldn't fly back. My hand went to his shoulder, the other to his hair, feeling it prickle. One of his hands was at my ass, the other went up my back and into my hair. Then he tugged my hair to tilt my head while his went the other way. The kiss was hot and wild. He started walking and I felt the wall at my back and his heat hit my center. As I moaned into his mouth, he was grinding into me. He pulled his mouth away and set his forehead to mine.

"I fucking love your mouth, baby," he said against my lips.

"I kind of like yours too," I told him and laughed when he growled at me, grinding his hips into mine, making me whimper even more.

"Well, good thing I've got all night to make you love it." Oh, crap. With everything that has happened, I forgot that I'm going to be sleeping at his house again.

"We need to talk about tonight," I blurted out then bit my bottom lip. I mean, I'm okay with making out but sex…I wasn't sure about that.

"Listen," he said, grabbing my face while holding me up by his waist and the wall. "We don't have to do anything. We can go slowly."

"Okay," I whispered, feeling the tension leave my body.

"Okay," he whispered back then kissed me softly on my lips then my nose. My hands went to his shoulders and his to my ass then he slid me down and smiled. "I'll see you at my house. The key will be on your car key ring and I'll bring pizza back for dinner." He kissed me quickly and was gone before I could get out of my Asher fog and remember that he's a caveman and I should really question why the heck that turns me on.

After Asher left, the rest of my day was quiet. I packed a bag with enough stuff for a couple days. Dad and I hung around and I told him about the lawyer. He offered to take me if I wanted him to. I asked him how he felt about me and Asher and he said that he trusted him. It made me feel better that my dad approved. I was just going to have to try and take things slowly.

I spent the rest of the time begging him to teach me how to ride a motorcycle. Once he agreed, he had to go to bed so I decided to go into town. I wanted to look around at some of the antique shops to see if they had anything interesting.

I found a small side table that had a large round top with three legs that curved up and in. I couldn't wait to get the old white paint off it to see what kind of wood was underneath.

After I stowed the table in my car, I wandered into a small boutique on the square in the center of town. The window display was what caught my eye. They had a cool metal mannequin that would look perfect in my dream closet. When I walked in the store, there was an older lady behind the counter talking on the phone.

As soon as she saw me come in, she gave me a smile and a wave then went back to her conversation. Looking around, they had large and small mannequin stands. They also had all kinds of cool handbags, scarves, socks, jewelry, and other odds and ends that women don't really need but want anyway. I was in the back of the store looking at a mannequin stand. It was a metal frame painted pink with no head or arms. It was just the torso in the shape of a dress with a long pole out the bottom and three legs like a Christmas tree stand. I loved it. I could picture it in my dream closet or even just the corner of my bedroom.

"Can I help you?" I heard a small voice ask. I turned my head and a woman my age was standing next to me. She was about my height. Her long, blonde hair was pulled away from her face with a clip and she was very pretty, even without any makeup. She had on a pair of dark jeans and a green wrap shirt and cowboy boots.

"Yeah, how much for this stand?" I asked her, smiling.

"This is one hundred and twenty five," she mumbled like she didn't want to actually talk to me but was forced to because of her job.

"Really? Wow, I love it. Don't you love it?" Her head flew up and she looked me in the eye for the first time. They were light green with a ring of dark green. She had the most beautiful eyes I had ever seen besides Asher's.

"Yeah, it's nice," she said so quietly that I almost didn't hear her.

"I'm November," I said, sticking out my hand. She hesitantly shook it.

She looked a little surprised before she answered. "I'm Liz. Are you Mike's daughter?"

"Yeah. You know my dad?"

"He and my dad were best friends," she said quietly. I saw the look of sadness cross her face and I realized that she said were and not are.

"Well, it's nice to meet you, Liz. This is an amazing store. I can see where my paychecks will be going," I said, trying to change the subject and hating that she looked so lost. She laughed and the sadness was replaced with pride and her whole face became stunning.

"My mom and I own it. We just opened a few weeks ago. I grew up around here so if you ever want me to show you around, let me know," she said. Then she froze when we heard laughing from behind us. Two women were there. One I recognized from the bar.

"Oh, how cute. Liz is trying to make a friend," the taller of the two girls said.

"Some people never grow up," I mumbled under my breath, shaking my head. Having dealt with my mother, who was just like these women, I did what I always do. I ignored them. "I don't know many people in town. We should get together and have coffee sometime."

She looked a little surprised but recovered quickly. For some reason, I was proud of her. I got the feeling that she usually let what people said get to her.

"Um…sure. That would be nice. I'll give you my phone number when you finish shopping," she said, turning and going through a curtain into the backroom of the store. I looked around for a few more minutes and the girls were still in the store. I heard them whispering and could make out Asher's name a few times but I couldn't be bothered with them so I went to check out. I found a very pretty scarf that had a bold paisley print in lots of bright colors and a pair of wide silver hoops with a cool design etched into them. I set my stuff on the counter and the woman looked up to me.

"Did you find everything okay, dear?"

"Yes. I would also like to buy that stand in the back. The pink one," I told her with a smile, thinking about my new treasures.

"Sure. I'll have Liz pull it out for you."

"Thanks." She gave me my total and when Liz came back out, we exchanged numbers. I told her that I would call. I went to my dad's and dropped off my new stuff and packed up Beast. I quickly left my dad a note telling him to call me later and drove to Asher's.

Now, I'm enjoying the sun that is slowly setting. There is a slight chill in the air but I put on my knit hat and giant wool sweater so I feel nice and toasty. My hair slides across my neck and then lips kiss the sensitive skin under my ear. I open my eyes to see Asher smiling down at me.

"Hey, baby. I've been looking for you," he whispers.

"Hi." I stretch, sitting up and looking around. "I guess I fell asleep," I say quietly, realizing that I'm still sitting outside but it's dusk and really cold.

"Yeah, I got worried when I couldn't find you in the house. Where is your phone? Your dad and I tried calling you."

"Oh, crap. I think it's still in my bag. I wasn't planning on being out here so long."

"Let's get you inside," he says, picking me up. My arms go around his shoulders and I lay my head on his chest. His body is so warm and he smells so good.

"I can walk," I mumble into his chest.

"I like carrying you. You're so tiny," he says and I feel him kiss my forehead.

"Ha! Only to you because you're a giant," he laughs and I can feel it rumble against my cheek as he carries me into the living room and sits with me in his lap. I curl into him for a few minutes just absorbing his warmth and the feel of his steady breathing. It should feel awkward to be with him like this but it feels completely normal. How creepy is that?

"What do you want on the pizza, baby?" he asks, rubbing my back. I feel like I could fall back asleep.

"Um, mushrooms, peppers, olives, and pepperoni, unless you want something else."

"Nope, sounds good." I feel him lift his hips and his hand leaves my back. I can hear the beeping of his phone before he places our order. After he hangs up the call, I hear the phone hit the coffee table.

"Did you have a good day?" I ask into his chest.

"No. The fire inspector wanted to close the site and Cash had to go to the hospital to get stitches." The second the words are out of his mouth, I'm up, trying to pull out of his arms.

"Oh my God! What are you doing? You should be with him. Is he okay? Who's taking care of him?" I yell, trying hard to pull away.

"He's fine. Mom's with him. He just cut his hand. Calm down."

"How many stitches did he need?"

"Just three. Why are you so worried?" he asks, narrowing his eyes. Suddenly, he looks angry.

"He was hurt and he's your brother," I say slowly. "What do you mean, why am I worried?" I ask. I'm confused. He doesn't say anything.

He just stares at me then I realize why he's asking that question and I want to kick him. "Seriously? Your own brother?" I ask, shaking my head in disbelief and again trying to pull away.

"Let me up," I say but his arms only tighten. "I'm serious, Asher. Let me up right now. I cannot believe you would even think that I would be sitting here with you if I was even a little interested in your brother. I mean, obviously we don't know each other very well but if you want to get to know me, you're going to have to trust me. Otherwise, don't waste my time." I pull away and am finally able to stand. I leave him sitting on the couch and go into the bathroom. I hop up on the counter, wondering what the hell is wrong with him. First Nick, now his brother. I want to scream at the top of my lungs.

The door opens and I look up. He's just standing there, looking at me, and not saying anything. I'm beginning to feel like I shouldn't be here anymore and should risk respiratory failure and stay with my grandma.

"I think I should go stay with my grandma," I say quietly.

He still doesn't say anything and I start to squirm on the counter under his stare. Then I see him take a deep breath and he lunges at me his mouth crashes into mine. His hands go to my ass, pulling me to the edge of the counter.

I'm caught off guard but my body takes over and my hand goes to his back. My other hand digs into his hair as he bites my bottom lip, then lightly bites my chin and then comes back to my mouth where he devours me.

His tongue is in my mouth and playing with mine, nipping and biting my lips. I feel one of his hands leave my ass and travel around and up the front of my shirt, cupping my breast through my bra. I whimper into his mouth and try to press closer, knowing my panties are soaked. I don't think I've ever been so turned on in my life. Then he pulls away, kissing me softer and setting his forehead to mine.

"You're not going anywhere," he rumbles and I feel the vibrations of his words straight between my legs.

"I don't want to go anywhere," I tell him truthfully, knowing that I should leave because this situation has heartache written all over it.

He presses his forehead to mine and takes a breath. "Almost every woman that I've fucked has also fucked one or more of my brothers," he says quietly.

I can feel bile crawling up my throat and a horrible pain hits my chest at his words. He is actually opening up to me but I'm not sure I want to know this.

I don't know why, but I feel like I need to share something about me to make us even, to make him understand that he isn't the only one with baggage.

"I was engaged and found out that my mother had been sleeping with my fiancé during the whole time we were together," I blurt out and immediately wonder why the hell I said it like that. Why can't I just keep my damn mouth shut? "I'm sorry. I shouldn't have told you like that. It's just...I know how you feel. Well, not that I have sisters but if I did I would tell them that it's really gross. I mean who does that?"

I feel his body start shaking and I wonder what the hell could be funny about this conversation. "Are you laughing?" I feel his body still and he takes his face out of my neck. He gently wraps his hands around my neck, running his nose along mine.

"I'm not letting you go, November." His eyebrows pull together and I can see something working behind his eyes. It looks like hope but I don't know him well enough to be sure.

"Just try to trust me, okay," I say, watching my finger travel across his bottom lip. He places his forehead against mine again and doesn't say anything for a long time. What is he thinking?

"I'm gonna try," he says softly, taking a deep breath.

"I'm going to try too, you know?" I say, trying to lighten the mood. "I feel like I have a lot of competition to deal with. All those women constantly throwing themselves at you." He opens his eyes and looks at me seriously.

"I promise that it's you, only you, for as long as this lasts. Now, we need to pick up the pizza so get your ass in the jeep." And just like that, the conversation's over and he's pulling me off the sink and onto my feet. He kisses my nose and walks out of the bathroom, leaving me there with his words replaying in my head.

It's you, only you.

I smile to myself in the mirror and walk out to the living room. I grab my bag then get my ass in his jeep.

I WAKE UP wrapped around Asher. My thigh is over his, my arm is across his waist and his arm is holding me close. Last night, after we got the pizza, we came back to his house, put in a movie and lounged on the couch while we ate. Then he moved the pizza box, got us both another beer, and stretched out with his bare feet up on the coffee table and dragged me by the hand until I was pressed into his side with my leg wrapped over his thigh and my arm around his waist, holding my beer and my head on his chest. After the movie, we got up and Asher pushed me toward the bedroom, telling me to get ready for bed and that he would let Beast out.

I did my normal nightly routine, brushed my teeth, moisturized, took my hair down and brushed it out. I dug out my pajamas. This time it was a nightgown with slim straps and a built-in bra. The cotton material gathered under the breast and went to above the knee. It was cute and not too sexy for sleeping with a new boyfriend. Well, I thought so anyways until Asher walked in. "Jesus," he mumbled and I watched in fascination as his eyes got dark.

Without saying anything else, or touching me at all, he pulled out something from his dresser then went into the bathroom and closed the door. As soon as the door closed behind him, I ran to the bed and jumped in, pulling the blankets up around my waist. Then I reached over to turn on the lamp. When he came back out, he was shirtless and wearing a pair of flannel pajama pants that looked hot on him. They hung low, showing the V of his hips and I could feel my mouth water just watching him.

He turned off the bedroom light then walked to the opposite side of the bed and got in. I sat there for a second then leaned over and turned off the light next to me. I laid down and pulled the covers up over my shoulder. The next thing I knew, I was being pulled across the bed, my back to Asher's front, his arm around my waist and his legs bent into mine. He moved my hair off my shoulder gently.

"Night, baby," he whispered then kissed me where my neck and shoulder met.

"Night," I whispered, cuddling closer and listening to his breathing even out. I felt his body relax a few minutes later and I quickly followed him to sleep.

I PLACE MY nose against his ribs and take a deep breath, absorbing his smell. It's earthy and spicy and all Asher. I feel his hand flex on my hip where he's holding me and I scoot closer. Suddenly, I'm on my back, looking up at his face. Rumpled with sleep, he's still beautiful.

"Morning." His voice is scratchy and rough and does serious stuff to my insides. His eyes are warm as he leans down and kisses me softly. Moving his face away, he holds my face in his hands.

"Morning." I breathe deeply, looking up at him and wondering what he's thinking. "Are you okay?"

"I like waking up to you." I don't say anything back but I can feel my face get soft. I like waking up to him too. "So what do you want to do today?" he asks as he nuzzles my neck. I wrap my leg around his hip and my arm around his back, feeling the hardness of his muscles and the smoothness of his skin.

"Will you take me out on your four wheeler?" I ask. He lifts his head and smiles down at me.

"How about we load 'em up. Mom and Dad have two-hundred acres and a few ponds on their property. I'll call the guys and see if they want to go four wheeling."

"Oh my God, yes!" I scream excitedly then I roll him over, straddling his hips. I bend down and kiss him quickly then go to jump off him but I'm held down by his hands at my hips. I look at his face and see his eyes are dark and hooded. I know I'm in trouble when his hands slide from my hips, down my thighs, and up under my nightgown.

I feel the length of him pressed to my core and become instantly wet as his hands travel over my ribs. His thumbs move over the sensitive skin under my breasts and my breathing becomes erratic. My nipples go instantly hard. He sits up and kisses me as one of his hands move to my ass and the other grabs my hair, tilting my head. He tastes so good that my hands go to his head, holding him close. He bends me back so I'm under him. My legs go around his waist and he kisses me deeply then sits back, looking down at me.

We are both breathing heavily and I want his mouth back. I whimper as I feel his fingers at my hip, running down my thigh. He's watching them travel over my skin. When his eyes lock with mine, he bends his head and takes my mouth again. His tongue is against mine briefly then moves to my neck, licking and biting. His hand travels up my side to my breast, and I feel the air against my nipple just before his mouth is on me, sucking hard. My back bows off the bed and I hold his head against me, trying to pull him closer. I'm shocked when I feel like I might orgasm just from this.

I moan and he growls, releasing my breast then attacking my other nipple while his fingers roll and pull the one he just left. My hips lift into his and the friction hits me just right. I shatter into a million pieces, moaning his name as my legs tighten around him. My fingers are gripping his head while I come back slowly.

Opening my eyes, I see that he's looking down at me. "Fucking beautiful," he says, kissing me again. This time, it's much harder.

I kiss him back while my hand goes to his stomach. I can feel his muscles tense under my fingers and I drag my nails along his skin. Then my nightgown is gone, over my head, and Asher's body is covering mine. His chest is against mine, his mouth is devouring mine and I roll him over and straddle his hips. His hips rise up as mine go down and I moan. My head flies back and then his mouth is on my nipple. He rolls me back over and his fingers go inside my panties and press in.

"Fucking soaked." He growls and that just makes me wetter. "Jesus, I can't wait to taste you." His fingers swirl over my clit and I grab onto his bicep, my head flies back. His fingers fill me so perfectly that my hips lift off the bed.

I pull his head down to mine and kiss him deeply. "Please," I beg. I need more.

"I'm not letting you come again until I can taste you doing it, baby." I feel my self-contract at his words and he starts sliding my panties down my legs.

"Yo! Get your lazy ass out of bed." My head jerks up. "What the fuck," the person says then I hear barking and growling coming from Beast.

"What the fuck?" Asher growls then the alarm starts going off. "Jesus Christ," he mutters, rolling off the bed and I sit up, trying to find my nightgown. He puts an arm on each side of my waist then kisses me like my dog is not about to kill someone and the alarm is not going off. It's wet and deep and I'm breathing heavily when he pulls away. "Come to the kitchen, baby," he says, putting a shirt on and walking out of the room. The alarm stops and I jump off the bed, pull my nightgown down over my head, and then run to the bathroom.

I brush my teeth, dig through my bag to find a hoodie, and put it on over my nightgown then go to the kitchen. Asher is standing near the coffee pot and there is a guy sitting at the island. He's slim but you can tell that he's also muscular. His dark brown hair is messy and his face is model perfect with long lashes, dark eyes, and full lips.

He's looking at me strangely then his eyes drop to my legs. I feel so uncomfortable that I know I'm not going to be able to stand in the same room as him wearing what I have on so I turn and run back to the bedroom. I find my sweats and tank and put them on quickly. When I go back out, the guy is smirking at me but Asher is just smiling. "Come here, baby," he says quietly, lifting his arm as I walk to him. My face goes into his chest and I feel his lips at my hairline. "November, this is Sven. Sven, November."

"Hi. Nice to meet you," I say and he's looking between Asher and me. I can tell that he is guarded, and that's okay. I feel the same.

"You too, November."

I smile at him then look around for Beast. I hear his paw on the door so I leave Asher's side and slide the door open.

Once again, I'm trampled by my dog. I fall on my butt and he's licking me and standing over me. I try to push him off but he's too excited and I'm laughing so hard that tears start to fall from my eyes. Then Beast is pushed away and Asher is there, smiling down at me.

"Baby, we need to get you a smaller dog," he says, picking me up off the floor.

"He just gets a little excited." I laugh and Asher runs his nose along mine.

"Beautiful," he whispers then kisses me softly and puts me back under his arm. He walks me back around the island and I'm in such a fog that I forget for a second that someone else is here with us.

I look up at Asher and smile big, biting my lip and realizing that I could fall in love with him. I look at Sven, he smiles and winks like he's reading my mind. I smile back.

"Coffee?" Asher asks, giving me a squeeze.

"Yes, please. Can I, um, make breakfast?" I ask, unsure if that might cross a line.

"If you want." He shrugs.

"Okay," I say and go about getting everything ready for French toast. Once it's done, I slide some on a plate for Sven, Asher, and myself. I find syrup and butter and put them out on the counter in front of the guys then grab the coffee pot and fill their cups. Everything has gone silent so I look up and both of them are staring at me like I'm crazy. "Um…"

"You gonna eat, baby?" I nod my head. "Come here, November." I walk towards him even though I want to run and hide in the bathroom. Once I'm in front of him, he pulls me onto his lap and pulls my plate toward us so mine and his are next to each other then he hands me my fork.

"I can sit on the other stool," I say quietly.

I feel his lips under my ear. "I want you close." He kisses my neck and goes about eating and talking to Sven. "I'm taking November to Mom and Dad's to go four wheeling. I'll call the boys and see if they want to meet there. You wanna go?" he asks Sven. Sven just looks at me.

"You want to go four wheeling?" Sven asks with a look of shock written all over his handsome face.

"Yes! I'm so excited," I squeal and clap, which makes him and Asher chuckle. "Hey, can I invite Liz?" I turn, looking over my shoulder at Asher.

"Who's Liz?" he asks.

"I met her yesterday. She owns a store on the square with her mom. She's really sweet. Some of your harem were there giving her a hard time." I roll my eyes and I hear Sven chuckle.

"Harem?" Asher questions with his eyebrow raised.

"The girls from the bar that were all gathered around the pool table waiting to be chosen like a bad episode of the bachelor," I say, giggling when Asher starts tickling my sides.

"Well, I chose you, so I guess you get my pool stick."

"Did you seriously just say that?" I ask, scrunching up my nose, laughing. I look at Sven who is also cracking up.

"Call your friend. Just have her meet us there. I'll give you the address." He, smiles and kisses my neck.

"Cool," I say, smiling back.

After breakfast, Asher and Sven leave to load up the four wheelers while I clean up the kitchen and jump in the shower. I'm standing in Asher's bedroom, wrapped in a towel, when Asher walks into the room. I automatically feel like prey to a very large, very hungry predator.

"Jesus, I feel like I'm living a fucking nightmare."

"What?" I whisper, feeling uncomfortable all of the sudden, wondering if I read his expression wrong.

"Having you wrapped around me all night, feeling you come around my fingers, now wrapped in a towel and knowing what's under that shit and not being able to do a damn thing about it is my worst fucking nightmare."

Oh my God, my nipples go hard and my breath hitches at his words. I want him to do something about it and I am trying not to run across the room. He lunges before I can make a move and I am in his arms with his mouth on mine. I go into an instant Asher fog. He breaks away, shoving his face in my neck.

"Tonight," he growls, biting my neck then letting me go. He goes straight into the bathroom, closing the door behind him. I can hear the shower turn on. I run to my bag and pull out jeans, a plain red T-shirt, and a red lace bra and matching lace cheeky panties. I dress fast and am braiding my hair when Asher comes out with a towel wrapped around his waist and water dripping down the contours of his body. I am completely lost and know what he was talking about when he said he was living a nightmare. Part of me wants nothing more than to throw myself at him but the other part of me is afraid that once we have sex, he will get bored and lose interest.

"I'm gonna get dressed, baby, so unless you want to watch, you should go wait in the kitchen."

"I'll be in the kitchen," I squeak then walk quickly out of the room.

Chapter 5

I CALL LIZ and ask her to come four wheeling. She says she is working at her shop and can't make it so we make plans to meet up Monday after my meeting with the lawyer.

Asher drives us out to his parents' house. Everyone is standing outside a huge, steel building when we arrive. They're gassing up the four wheelers and bikes.

I've never ridden before, so Asher shows me what to do. I really only hear half of what he says because my excitement is taking over. We take off on the trails around his parents' place and ride for a couple hours.

Eventually, the guys start racing, so Sven say he will teach me how to ride his dirt bike while Asher is racing his dad. I am practicing my balance when Asher comes around the corner and sees me on the dirt bike. I watch Asher walk over and shove Sven then he slings his hand out in my direction. I can see his mouth moving but I have a helmet on so I can't hear what is being said.

I stop the bike and Cash holds it up while I get off. I walk towards Asher. His mom and dad are standing to the side while he yells at his friend about how in the hell he let me get on his bike. Hearing what he is saying pisses me off. I'm not some helpless child who needs constant supervision.

"Is everything okay?" I ask, crossing my arms over my chest. I look around and notice everyone is watching.

"What the hell are you thinking?" Asher glares at me. "That bike is too big for you. Do you realize you could be seriously hurt?"

"Are you serious?" I ask, looking at him like he grew a third eye. I can hear the guys chuckling behind us.

"Deadly fucking serious," he growls.

"You listen to me, Asher. You are not the boss of me. I'm going to learn how to ride a motorcycle and then I'm going to buy one so I can ride it whenever I want, and there is not a damn thing you can do about it," I say, poking him in the chest.

"Fuck, no, you're not."

"My dad's teaching me on his next day off," I say, smiling sweetly.

"Baby, I'm telling you right now, if you think I'm going to let you ride, you're crazy."

"And, baby," I say sarcastically, "I'm telling you that I don't need your permission to do anything."

"We'll see," he growls then pulls me into his chest and kisses me hard with tongue while everyone watches. When he brakes the kiss, I am in such a fog that I don't even yell at him for kissing me in front of his parents. He puts his arm around my shoulder and pulls me into his side. I look around and everyone is smiling. I am wondering what the hell just happened. We were arguing then we weren't…is that normal?

"Alright, kiddos. Let's go eat," Asher's mom calls loudly. I start giggling and Asher just looks down at me, smiling.

"What?" I shrug my shoulders. "She makes me feel like I'm five years old."

Asher's mom makes amazing BBQ pulled pork in her crockpot then toasts giant potato buns and loads them with meat. She even makes sweet potato fries and homemade coleslaw. It is delicious.

We sit around a large fire pit, drinking and eating, then she brings out marshmallows, graham crackers and chocolate bars so we can make smores. It is perfect.

I am tucked close to Asher with my belly full and my favorite hard apple cider in my hand. Life can't get any better than this. The guys start telling stories about tricks they played on each other when they were younger and other stupid things they did.

"So Asher and me used to skateboard when we were in high school," Sven says, starting his story. "One time, we were out riding around when Asher fell while trying to do a trick off a set of stairs near the library.

Well, he missed his landing and ended up doing the splits down the stairs, hurting his groin muscle. We went back to my house so he could put some ice on it. I was in the kitchen getting ice out for him when I heard him screaming from the bathroom like a damn girl. I ran to the bathroom to figure out what happened. I banged on the door and he didn't answer. All I could hear was moaning and crying. So, I said fuck it and walked into a scene that, to this day, is still burned into the back of my eyelids. Your man," he says, looking at me and laughing, "was laying on the floor in the bathroom with a jar of icy/hot He decided to put that shit on his groin, thinking it would help. He got that shit on his balls and almost passed out from the pain."

I am laughing so hard, I fall backwards off the log that we are sitting on. I haven't ever had this much fun and I am dirtier than I have ever been in my life. I have mud in my hair, on my face, and all over my clothes. I'm sure I look like a homeless person but everyone else is just as dirty. Even Asher's mom is covered in dirt. I love all of them and I love Tennessee. The laid-back lifestyle and the friendly people are so different from New Yorkers.

I realize, lying on the ground in the dirt, that I am happy. Really, really happy for the first time in my life. Asher leans over and helps me back up on the log. He puts me back under his arm and kisses my nose, smiling.

"I'm stealing your girl," Sven deadpans.

"Fuck, no," Asher says, smiling at him. The guys go back to talking about the jobsite and things they have to get done before the next inspection, while Susan and I plan our trip to Nashville the next day.

"So, I'll pick you up around nine," she tells me.

"Okay, sounds good."

"Twelve, Mom. No earlier," Asher says, breaking into our conversation.

"Nine," his mom says, looking at him, daring him to disagree.

"Twelve. Tomorrow is Sunday and we're sleeping in."

"Ni—"

"Susan," Mr. Mayson says in a warning tone to his wife then he pulls her into his lap and whispers in her ear. She melts against him then looks over at me.

"I'll be there at twelve." I nod my head in agreement then giggle when she laughs. Apparently, Asher takes after his dad.

I crawl into Asher's lap and cuddle into him while everyone sits around talking. I must have fallen asleep because the next thing I know, I am being put into the front seat of Asher's jeep.

"We'll be home soon, baby," he whispers and I feel his lips at my forehead. I am back asleep before he shut my door.

I feel the car come to a stop and I lift my head from Asher's shoulder, where it had fallen.

"Hey, sleepy head," he says, looking over at me.

"This was the best day ever," I say, smiling. I grab his face and kiss him hard.

"Yeah," he says with his eyes running over my face. He kisses my nose and opens his door to let Beast out on his side. I meet him in front of the jeep and we walk into the house with me leaning into his side. I don't pull away until we are in the living room.

"I'm going to shower," I tell him and stumble my way to the bathroom. I take off my dirty shoes and socks but am waiting for the water to get hot before I fully undress.

I turn on the shower and feel warmth hit my back and Asher's hand slides along my belly. I turn my head to ask what he is doing when I catch the look in his eyes. He uses his hands to turn me by my waist, his fingers at the edge of my shirt as a shiver runs down my spine and heat floods my center. He lifts the edge of my shirt and pulls it up over my head. His eyes are on my red lace bra and his finger trace the edge of it. I put my hands up the front of his shirt, feeling his smooth skin. He takes my hands away from his body and puts them on the wall behind his head. Dragging his shirt up and over, his hands then come to the button of my jeans. My stomach muscles contract at his touch. My breaths are becoming erratic from having him this close to me, touching him. Asher touching me. I pray that no one interrupts us this time and quickly move my hands to the front of his jeans.

Without warning, he captures my hands and pulls them away from his skin. Startled, I look up at him. His mouth crashes into mine; his tongue sweeps the seam of my mouth and mine opens under his. My hands grab his head, holding him closer, deepening the kiss. His hands slid down my waist to my ass and he picks me up. My jeans fall to the floor and my legs circle his hips. He walks five steps to set me down on the basin of the sink. His hand go to my hair and he tugs out my hair tie. My hair falls down around me and he wraps a fist in it, tugging my head to the side so he can kiss me harder.

My body is on fire and my panties are soaked. I tighten my legs around him, trying to get some friction to relieve the ache that he created. He growls and pulls his lower body slightly away from me. I whimper and my head falls back against the mirror. His lips trail down my neck, breathing heavily. My thighs start shaking as he kisses down my neck, over my collarbone, to the edge of my lace bra. Then his mouth is sucking my nipple through the lace. The friction is intense. "Asher," I whimper.

"I know, baby." Then he sucks harder and I can feel his teeth scrape against my sensitive flesh. His hand travels down my side to the edge of my panties. Near my hip, I feel his finger sliding under the edge and traveling along the inside of my thigh. He is approaching my core and I start panting. His hands and mouth feel amazing on me but I need more.

Biting my lip, I look down at him. It is the most erotic thing I've ever seen. His hand pulls down the cups of my bra then his mouth latches back on. His hand goes to my other nipple, pulling and rolling it between his fingers. My head thrashes then his mouth is back on mine. My hands travel down his back, around to the front of his jeans so I can get his button undone.

I use my toes to shove his jeans and boxers down his hips then I watch as he springs free. His cock is as beautiful as he is. Long and thick.

I just want to wrap my mouth around it but I am pinned to the counter. I wrap my hand around him and pump once.

"Shit!" Asher growls and pulls away from my grasp. His mouth is trailing down my body, licking and biting. His hand goes to my panties and he grabs the material at my core and rips it away. "You're soaked, baby. Do you want my mouth or my cock?" This is such a complicated question.

I want both but all I can say is, "Please." Then his hot mouth is on me sucking, licking, and consuming me like he is starving. His hands go to my ass, pulling me closer. My hands go to his head, holding him to me. His fingers slide in and I shatter, screaming out his name. My body is shaking. Never have I felt this way in my life. It is one of those mind blowing, body shaking orgasms that everyone talks about. I float slowly back to earth.

When I open my eyes, Asher is leaning over me. "Please tell me you're on birth control."

"Yes," I cry, feeling the length of him against me. Then he slams into me. I scream his name and his forehead drops to my chest and he stills his movements. I roll my hips, trying to get him to give me what I need.

His head comes up. "Don't move, baby," he whispers. I watch as he takes a deep breath then he pulls out and slides back in.

My back bows. "Please, Asher," I cry, digging my nails into his back.

"Hold onto me, baby."

I grab on to him and wrap my legs around his waist. He carries me to the bed. Once he lays me down, he grabs my hips and slams into me over and over. My head goes back and my eyes close. He is hitting the perfect spot and his fingers are digging into my hips. The pain and pleasure I am feeling is making me cry out with each thrust.

"Look at me," he growls. My head tips down and he kisses me deeply. I take my mouth away and my head flies against the mattress as I feel myself start to come. "Look at me, November," he growls again and my eyes come to his. "You don't come until I come with you," he says, pounding into me.

"I'm going to come now," I tell him, feeling my insides tighten.

"Not yet. Hold it." Oh God, I don't know if I can hold it. My body is on fire. I bite down on his shoulder, trying to control my orgasm.

"Fuck, come now," he roars and I feel him swell as my body explodes around him.

I am floating with a million colors dancing around me. My face goes into his neck, my arms and legs tighten around him, holding him close. We stay like this for a long time, just holding each other close. Our breathing evens out and he lifts his head. I pull my face out of his neck.

"Are you okay, baby?" he asks, his eyes searching my face.

"Amazing," I say, leaning in and kissing him softly.

"Fuck, your pussy is as beautiful as you are." He tightens his arms around me. "And as sweet as your mouth." I have never had a guy go down on me before. I thought it would be uncomfortable but it was amazing. All I can do is smile. "What's that look?" he asks.

"Um, I've never done that before. I mean, I've done it but never had a guy do that to me." He starts chuckling. His body is still surrounding me and I can still feel him inside me.

"You're kidding, right?" he asks. I feel embarrassed and my body goes tight. I look over his shoulder, wondering why I have no filter with him. It is like whatever is on my mind comes out like word vomit.

"We should…um…turn off the shower," I tell his shoulder. That isn't a lie. There is steam rolling out of the bathroom.

"Baby, look at me."

"I'm just saying we don't want to run out of hot water."

"November, look at me." At his tone, my eyes go to his. He cups my cheek in his big palm and kisses me softly. "You never have to be embarrassed. Trust me, I'm fucking thankful that I'm the only one who has gotten to see you like that." I feel my nose sting and I shove my face in his neck.

"Okay," I whisper. He makes me feel beautiful and special, like I have known him forever rather than just a few days.

"Now, let's have a shower," he says, picking me up. My legs are still around him and I can feel him inside me. The movement causes me to moan. "You're going to get soapy and play with yourself while I watch."

"What?" I whisper, feeling nervous and excited.

"You heard me," he says, nipping my neck. He stands me up in the shower and hands me a bottle of body wash and a sponge. As directed, I get soapy and play with myself. Then, he plays with me. Then, I play with him.

When we get out and dried off, he carries me to bed without bothering with clothes. He wraps his body around mine and we fall asleep. It is definitely the best day of my life.

SO MAYBE, I'M more like my grandmother than I thought. I love shopping as much as the next woman but seriously, it's almost ten at night and we're just now heading home from our girls' day out.

The day started with Asher waking me with his mouth and fingers then he had me get on top and ride him until we both collapsed back into bed, breathing heavily. We made breakfast and drank coffee out on the deck while watching Beast chase wild turkeys around the yard.

Asher's mom showed up at eleven thirty when I was in the bathroom putting on makeup. I still had to put my clothes on so I chose a pair of dark jeans and an empire waist floral tank top and a mint green cardigan over it with knee high brown boots. They have a low heel so they're comfortable for walking.

I walked into the kitchen and Asher was standing near the sink in jeans, bare feet, and a black thermal long sleeve shirt that had buttons at the neck that were undone. His face was extra scruffy so he looked exceptionally sexy. I wanted to send his mom home and drag him back to bed for the day.

His eyes came to me and he did a head-to-toe inspection and gave me a sweet smile. His eyes were warm, and as I bit my lip, they dropped to my mouth and I got the dimple.

"Are you ready to go, beautiful girl?" his mom asked, making me jump. I felt heat hit my cheeks because I forgot she was there the minute I saw Asher.

"Um, yeah. Can we stop at my dad's so I can drop off Beast?" I asked, looking at her.

"Beast is going with me, baby. I'm meeting Trevor to help him with some shit at his house."

"Are you sure?" I asked.

"Yeah, now come kiss me before you leave."

"Asher," I said in a warning tone.

"Baby, get your ass over here. If I have to come to you, you're not going to like it." I felt my nipples tighten at his tone. I wasn't so sure that I didn't want to see what he would do.

"You do know that you're not the boss of me, right?" I asked, crossing my arms over my chest to hide how turned on I was. He didn't miss the gesture and a smug smile slid across his face. "Whatever," I muttered and grabbed my bag off the island.

Looking at Asher's mom, I asked, "Ready?"

Before I could make it five steps, I was spun around and Asher's mouth was on mine. I tried to fight him but his hand twisted into the hair at the back of my head. I gasped then his tongue was in my mouth. I couldn't help but to kiss him back.

When he tore his mouth from mine, he moved his lips near my ear and whispered, "You're mine. Every inch of you belongs to me. From your sweet mouth to your even sweeter pussy and when I want it, you better give it to me."

He bit my earlobe then kissed my nose. I was in a complete Asher-fog when I heard Susan call my name. I looked at her and she was smiling. I looked up at Asher and he kissed my nose again. "Have fun, baby."

I narrowed my eyes on him, praying for magical powers that would set him on fire. This didn't happen and I rolled my eyes. Susan moved to stand in front of Asher.

"Have fun, Ma, and take care of my girl," he said, bending down to kiss her cheek. He walked us to the door. His mom walked out before me so I slowed my steps and turned around.

Standing on my tiptoes, I kissed Asher and quickly ducked my head before he could get his arms around me. I ran out the door to his mom's truck. "Bye, honey. Have a good day," I yelled, looking over my shoulder and laughing.

Asher was standing on the porch with his arms crossed and feet planted apart. His dimple was out. I hopped up in the truck and shut the door. I heard Asher call Beast over to him. I waved as we backed out of the driveway. Asher didn't wave but I did get a chin lift so that's pretty much the same thing.

"I never thought I would have a front row seat to my eldest son falling in love," Susan said. I looked over at her, dumbfounded.

"What? I don't think so," I said, looking out the window and trying to fight my smile.

"Oh, yes, honey. I know so. You know, James grew up in this town. I moved here after college to work in the hospital. When I got to town, I was warned by dozens of women about him. They all said he was so good looking that he had a different woman in his bed every night. Well, I made it my mission to stay away from him. Why would I want a man who obviously wasn't faithful and never wanted to settle down? Then one night, I got a flat tire on my way home. A very handsome man pulled up and helped me get the spare on my car. I had no idea who he was until after he finished and introduced himself. When he said his name, I got out of there as fast as possible.

"The next day, I ran into him in town and he asked me out. I said no and he walked away, so I thought that was it. But then everyday he would be somewhere that I was. He would ask me out and I would say no. This went on for about two months. Then one day, I finally said yes but made him promise to never ask me out again. He agreed so we went out on one date. Next thing I knew, I was staying at his house, he put a ring on my finger, and I was planning a wedding. All of that happened in just a few months. And if you talk to his mom, she will tell you a similar story about her and James Sr. I think the Mayson men don't bother getting serious until they see someone that they can't live without."

"Um, Asher was already married," I reminded her. I liked Asher a lot but I was not going to get my hopes built on false dreams.

"He was for about three months. I never met the girl and didn't even know she existed until a couple weeks after they were married when she answered the phone at Asher's apartment. I'm not a man but I would think that if I found a woman I was going to spend the rest of my life with, I would want my family to know about her."

"Can we talk about something else?" I asked, trying not to sound rude but wanting to change the topic. The thought of Asher in love with someone enough to marry her made my stomach turn.

"Sure, beautiful," she said, grabbing my hand and giving it a squeeze.

"Thanks," I whispered, squeezing her hand back.

We stopped for coffee on our way out of town then headed to Nashville for a day of shopping and manicures.

Asher

WATCHING NOVEMBER PULL away with my ma, I get that feeling in my chest, the same one I get every time November smiles at me. It's like taking a shot of whiskey. After the burn, you're left with the warmth. I wait till I can't see the truck anymore and drag my hands down my face. Beast barks, getting my attention.

"Come on. We got shit to do," I tell him, walking into the house. Fuck me if I'm not starting to sound like her. She's always carrying on one-sided conversations with the dog like she expects him to talk back.

I walk into the bedroom and see that she made the bed while she was in here getting ready. She left the bathroom light on so I go to turn it off. There is girly shit all over the counter. I wait to see if I feel panic and none comes. Not that I actually expected it to. Shit, when she told me that she couldn't do casual, I had to laugh.

If I could put a ring on her finger right now, I would, but I don't think she would consider that to be slow. Grabbing my boots and socks, I head out to the living room and call Mike.

After what November told me about her childhood, I am done. I don't care what I have to do, she is mine and I will never let her feel second best again.

Remembering the tone in her voice when she opened up about her childhood—the neglect and the abuse—has me in such a rage that I have to remind myself that she is here with me and it will do neither of us any good if I get sent to prison for murder. We were in bed and November was lying on top of me as I played with her hair when I finally asked the question that had been nagging me.

"Tell me about your mom," I said, feeling her whole body go tight. It made my stomach clench knowing that whatever she was about to say was bad. So bad that she was not breathing and her nails were digging into the skin on my arms.

"My mom was an illusion," she whispered, her body getting closer like she was trying to press her way inside of me. "She was one person to the world and then with me, she was someone completely different." I squeezed her to encourage her to keep going.

"When I was around seven, I had a school show coming up and was so excited because I had gotten the main part. I ran home to tell my mom, hoping this was something that we could share. She lived to be on stage and was always away following her dream, so I couldn't stop thinking that she would finally be proud. She would finally see that I existed as more than just some kind of obligation. When I got home, she had already gone out so I went to Miss B. like I always did. I was so excited about the part that I spent all night making sure I knew every line, word for word, so when my mom got home, she would see how hard I'd worked.

"Later that night, my mom called Miss B. and told her she was going out after her performance and to just put me to bed. So, like always,

Miss B. took me across the hall to our apartment and put me to bed in my own room. It was the middle of the night when I was woken up by being beaten with a broom. I thought someone had broken in and was trying to kill me until my mom started yelling about me not doing my chores. She kept hitting me over and over again. I remember begging her to stop. Finally, after what seemed like hours, she made me get out of bed and clean the house from top to bottom."

She took a breath and pushed closer to me. "When I told her why I had forgotten about doing my chores, she told me that I wasn't allowed to do the play because I was too irresponsible. Then, she made me kneel on dry rice for an hour while apologizing for being so stupid and unappreciative. The night of the school play, my mom, who had never gone to a school function, made me go and watch another girl play the role that I had been chosen for. When the play was over, my mom dragged me backstage and gave flowers to the girl, hugging her and telling her how amazing she was." I could feel her tears wetting my skin.

"My whole life she did things like that," she whispered so softly that I almost didn't hear.

"Why didn't you live with your dad?" I asked, pulling her closer.

"She told me he didn't want me either." I couldn't handle any more about her mom so I pulled her tighter against me, rubbing her back until her breathing evened out and I knew she was asleep.

"Asher? Where's my daughter?" I hear Mike ask on the third ring.

When I met November at the strip club, I was only there to make sure the new guy we hired was doing a good job. I saw her with Mike at the bar and wanted to walk over and take her from him. Then Justin, a new bouncer, caught sight of her walking out to her car alone and was headed to tell her about the rules, but I told him I would take care of it. I was pissed at myself for wanting her and disgusted with her for dating someone old enough to be her father.

Obviously, the joke was on me. When I walked up to her and she turned her keys over in her hand to use them as a weapon, I was instantly proud. She was so small that it wouldn't take much to hurt her, but she didn't back down. Then she argued with me and I saw her cheeks flush. It took everything in me not to wrap her hair around my fist, press her against the car, and kiss her.

When Mike called from the other side of the parking lot, she said, "Over here, Daddy," in a way that had me biting the inside of my cheek to avoid asking her what the fuck she was doing with someone as old as Mike.

Then Mike came over and patted me on the back and introduced November as his daughter. You could have pushed me over with a feather. One, I'd known Mike my whole life and he never mentioned a daughter. Two, she was the most beautiful woman I had ever seen. When she laughed at me, I swear I felt that shit in my soul. Then she shook my hand and electricity went through me. I knew I had to get out of there. I said her name, turned around, and walked off.

Then, a week later, I go to visit Gran and I see her there. I was in shock, and a dick, as usual. So what do I do? Force her to walk out with me then crowd her until she agrees to meet me at the bar.

I knew she was as attracted to me as I was to her. When I was standing in front of her and her eyes glazed over and her lips parted, I knew she was mine.

"Asher?" Shit, I spaced out.

"She's out with Ma. They went to spend a girls' day in Nashville. You get any word on the break-in or have any idea who may have done it?" I ask, putting on my boots.

"No. I made an appointment to have a security system put in on Monday. I have no idea who she could have made an enemy out of or who would hate her enough to follow her to Tennessee from New York. That shit doesn't make sense. She hasn't dated much. Her mom kept her under her thumb. She got free when she went to college and that's when she got engaged. I think that situation fucked with her head so much, she stopped dating all together." I know it's irrational, but every time it's mentioned that she's been engaged, I want to find the fucker and slaughter him.

"Yeah, she mentioned him. Do you think he may be trying to find a way to get her back?"

"Not sure. All I know is they were engaged and she called it off not long after he proposed. She never told me why it didn't work out, just that he agreed with her." He was fucking her mom and got caught, I'm sure he didn't have much choice but to agree. Not that I could tell Mike that shit.

"Well, I called a buddy of mine who was part of F.A.S.T. with me in the corps. He works in New Jersey now and is in the DEA. He has a few friends on the force in New York that he's gonna check with about her case and see if there were any other crimes that happened in the same area that match what happened to her."

"Good. I don't know what's going on, but I feel like I'm missing something." Yeah, I know the feeling. Being beaten in New York, then the strange car at the rest area, and now the break-in here. Something is going on.

"I'm going to bring out some motion lights and set them up around your place and do the same at mine. I don't like her staying at your house alone at night while you're at the club, so I'm going to continue keeping her here with me. I would appreciate your agreement. She's the most stubborn woman I have ever met, so the only way she's going to agree is if you tell her she can't stay there unless you're home."

"Really? The only reason you want her staying with you is because you don't want her here at night by herself?" I hear Mike chuckle through the phone. It's not the only reason I want her here. I like her in my bed, wrapped around me. She has the sweetest pussy I've ever tasted. She gets wild the minute I touch her, and I like knowing she's in my space, but once again, I'm not going to tell him that shit.

"Never thought I would choose you for my baby girl, but fuck me if I'm not glad about this shit now."

I know everyone judged my lifestyle before, but Jesus, I was single, and every woman I fucked knew I was going to stay that way. Now, November is different. She isn't trying to impress me or get to my money. She laughs at herself and has a good time no matter what we're doing. That's why I know she's it for me.

When I married Joan, I felt like I was doing the right thing when she claimed to be pregnant. I was going to be involved in my child's life, regardless of how I felt about the baby's mother. It helped that she was hot and had a mouth like a fucking cyclone. I was on my way home from an assignment, a man I considered a brother, stopped me and completely broke down.

First, I thought someone we knew died but then he told me that he'd slept with Joan. When I went home that night, I kicked her ass out and told her my lawyer would be in touch.

A week later, she came to me crying, saying that she miscarried the baby. I knew right then that she played me. When I asked her for paperwork from the hospital, she couldn't give me any. Fucking cunt.

"I'll let November know she can't stay here unless I'm home," Mike said, bringing my mind back in focus.

"Thanks, Mike. I'll hit you up later this week if I hear anything from New York."

"Sure thing, bud. Talk to you then."

I hang up with Mike then grab my keys and a water bottle from the fridge.

"Jeep, Beast." I see him waiting at the front door when I get around the corner. I never thought I would want a dog again, but I like having him here. And I know how loyal he is to November. We just need to work on him knocking her down every time she lets him inside. That shit would not be funny if she were pregnant. An image of November, round with my child, filters through my head and I stumble into the wall.

"Holy shit," I say out loud, leaning into the wall and trying to pull myself together. I take a few deep breaths then push away and walk to the door, stumbling out to my jeep. I open the door for Beast to jump in then I stand outside for a few minutes, letting the cool air help calm me. The fucked-up part is that I'm not even afraid.

"Shit," I say, shaking my head. Part of me wants to make her that way as soon as possible.

"TREVOR!" I YELL as I walk into my brother's house. I head into the kitchen, grab a beer and take a drink when Jen walks in. Now I know what the fuck my brother's been doing.

"Hi, Asher," Jen says, running her hand along my arm. I turn around and hold her wrist.

"Don't." I drop her hand, taking a step back.

"So, the rumors are true? Never thought I'd see the day that Asher Mayson was pussy whipped. Though, for the life of me, I don't see—"

"Time for you to go, Jen," Trevor says, cutting her off while putting on his shirt.

"What? I thought we could hang out for a while. You know, watch a movie or something…" she says in a whine. I almost feel bad for this bitch. Then I remember that she's a bitch and will never be more than an easy fuck. The same thing she was to me.

"When have we ever watched a movie?" He shakes his head. "You drove out here to fuck. I gave you what you wanted and now you need to leave."

Shit, my brother was harsh, but then again, I never had to deal with kicking chicks out of my house. That was a lesson I learned early on. Unless you want them showing up at your house at all hours of the day and night, never invite them there.

"Okay. Will you walk me out?" she asks and I see my brother's face change. I know exactly what he's thinking.

"Look, Jen. You and I know this will never be anything more," Trevor says softly. I see her face go hard.

"You're a fucking joke," she says, poking him in the chest. "I had to fake it every time we were together," she yells, her voice getting louder.

"That's why you keep coming back? Look, I don't have time for this shit. Now get the fuck out of my house and don't come back." I watch as my brother crosses his arms over his chest and glares down at her. Then, she turns and looks at me and I know I'm next on her tirade.

"I hope you know that your bitch is going to find out the way you guys treat women," she says, glaring at me. "And when she leaves your ass, I will be there cheering her on."

"She knows how I treat bitches, and trust me, Jen, you were one of the biggest. Now, I suggest you get the fuck out of here like Trevor asked you to, or I will call the sheriff and have you removed." I watch her stomp to the counter and grab her bag, and hear her stomp down the hall. Then I hear the door slam.

"Jesus, she's a pain in the ass," Trevor says as he scrubs his hands down his face. "You do know that the women in town are in a fucking tizzy because of your ass, right?" he asks and I raise my eyebrow at him. "Seriously, they think now that you've settled down, we're all going to follow in your footsteps and start handing out rings. I mean, if I had a November of my own, I might consider it, but there's only one of her and I don't see you being done with her anytime soon, so that doesn't give me much hope."

"I'm never going to be done with her. And if by some chance this shit doesn't work out, she's off limits," I say, being one-hundred percent serious. I have never cared if my brothers went after a chick I fucked. But if one of them even thinks about getting with November, I will kill them, brother or not.

"I fucking knew it." He claps his hands. "So the Mayson curse is real. Fall in love on sight and all that bullshit." I want to laugh. From the time I was young, my father and grandfather told me and my brothers that we were cursed. They said that we would only find one love. When we met the woman who was ours, it would be like an explosion. Nothing else would matter but her. We all thought it was bullshit. Now I'm not so sure.

"The moment I met her, I knew she was the one, as cheesy as that shit sounds," I say, taking a slug from my beer.

"Wow," Trevor says, looking stunned. "I don't blame you, man.

She's fucking hot and funny." There are a lot of things that November is; hot and funny are only a couple. She is also a good person and that is hard to find in a woman these days.

"So, are you ready to get this shit done or did you call me out here to gossip with you?" I ask, done talking about her. Part of me wishes I was the only person who knew her. I don't want to share her with anyone.

"Let me get my boots and we can go. The truck is in the garage. It shouldn't take long to pull the engine."

I take a swig of my beer and watch my brother leave the room. I can't wait for this day to be over.

Chapter 6

I WAKE TO a ringing off in the distance. I know it's the alarm. I'm silently praying that Asher turns it off before I'm so awake that I can't fall back asleep. I cuddle deeper. He's pressed into my back. His arm leaves my waist, and finally, beautiful silence. His arm comes back around me, pulling me even deeper under him, and I feel his breath on the back on my neck.

The goose bumps he's causing are bringing me to the surface of consciousness. It's Monday, the day after shopping with his mom. I got back to his house at around eleven. He and Beast were waiting out on the porch when we pulled up. Asher kissed his mom then helped me carry all my new stuff into the house, where he threw them into his closet. Yes, threw, not set them down nicely. He swung his arm back and tossed them through the open closet door. When he turned around, I could tell he missed me as much as I missed him.

The next thing I knew, my clothes were gone. He picked me up, threw me onto the bed, and made slow love to me. It was so beautiful that it brought tears to my eyes. I was glad the darkness hid them from him. Afterwards, he pulled me close and dragged the blanket over us. I had my head in the crook of his arm and his fingers were at my hip.

We both talked about our day. He told me that he helped Trevor pull an engine from a truck he was rebuilding. I never knew that you could pull an engine from a car, or truck, for that matter, and I really had no idea why you would ever want to. Our conversation went something like this:

"Did you have fun with Trevor?" I asked, running my fingers along the ridges of his abs.

"No, but we did get the engine pulled from his truck."

"Why would you take the engine out? Doesn't a car need that to run?" Yes, I'm stupid, I know, but hey, I'm a New Yorker. We hardly drive. We take the subway or a taxi to most places, and if my car needs a mechanic, I take it to Juan and leave it with him. I don't hang around to see what he's doing while my car is in the shop, which is probably why my repair bill is always a lot…hmm. I could feel him laughing silently, then he couldn't hold it and burst out in a loud laugh, and I started to get offended.

"Yeah, your car needs an engine to run. He just wants to put a stronger one in his truck." This fascinated me. I mean, who knew that you could change your engine and get a faster one?

"Cool," I whispered, thinking that I should get a faster engine for my bug.

"Not gonna happen," he said, looking down at me. Then he kissed the top of my head. I grinned into his chest. It was funny that he thought he could boss me around. I seriously couldn't wait to pull up to meet him on a motorcycle.

"How was it shopping with Ma?"

"Um, let's just say that I will only be going shopping with her every few months. I felt like I should have prepared better. Maybe ran around Target a few times, or even went to the strip mall and marched into each of the stores a few times. She's a serious shopper, and if they had a competition, I'm sure she would come in first place."

"Yeah, that's Ma," he said through his laughter. Then, I wrapped myself tighter around him, listening to his heartbeat and feeling him run his fingers through my hair. I fell asleep feeling like this was exactly where I was supposed to be.

I doze off again, only to be woken by the sound of the alarm for the second time. I feel his lips kiss my shoulder, and his tongue run up my neck just below my ear as he kisses me again. Then he squeezes me into him. His warmth leaves me and I feel the cool air rush in behind me, and hear the alarm go off yet again. I roll over until I am lying where he had been. I pull his pillow down and wrap myself around it. I can hear the shower, and I open one eye and look at the time. It is dusk out, and the alarm says it is five thirty. I can't believe he has to get up so early. I have to get up by nine so I can get ready and go see the lawyer. I see the closet light come on and I lift my head.

Asher is wearing a towel, and I watch in fascination as he pulls it off and pulls on a pair of black boxers that mold to his thighs and ass. He seriously has the most amazing body of anyone I have ever seen. He must have felt me looking because he turns around, smiles, and shakes his head.

"Go back to sleep, baby. It's too early for you to be up."

"Do you always wake up so early?" I ask, cuddling back down into the bed.

"Depends on the job."

"Hmm," is all I am able to get out before I fall back to sleep. I feel my hair slide off my neck and lips just below my ear.

"I'll be home around six, and I'll call you when I take lunch, baby." I feel him kiss me again, but I am too far gone to get any words out, so I just grunt my agreement. I hear him chuckle then he kisses me again before he leaves.

STANDING WITH MY hip resting against the side of Asher's kitchen sink, I am drinking coffee while watching Beast eat. More specifically, I am watching Beast eat out of a very nice dog bowl that is next to a very nice water dish, neither of which I bought. They are the large ones that hold an endless supply of food and water so your dog can enjoy food and clean water whenever they want.

I have no idea when Asher bought them. All I know is he must have done it yesterday. Then I watch as Beast finishes eating and walks to the sliding glass door. He lays down in a giant dog bed that is also new, and proceeds to chew on a very large dog bone. I smile and let the feeling of warmth run through me. He obviously likes my dog, and plans on us being here with him often enough that Beast will need food and water dishes and a bed for when we come to visit. I'm not ready to start staying over all the time. I mean, I am, but at the same time, I don't want to over stay my welcome. I know Dad has people coming out to put in a security system today, so I will be sleeping at home tonight without Asher.

On that thought, I go to his room and make the bed, clean up the bathroom where all my stuff has gathered then I collect all of my clothing from his closet and pack up. I gather Beast and we go to my dad's place so he can go with me to the lawyer.

I AM STUNNED. I mean, this kind of thing doesn't happen to people every day. I am sitting across from Mr. Stevenson and I can't find my voice. My mouth is moving and I'm sure I look like a fish out of water.

He sits forward in his chair. "Are you okay, darlin'?" Mr. Stevenson asks. It has to be a trick question. I mean, I am a millionaire. That's good, right? Everyone wants to be rich. I just don't know what to think about being told that I will be one million five hundred and thirty-six thousand dollars richer by the end of the month. Part of me wants to tell him that I can't take it, but then a bigger part of me realizes how many people I can help with that money.

"Um, I—I just need a minute to process this," I tell him honestly.

"Take your time."

I look at him then over at my dad. He is holding my hand and his face looks shocked as well.

"Can I ask a question?"

"Of course," he says, sitting back in his chair. He looks like he belongs in an old movie. He has on black slacks with a button up shirt but instead of a tie, he has one of those silver pendants that have two pieces of leather hanging from it. On his feet, he has cowboy boots and I know that he wore a cowboy hat because it is sitting on his desk.

"Why did they leave it to me and not my mom?" Why would they leave me anything when I don't even know them?

"I'm not sure of their reasoning. A few weeks before the car accident, they came in and changed their will so that you would be the sole beneficiary of their estate at the age of twenty-five. Now, your mother contacted me about their estate shortly after the death of her parents and I explained the situation to her. She was upset, but said she understood why her parents left their estate to you. I'm surprised that she never told you about this."

I'm not surprised she didn't tell me. We aren't close and she never talks about her parents. Maybe she doesn't talk about them because they left me the money. That might also be why she treated me so poorly growing up. She feels that I took something away that should be hers. I decide I am going to call her later and tell her I will give her half of the money. They were her parents and I'm sure they would want her to have some of it.

"Are you okay, baby girl?"

I turn towards my dad. His eyes are concerned, and I know I'm so lucky to have him. His love is unconditional. No strings, no stipulations. He just loves me. He doesn't even care that I now have money. And I know that if my mom was sitting where he is, she would be mentally spending every penny.

"Yeah, Dad. I think I need to call Mom later and talk to her about this." I squeeze his hand. I can tell by the look on his face that he wants to say something.

"I'm not sure that's a good idea, baby girl."

"Dad, I want to tell her that I'm going to give her half the money."

"No, that's your money. You are going to keep every fucking penny. That bitch is not getting one cent of that money."

"Dad," I whisper. "They were her parents. No matter how you feel about her, they gave her life. I feel like they would have wanted her to have something from them."

"Fuck, no. They left it to you, not her, and they did that shit for a reason."

"Dad—"

"Baby girl, I want you to think about this for a week. Seven days. Then, you decide what to do about it. But don't call her yet. Wait a week and see how you feel." I feel tears sting my eyes and I know my dad hates my mom for what she took away from him. I also know he wants me to make a good decision.

"Okay, a week," I agree. He pulls me into his arms and hugs me close.

"I love you, baby girl. Never forget that."

"I know, Daddy." I hug him tighter.

"Okay, November," Mr. Stevenson says, bringing my attention back to him. "Since that is all out of the way, I'm going to have Nick call you in a few days when I have all the papers ready to be signed. Once that's done, we can talk about the accounts and I can help you get things sorted so that it's more manageable for you to handle on your own."

"That would be great," I tell him. He stands and Dad and I follow. Mr. Stevenson comes around his desk and shakes my hand.

"We'll be in touch," he says, walking us out to the front of the office where Nick is sitting behind a desk, typing away at a computer.

"Son," Mr. Stevenson calls out and Nick's head lifts, "I'm going to need you to pull all the papers for the Armsted estate then gather the transfer papers."

"No problem. How are you, November?" Nick asks. He has on a suit and he looks good in it. He also has on a pair of black rimmed reading glasses that make his eyes stand out. His hair is a little shaggier than the last time I saw him and it fits him well.

"I'm good. How are you?" I ask, starting to get uncomfortable about the way he is looking at me. I have on a pair of black leggings and a cream scoop neck sweater. I'm also wearing black knee high wedge heels and the scarf I got from Liz's store.

"Good. I was just getting ready to have lunch. Do you want to join me?" Nick asks me.

His dad takes a step back and I feel awkward that he is asking me out in front of his father. Plus, he knows I am seeing Asher, who has made it perfectly clear that I'm not available.

"I'm sorry, but I'm meeting Liz for coffee." His face falls and I feel bad. I've never liked hurting people's feelings. "But I'm sure she wouldn't mind if you joined us."

Even though I am sure that she will mind. I invite him anyway She doesn't seem like a people person. I am actually surprised that she even agreed to have coffee with me. Then an idea forms in my head. Nick is cute and Liz is pretty. Maybe they could get together.

"Sure." He smiles and stands. He takes off his glasses and lays them down then grabs a file and hands it to his father, who looks shocked.

"I'll be back in an hour. Do you want me to get anything for you while I'm out?" he asks his dad.

"Coffee," his dad tells him. Mr. Stevenson turns towards me. "It was nice meeting you, November. See you next week," he says, smiling big. EEEKKKK!!

"Nice to meet you too," I say, walking out the door. "Um, Dad, I'll see you at home, I guess," I say, almost wanting my dad to offer to stay. I don't want Nick to get the wrong idea that this is a date or anything close to a date.

"Sure, baby girl. See you at home." We are all standing outside on the sidewalk a couple blocks away from Liz's store. I watch my dad walk to his car. His head is bent towards his boots and he is shaking his head.

"Um, we can just walk to get Liz, and then go to the coffee shop next to her store, if that's okay with you?" I say, looking up at Nick.

"Sure, lead the way." He smiles and I smile back, and then I pull out my phone. I debate about calling Asher. I feel guilty and I don't want him to find out that Nick is with me by someone else, but at the same time, I don't want to call him in front of Nick, and have him freak out and get into an argument with him while on the phone.

"So, are you still seeing Asher?" he asks. I put my phone away, deciding I will just call him later.

"Yeah," I say, smiling.

"Oh." His eyebrows shoot together in surprise, and worry crosses his face. "Look, November, I know you're new but you should know—"

I cut him off before he can make me mad. "What? That he has bagged almost every girl in town? Tell me something I don't know. Do I like knowing that?" I ask, looking up at him. "No, but it is what it is, and I'm giving him a chance. He is sweet to me, and if there comes a time when he is not sweet to me, I will deal with it. Got it?" I narrow my eyes.

"Got it," he says, his lips twitching. I am still looking at him when I'm grabbed from behind and pulled off the ground. I scream and start kicking, trying to throw a punch. I can hear someone telling me to calm down, but I can't stop fighting. I won't let myself be dragged down an alley and beaten again. I kick, scratch, and scream then arms wrap around me, and I am being rocked back and forth. Someone is whispering to me that it's going to be okay. I start pulling myself together.

I open my eyes and see Nick standing further down the sidewalk with Cash blocking him. I take a breath and realize that I'm sitting on the ground. Not only that, but I'm in someone's lap. I hold my breath and lift my head. Yep, it's Nico and he has a bloody nose and a mark under his eye.

"I'm sorry," I whisper. I swallow hard and shake my head. "I don't know what happened." I shake my head again, trying to clear the adrenaline.

"Do not apologize," he says, framing my face with his hands. I can feel the tears sliding down my cheeks.

"Jesus, Asher's going to kick my ass." He leans in and kisses my forehead then pulls my face back into his neck. I let him hold me for a minute and feel so embarrassed about what just happened.

"I'm okay now," I tell him, wiping my face on his shirt.

"Did you just wipe your face on me?"

"Nope," I say, smiling into his shirt, remembering Asher and the fake blood.

"Just checking," he mumbles. I look up to see his lips twitching. His eyes scan my face and his thumb sweeps my cheek. "Have you talked to anyone about what happened?" I can't talk. I just shake my head.

"Babe, you need to talk to someone." I swallow and look down. I feel tears pooling in my eyes again. "Ah fuck," he growls and hugs me tighter to him. Then he stands and pulls me with him, and then Cash is here hugging me.

"Hey, sis, you scared the fuck out of me."

"Sorry," I mumble while I try to smile. I like that he called me sis. He pulls back and Nick steps closer. Nico steps in front of him then I see the damage I caused. Nico's shirt is ripped, his nose is bloody, and there are a few bruises under his eye.

"Oh my God," I whisper. I walk to Nico and grab his hand. "Come on, we have to go to the bathroom."

"What?" He stops and pulls his hand away. He looks at me like I'm crazy.

"We have to go to the bathroom," I say slowly.

"This may have escaped you, but I have a dick. The only time I go into the bathroom with a chick is for a quick fuck, and that's not happening, so no, we don't have to go to the bathroom."

"Yes, we do," I yell. I grab his hand again and drag him down the sidewalk. When we get to the café, I see Liz. We make eye contact and her eyes almost pop out of her head.

"Hey, honey, I'm going to take Nico to the bathroom. I'll be right back. Can you order me a coffee and a cinnamon roll?"

"Take Nico to the bathroom? What am I, five?" I hear him mumble beside me and I giggle.

"Um, sure," she says, her eyes large from shock then I hear her gasp and look behind me. Cash and Nick are walking in.

"Oh right. Liz, meet Nico," I say, pulling his hand up, which I am still holding. "Cash and Nick, this is Liz. We will be right back." I drag Nico with me down the hall and pull him into the bathroom. I see Liz give a slight wave to the guys and can tell she wants to bolt.

"Stay here," I mumble, standing him in front of the mirror. I go into the stall to get toilet paper.

"We have to make this fast before Liz bails on me."

"Are you this bossy with my brother?" Nico asks, his lips twitching. I smile and shrug my shoulders. He laughs.

"So, how do you know Liz," he asks as I wet a paper towel and start wiping the blood from his face.

"I don't really know her. I just met her the other day when I went into her store. She seemed sweet and some of the Mayson boys' harem were there," I say, glaring at him.

"We don't have a harem." He smirks, so I just shake my head.

"Yes, you guys do but anyway, they were rude to her, so I figured that if they didn't like her, I most likely would. No offense."

"None taken," he chuckles and I finish cleaning him up. Then, I turn toward the mirror and wipe the mascara off my face.

"You're going to need ice for your eye," I say to him through the mirror then turn to throw the garbage away. He ignores my comment and opens the door. "You need ice," I repeat and he just shakes his head.

"I'll be fine," he says and my phone starts ringing, saving him from a lecture. I pull it out of my bag and see Asher calling. *Crap!*

"Hey," I answer.

"Are you okay, baby?"

"Um, yeah. I just freaked and beat up your brother," I whisper into the phone.

"I'm going to kick his ass. What the fuck was he thinking, doing that shit?"

"It's fine. He was just joking around and I don't think he will ever do it again."

"Yeah, I heard. So, how was the meeting with the lawyer?"

"Oh…um…it was okay."

"Well, what did he say?"

"Oh, you know, this and that, typical lawyer stuff." I cross my fingers, praying that he doesn't ask me anymore about it. I want to tell him everything but money always changes people.

"What the fuck?"

"I'd rather not talk about this over the phone."

"Okay. You can tell me tonight. Should we do takeout?"

"I'm staying at my dad's tonight."

"November, you're not staying there. It's not safe."

"I'll sleep in the guest room upstairs. My dad will be in the next room."

"Have dinner with Mike then I want you in my bed tonight."

"I don't know if that's a good idea."

"Why the fuck not?"

"Don't you think we should have a break? I mean, we have been together all weekend."

"A break?" he yells and I know that was the wrong thing to say. "Careful how you word shit right now, November. I'm already pissed off about you being out with Nick then you say you need a break. I might get the wrong idea."

This is when I remember that he can be a total jerk. "Are you serious right now? Wait, don't answer that. I know you are," I yell back. "I also told you that you have to trust me. That is not optional, Asher," I whisper into the phone, knowing my temper is going a little crazy. "Liz is waiting for me. I'll talk to you later." I hang up and turn my phone to silent.

I walk to where Liz is sitting with Nick. Her head is bent, studying the coffee cup in front of her like it holds the secrets to the universe. I feel guilty for leaving her out here for so long. She looks up as I sit down across from her.

"I'm so sorry," I tell her honestly. I feel bad that I made plans with her and they got completely messed up.

"It's fine." She smiles and looks over her shoulder at Cash and Nico, and I know that she is in hot-guy heaven. I laugh and she starts laughing too. Yep, we are going to be great friends.

I look up from her to see Nico and Cash walking towards us. Both are carrying coffee cups.

"Alright, sis," Cash says, looking down at me. "We gotta go. We'll see you this weekend, right?" His phone starts ringing and he picks up. "Yo, yeah, hold on."

He pushes the phone in my direction and I know it is Asher. I look at it in his hand and feel like it is going to uncoil and strike out at me. Then, he shoves it closer and I have no choice but to take it from him.

"Hello?"

"Don't ever fucking hang up on me."

"I—"

"See you at seven." Then the line is dead.

"Crap," I whisper.

"Is everything okay?" Cash asks.

"I guess we'll see," I tell him truthfully, biting my lower lip. For the first time, I'm not looking forward to seeing Asher.

After the guys say goodbye, I debate on telling Liz I have a headache. I no longer feel like visiting. I want to go home and crawl into bed and cuddle with Beast, but I stay. Nick is really nice, no flirting, just chatting. Liz is watching him closely. They had gone to high school together but didn't know each other well.

After a while, we all say goodbye and I tell Liz to call me so we can meet up later in the week. I tell Nick that I will talk to him when he gets the papers ready for me to sign. Then, I get in my car and drive home.

WHEN I GET home, my dad and uncle cameo out on the front porch and had me follow them around the side of the house to the garage. When we got there, I have no idea what is going on until they pulled the tarp off a shiny, black motorcycle.

They explain that it's a 2011 Ninja 250r. It's a small bike—perfect for my height and weight. It also doesn't have as much power as a bigger bike, so there is less of a chance of me doing damage to myself or someone else. I only half listened to them. I mean, I have a motorcycle. How flipping awesome is that?

Uncle Joe tells me that one of his buddies bought it for his son when he wanted to learn to ride. Now, he is upgrading to a Harley so he's ready to sell it. I'm instantly in love. I love it. He also hands me a white helmet with hot pink and black airbrush writing that says *baby girl* on the back. I jump up and down when he hands it to me.

They show me how to ride for over three hours after I've changed into jeans, boots, and a leather jacket. Then finally, they let me go out on the road.

I feel free. It's amazing. The landscape passes by quickly as I drive down a long stretch of…

In the country, there is no traffic. You might come across a truck or two but normally you are the only car on the road for miles at a time. It is perfect. I am in love and know that I will be doing this often just to clear my head.

When I start up my dad's driveway, I see Asher's jeep and my good mood leaves just as quickly as it came. "Great," I whisper to myself. I pull up in front of the garage. I get off the bike, take off my helmet, and shake out my hair. Asher walks up with Beast following behind him. He is wearing a red thermal and a pair of dark jeans with his brown boots. He's also wearing a white baseball hat with black writing. I have never seen him in a hat before and he looks hot. Well, hotter than normal.

"Hey," I say and start pushing the bike into the garage. He takes over and pushes it all the way in then takes the cover from me and tosses it over the bike.

"So, I guess this is one more thing that I have to worry about?" he asks, and even though I know what he's talking about, I still ask.

"Sorry?"

"The bike," he says, crossing his arms over his chest and narrowing his eyes on me.

"My dad and uncle got it for me. I like riding it and I'm going to keep it." I cross my arms over my chest, copying his stance and daring him to say something stupid like, you 'can't keep it'." Then I will have to inform him that he is going to be the only thing not kept if he thinks he can tell me that I can't have my bike.

"Just promise that when you're on this shit, you'll always wear a helmet, jeans, boots, and a jacket."

"Promise," I smile and his eyes narrow on my mouth.

"Now tell me why you were out with Nick."

"I wasn't out with him," I say, completely exasperated. "I went to his dad's firm, he asked me to lunch and I said no thank you and that I had plans. I felt bad, so I asked him if he wanted to go with me and Liz for coffee."

"Uh huh," he says, pulling one of the belt loops of my jeans, forcing me to take a step in his direction.

"Uh huh?" I repeat with a raised eyebrow.

"Where are you sleeping tonight?" he asks, pulling me closer and dipping his head towards my neck.

"In bed," I answer but my brain is being dragged into an Asher-fog with the way he kisses the skin below my ear.

"What bed?" he whispers as he bites my neck.

"What bed am I supposed to sleep in?" I breathe deeply as he starts nipping on my earlobe.

"Mine."

"Hmm," I moan as he presses into me.

"So, where are you sleeping, November?" He growls and his hand is fisted into the back of my head, his mouth hovering over mine. My eyes flutter open. "Where are you sleeping, baby?" he asks against my mouth.

"With you," I whisper, feeling powerless against him.

"That's right. Always with me." My brain registers his words but before I can make him clarify what he means, his mouth is on mine and my brain goes deeper into the Asher-fog. His kiss feels desperate, like he is branding me with it. When he pulls away, he presses his forehead against mine. I run my hand along his jaw and his eyes open at my touch.

"Are you okay?" I ask.

"Better," he says and gives me his cocky grin. He thinks he's just gotten his way. I want to tell him that I have no problem sleeping with him. The only thing that worries me is that I can be a little clingy. My mom and my ex told me the same thing. They may have told me that so I wouldn't nag them about where they were going or how long they would be gone. But I know I'm a people person, and if I know someone is around, I want to be where they are. I worry that I might be what my mom and ex say I am, and I never want Asher to feel like I am crowding him.

"Will you promise me something?" I ask.

"What?"

"Just promise that, when you start feeling like I'm around too much, you will let me know."

"That's not going to happen," he says, cupping my cheek. His thumb slides across my lower lip.

"Just promise, okay?" I say again, feeling desperate for him to understand how much this means to me.

"Promise, baby."

"Thanks." I grin and he kisses my nose.

"Now, do you want to eat here or do you want to pick up something on the way back to my place?" I bite my lip, thinking about it, and his eyes drop to my mouth.

"Never mind. We're picking something up." He bends down and my belly goes into his shoulder as he picks me up and carries me out of the garage.

"Um, I have to go inside and get some stuff," I say from my upside down position.

"You have shit at my place."

"I packed everything." He stops and my feet hit the ground. Luckily, his arms come up to my shoulders or I would have fallen on my ass.

"You packed everything?" he growls.

"I didn't want you to feel like I was suffocating you," I say in a huff.

"Don't do that shit." His hands go to my neck, his thumbs sweeping under my jaw then his face gets closer to mine. "Unless I tell you I want space, don't read into non-existing shit and create problems. I swear," he says, looking into the sky, "if I don't want you around, I will tell you that shit straight out. No games, no bullshit."

"Okay," I whisper, never wanting to hear those words from him.

"Okay, now go pack your shit," he says and I glare at him.

"Don't tell me to pack my shit. It's rude."

"It's rude?" he asks, tilting his head to the side. "Baby, I promise you when I get you in my bed, I'll show you how much you like it when I'm being rude." This makes me tingle in a couple different spots. I definitely want him to show me how rude he can be. "Just for that look right there, I'm going to make you beg me to be rude to you."

Oh my God, I just had an orgasm standing outside my dad's house in the daytime. I look around, hoping no one saw me have a mini orgasm. I know I have to play this off, so I do what any woman would do.

"Whatever." I roll my eyes, and then run into my dad's house as quickly as I can with his laughter following me the whole way.

Asher

As I watch November pull up in front of the club on that damn bike, I look over and see a group of guys staring at her too. She puts the kickstand down, takes the helmet off, and shakes out her hair. She looks like a fucking wet dream sitting on that bike. Her legs are covered in tight denim with black boots laced up to mid-calf. She has a leather jacket on and it's zipped up half way, showing off a good amount of cleavage. I hear one of the guy whistle and her head comes up, spotting me.

"Hey, babe," she calls and the guy goes to step in her direction. Her nose scrunches and I shake my head at him, walking toward my girl.

"You just had to ride the bike, didn't you?" I ask, not at all surprised.

She smiles, shaking her head. "Uncle Joe would be disappointed if I didn't ride it," she says, lifting her leg over the seat and putting her helmet under her arm. I look at her and know she's right. Joe loves his boys, but neither of them ride. Now that his niece has shown an interest in riding, he feels like he has someone to share it with besides Mike.

"Did you ride with him today?" I ask, taking the helmet from her.

"Yeah, we went out to the park and stopped for lunch."

"Good," I say and kiss her nose. We walk inside the club, past the group of guys standing near the door. It used to bug the shit out of me when men openly checked her out but not anymore. She never even notices. I spot Nico and Cash. They already have a table waiting for us.

"Hey, guys," November says to Cash and Nico. They both stand to hug her. "Where's Trevor?" she asks, looking around.

"He's picking up Liz," I tell her and her eyes light up. I shake my head. I have no idea what's going on with Liz and Trevor. I know he likes her, but I think her innocent-vibe is throwing him off. He doesn't know how to deal with a girl that has no experience. When he found out she needed a ride, he quickly volunteered to pick her up. Maybe they just need some time to get to know each other.

"Liz is coming?" Cash asks, rubbing his hands together. He's been fucking with Trevor every chance he gets. Anytime Liz is around and any guy even looks at her, Trevor looks ready to snap.

"Be nice, guys," November says quietly, taking off her jacket and revealing the low cut shirt she's wearing under it. I feel my pulse speed up and I look around.

"You're not cold, baby?" I hint for her to put the coat back on. I know if I tell her to put the coat on, she's going to tell me where to shove it.

"Nah, I'm good." She smiles sweetly. Her eyes go over my shoulder and I see her body get stiff. I turn to see Becky making her way over to us.

"Fuck," I mumble, pulling out a stool, trying to get November to sit down.

"Asher!" Becky squeals, throwing herself at me. I remove her arms and hold her back.

"Where have you been?" she asks, looking around the table. Her eyes land on November and her face goes hard. "Oh, never mind. I see you're still roaming the streets with the pussy peddler."

"Excuse me?" I feel November stand beside me. "What did you just say?" she asks, trying to get around me.

"You need to leave, Becky," I say, blocking November. Cash and Nico are now standing on either side of November, showing where their loyalty lies.

"Your daddy sells pussy," Becky snarls.

"No, my dad sells entertainment."

"You know some of the girls there sell pussy to their customers when no one's looking," Becky says, glaring at November.

"What's your last name?" November asks and Becky puts her hands on her hips.

"Hudson," Cash says. November looks at him then back at Becky.

"So, you were one of those girls who was selling pussy while no one was looking, weren't you, Becky Hudson?" November smirks and Becky takes a step back. "My dad's club is clean unless trash like you comes in to dirty it up. But then, you know what happens to trash, don't you, Becky? It always gets thrown out. Don't talk about my dad's club again. You worked for him until you tried to make money on the side, and he threw you out like the trash you are." After landing her final blow, November walks to the bar.

"I can't believe you're with a girl like her," Becky says, shaking her head.

"You need to go and don't come back," I say, turning to the bar. When I reach November's side, she's already got her Corona.

"I hate women like that," she says, shaking her head and not looking up from her beer.

"Yeah," I agree, thinking that I wasted a lot of time on women like that. "You okay?" I ask, pulling her into my side and tilting her head back to kiss her.

"I will be when I finish this Corona and can order another one," she mumbles against my lips and I smile against hers. I want to tell her so badly that I love her, but I keep telling myself to let her set the pace. "Let's go back to the table and enjoy the rest of the night."

Chapter 7

I T IS CHRISTMAS Eve and I'm standing in the bathroom, trying to finish getting ready to go to Asher's parents'. It's been a month since I found out that I am a millionaire. The only person who knows about my inheritance is my dad. I finally agreed with him that I wasn't going to give my mom half the money. She hasn't even called since I've been in Tennessee. I tried to call her and even left a couple messages but she never returned my calls. I'm sure if I had mentioned the money, I would have gotten a call back, but I didn't want that to be the reason she reached out to me.

My other dilemma is trying to find a way to tell Asher about the money. Every time I am going to bring it up, I wonder if it will change our relationship. I don't think it will, but you never really know.

We've been together for over a month and I still sleep in his bed every night, not that I have any choice in the matter. Anytime I mention staying at my dad's, he gets a look that tells me if I tried, he would drag me back to his house caveman style. But really, I don't mind. I love going to sleep with him every night and waking up to him every morning.

"Hey, baby. You okay?" Asher asks, coming to stand behind me and placing his hands on my waist and his mouth at my neck. My hands are rolling my hot rollers into my hair. I haven't even gotten dressed yet. I still have on my tank top and sleep shorts. We got up early and had breakfast, and then crawled back into bed.

"Yeah," I whisper as the scruff from his jaw runs down my neck to my shoulder. "Um, actually. I need to tell you something." I breathe deeply, hoping that I'm doing the right thing.

"Tell me." He bites my earlobe, distracting me.

"I, uh…um."

"Babe, uh and um isn't saying much."

"You're distracting me. I can't think when your mouth is on me." His head comes up and we make eye contact in the mirror. His dimple is out and he has a cocky grin in place.

"You like me distracting you with my mouth." He reminds me of something that I didn't need to be reminded of right now. Not when I'm trying to tell him something serious. I glare at him in the mirror and he chuckles. "Okay, baby. Tell me," he says, putting his chin on the top of my head.

"I'm a millionaire." Okay, I didn't mean to blurt it out quite like that, but now it is out in the open. I feel his body tighten around mine.

"What?" he asks. I swallow and bite my lip. There is no going back. I turn in his arms and put my hands on his chest.

"My mom's parents left me their estate and it's over a million dollars."

"When did you find this out?" I really didn't want to answer that question. I look over his shoulder towards the door.

"Eyes on me." I look into his eyes again. "When did you find out about this?"

"Um…I…" I bite my lip and look away again.

"Eyes!" He growls this time. "When did you find out about this?" I look into his beautiful eyes and see sadness there and my heart hurts.

"When I went to the lawyer," I whisper.

"Why didn't you tell me then?" he asks as he steps back, taking his warmth with him.

"I didn't want it to change us," I whisper again, looking down at the tiled floor of his bathroom.

"Have I ever given you that idea?" he asks. I feel like a horrible person for not telling him from the start about the money. It was stupid to hide it.

"No," I say, looking up at him. I can tell he's hurt.

"You're right. I haven't. And I have to say I'm fucking pissed that you would even think for one minute that money would change how I feel about you."

"I know it was stupid. I just wanted to make sure." His eyes narrow and I know that's the wrong thing to say.

"Make sure of what? That I wasn't with you for your money? Jesus, what the fuck? I don't understand what goes on in that head of yours sometimes." This kind of hurts, but I know he's right. "I've never asked you to pay for shit. I never want you to pay for shit."

This's i true. Anytime I've tried to pay for something, I get the look that promises I won't like what happens if I don't put my money away.

"You're right. I know. I should have told you."

"You should have but I understand why you didn't. It doesn't make me happy, but I understand."

"Thanks," I say, wrapping my arms around his waist and laying my head on his chest.

"Just don't keep shit from me. I don't like knowing you have kept that secret for over a month." Crap, I never thought about it like that.

"I'm sorry," I whisper into his chest, feeling like a total dork.

"When you move in, we'll talk about your money."

"What?" My head jerks back so I can look into his eyes.

"You heard me, and know that shit will be soon. I don't like you having to travel to your dad's every few days to go get clothes and shit."

"Asher," I say, glaring at him and putting my hands on my hips for the full effect. "You are not going to boss me into moving in with you."

"There will be no bossing, baby. You want to move in. Don't you love feeding me breakfast in bed every morning?" he asks and I shiver. Every morning, he has me for breakfast before he gets out of bed, and yes, I do love feeding him. "Don't you like lazing on the couch, watching movies at night?" I do love that too or even just lying on him while he watches a game. "Don't you love cooking in my kitchen?" Yes, I love his kitchen. It is my favorite room in the house. I love baking in there or just sitting at the counter and reading on my Kindle. "Don't you love me fucking you whenever you need to be fucked?" *Um, yes!* I bite my lip and look over his shoulder.

"Those are just a few of the reasons why I won't have to boss you to move in with me." He has a point. He won't need to boss me into it. It is just too soon. Maybe in a few months, but right now, I like knowing that I still have my dad's house to run to if I need it.

"Can we not talk about this right now? I need to get ready to go to your parents' house."

"Yeah, we can wait to talk about it, but we will be talking about it."

"Great." I roll my eyes. "Something to look forward to." He kisses my nose and gives me his dimple smile then leaves me to watch him walk away. I shake my head. He's such a jerk but I love him. Wait, what? I love him? Oh my God, I love him. Oh no, I love him. Crap! Oh my God, does he love me? I turn to look in the mirror. "So what, you love him. He doesn't have to love you back," I whisper to myself.

"What, baby?"

"Shit!" I jump and look through the mirror to see Asher watching me. "Um, nothing. I just, um, burnt myself."

"Are you okay?" he asks, smirking, and I wonder if he heard me admit to myself that I love him.

"Yeah, I'm fine. Great. Just fine." Great, now I'm blabbering like an idiot. He tilts his head and smiles. My heart starts thumping double time.

"Uh huh. I thought I heard you say something?" he says, taking a step closer to me.

"Nope, not me. I didn't say anything. Maybe you heard the TV or something." I cross my arms over my chest.

"The TVs are off."

"Hmm, that's strange. Maybe you have a ghost," I say, tilting my head.

"This house is built on an old graveyard, so I wouldn't be surprised if there are ghosts."

"What?" I whisper in shock. I hate ghosts. Not that I've met any, but I don't like the idea of them. I watched the first *Paranormal Activity* movie and got so scared that I had to sleep with the lights on for a month. Let's just say my college roommate was not happy about that. "We can't stay here," I yell. "We have to hire a ghost buster person to come get rid of it. Then, we have to bless the house, and if the ghost doesn't leave, we need to move." I am panting and Asher's lips are twitching. "Oh my God! This is not funny. We could end up dead, don't you know that? Haven't you ever seen the exorcist?" I yell.

He throws his head back, laughing. "Baby, there is no ghost. I was kidding. The house is not built on a graveyard."

I smack him in the arm. "That's not funny. Why would you say something like that?"

"You wanna admit what you said when you were in here talking to yourself?"

"I wasn't talking to myself," I snap at him. "I was talking to Beast." I'm a genius. I forgot about Beast. He's the perfect cover up.

His eyes narrow. "So, what were you saying to Beast then?"

"Nothing. Just that I love him and he's a good dog, even if he doesn't love me."

"Trust me, he loves you. Even though he thinks you're whacked." Does that mean Asher loves me? Wait, what the hell?

"I'm not whacked." I growl at him.

"Do you love me, baby?"

"W–wh–what?" I stutter, shaking my head. Then, he is crowding me against the counter.

"Don't piss me off, baby," he growls. I bite my lip to keep myself quiet. His eyes drop to my mouth and narrow. "Tell me you love me." I start shaking my head and he holds my face between his hands. "Tell me you love me so I can say it back."

"What?" I whisper in shock, searching his face to make sure he's telling the truth.

"Tell me, baby." I swallow the lump in my throat. "Say it, baby." He lays his forehead against mine.

Squeezing my eyes closed, I whisper, "I love you." My heart feels like it might beat out of my chest. I hear his sharp intake of breath then his hands fist into the hair at the sides of my head.

"Open your eyes." I swallow then open my eyes. "I love you too, baby. Jesus, I've loved you since I saw your beautiful face standing at the bar in your dad's club. I knew then that you were it for me."

"You were a jerk," I remind him, smiling.

"Yeah," he smirks. "I was pissed that I was gonna have to beat up Mike."

"What?" I say through my laugh.

"I was going to have you one way or another," he says, biting my bottom lip. "If that meant beating up Mike, I was willing to do whatever was necessary to stake my claim."

"You're serious?" I giggle and shake my head in disbelief.

"You're worth it," he whispers. I feel my nose start to sting and a tear slide down my cheek. His thumb catches it. He kisses me softly and lays his forehead back against mine. "Now I wish I had time to show you how much I love you. But if I did that, we would be late and I don't want to piss Ma off on Christmas Eve."

M nipples go hard as tingles race through my body. I want him to show me how much he loves me. He kisses me again, this time a little deeper but still not enough. When he pulls his mouth away, I want more. "We can be a few minutes late. I'll take the blame," I say breathlessly as I scrape my nails over his abs, watching his eyes grow dark at my touch. I lean forward and touch my mouth to his chest, running my tongue up to his collarbone.

One of his hands fist in my hair and the other pulls me closer to him so I'm on the edge of the counter. The hard length of him is pressed to my center. He takes my mouth in a hard, deep kiss then his mouth leaves mine, traveling down my neck. I wrap my legs around his waist, pulling him closer. He puts my arms around his shoulders then picks me up, carrying me out of the bathroom. I fly through the air, and then my body hits the bed so hard, I bounce twice. I hear my hot rollers hitting the hardwood floor. Then my shorts and panties are off. His hands travel up my thighs and my legs fall open.

"I love this pussy, baby. So pink, wet, and mine," he growls the words against my clit, making my pulse race. He licks me from top to bottom. "Jesus, so fucking sweet," he says, licking me again. This time, his tongue circles my clit, not making contact.

I whimper.

"Hush, baby." He licks me again, pulling my clit into his mouth. My hips shoot off the bed and my hands hold his head while my heels press into the mattress. He growls then throws both my legs over his shoulders and lifts my ass. His mouth is eating me like he's starving. My hips circle, pressing him deeper. I am close, so close.

"Asher," I moan. "Please." My back bows off the bed and my eyes shut tight. My hands fist the sheets at my sides. I am searching for it. I'm close. I feel it start then his mouth is gone. I whimper and he slams into me.

"Yes," I scream.

Asher looks down at me. "Give me your mouth, baby." My head is righted and his mouth is on mine. I can taste the salty sweetness of myself in the kiss. I wrap my legs around his hips, running my hands up his back, feeling the muscles contract as he's pounding into me.

"I'm going to come," I say, shoving my face into his neck and biting down. My limbs go tight around him.

"Not yet. Together," he says, lifting my hips higher.

"Asher," I cry.

"Fuck!" he shouts, pounding harder. My head flies back. "So fucking beautiful." His words make me hotter. I bite my lip, trying to keep from coming without him. His hands leave my hips and travel down to my breast, pinching my nipples. I'm trying so hard to hold off my orgasm that I can taste blood from where I'm biting my lip.

"Now." His words are like a trigger. I go off, feeling myself shatter into a million pieces. Two more stokes and he follows behind me, his mouth finding mine as he swallows my scream. I can feel myself convulsing around him. I tighten my limbs, holding him closer.

"Please don't leave me," I breathe, not ready to be separated from him.

"Never, baby," he says, and I know the emotion behind his words means more than just right now. He spends time kissing my jaw, neck, and lips. After a few minutes, he slides out and I feel the loss of him right away.

"We have to get ready, baby," he whispers, his lips close to mine.

I pout out my bottom lip. "I don't wanna."

He grins and bites my lip. "Sorry. Ma will kick my ass if we don't show."

"Fine." I continue pouting then I realize my hair is going to take forever to fix. Plus, I have to find all the rollers and clips that flew out of my hair. "You ruined my hair so I'm no longer taking the blame for being late."

"You love me, baby?"

"Yes," I whisper, melting under him.

"Good," he mumbles. He kisses my nose then slides off the bed, pulling me up with him. "You need to hurry your ass up, baby. Don't wanna piss Ma off," he says, smacking said ass.

"Whatever," I mumble, walking into the bathroom. My boyfriend is hot; he loves me, and I just had a really great orgasm. Even he can't piss me off right now.

I LOOK UP to see Asher watching me. I'm sitting on the floor with his cousin's baby girl, Emma, holding her little hands as she bounces on my thighs. She is so perfect. Her cheeks are chubby and her little lips are so kissable. Holding her makes me want a baby of my own. I wonder if Asher even wants kids. He would be a great dad. I've seen him with the kids in his family and they all love him. I look away, not wanting him to read my face. Emma giggles and grabs my hair, trying to pull it into her mouth.

"No, sweet girl. You don't want to eat that." I untangle my hair from her hand, and then tickle her, making her laugh louder. There is nothing better than hearing a baby laugh. There is something so pure and beautiful about it.

"You're really good with her." The rough voice startles me, and I look up to see a guy I've never met before standing over me.

"Um, thanks," I say, wondering who he is. He's about as tall as Asher but more bulky. His black hair is a little long, but it works for him, wisping out around his face in a messy '*I don't give a crap*' kind of way. His tan skin makes the golden color of his eyes stand out even more. He has full lips and a few days' worth of stubble on his jaw that is angled perfectly. He's not dressed up like most of the people here. He has on a pair of light jeans and a plaid shirt. I look away from him and back down to Emma, who is staring up at this guy, completely fascinated by him. I don't blame her. He is very good-looking. But he also has a vibe about him that seems almost dangerous.

"Kenton," the guy says.

"Sorry?" I say, looking back up at him.

"Name's Kenton."

"Oh, nice to meet you. I'm November."

"Pretty name. Never seen you before."

"I'm—"

"She's mine," Asher says, walking up with a beer in his hand.

"Shit, man. I didn't know you were here. How are you?" They do a man hug and I stand, bringing Emma with me. When I get to my feet, Asher pulls me to him, tucking me under his arm.

"I'm good. Ma would have my balls if I tried to skip out on Christmas Eve."

"True." Kenton chuckles, looking between me and Asher. "So, this is your girl?" he asks in disbelief and I giggle. Everyone is always so surprised that Asher has a girlfriend.

Asher looks down at me and smiles. Then, he kisses the top of my head. "Yeah, she's mine."

"Do you know how many hearts are breaking?" he asks, looking at me.

"Trust me, I know." I roll my eyes at him. I have become public enemy number one around here. You would think I went to the homes of all these chicks and personally stole their most treasured possessions.

"So, what are you doing in town? Last time we spoke, you were heading out to Mexico on a case?" Asher asks.

"I got back yesterday. The trail went cold. I came home for Christmas and to see if I can find any new leads. If I can't find anything, I'll leave again after the new year."

"I need your help with something while you're in town. I'll set up a time this next week when we can meet up."

"Is everything okay? Is it Joan?" Kenton asks. At the name Joan, Asher's arm tightens. I look up and see that his jaw is locked, and I wonder who Joan is. But before I can ask, Emma starts crying.

"Um…I'm going to find her mom," I say, looking up at Asher.

"Sure, baby. Come back to me when you're done."

"Okay," I whisper as he kisses my temple.

"It was nice meeting you, Kenton," I say, smiling.

He's looking at me closely and shakes his head, smiling, then says, "Yeah, you too. I'll see you around, I'm sure."

"Yeah," I mumble, feeling uncomfortable and wondering who Joan is and why that name would make Asher upset. I find Emma's mom and we talk for a few minutes and exchange numbers. She lives a couple towns over and is around my age. I like her right away and would love to spend more time with Emma. I walk back through the crowd and see Asher still talking to Kenton. It looks serious, so I make my way to the kitchen to find Susan.

"Hey, do you need any help?" I ask Susan after I find her in the pantry. She's standing on a ladder and it looks like it might fall over.

"Oh, thank God." She turns, looking down at me. "I need help getting some platters made up and set out. Are your dad and grandma here yet?" she asks, going back to looking on the shelf.

"Not yet. He said they were running late but they'd be here soon."

"Good. Here, grab these." She hands me three trays. "You can help me until they show up." She smiles, stepping down from the ladder. We walk into the kitchen. Their kitchen is a galley style. It's long and updated, but closed off from the rest of the house so you can't see anyone unless they walk into it.

"Can I ask you a question?" I ask, setting the trays down on the counter.

"Sure, you know you don't even have to ask. I'm always here anytime you need me."

"Thanks," I say. My voice is clogged from the lump in my throat. "Um, who is Joan?" Her face freezes and I'm not sure what that means.

"She was Asher's wife." Well, crap. That's not what I expected at all.

"Oh," I whisper, having nothing else to say.

"Why do you ask?"

"Oh, um, Kenton mentioned her," I say, cutting wedges of cheese and placing them on the platter. Susan comes to stand next to me, moving my hair off my shoulder. I look over at her and she smiles.

"You have nothing to worry about."

"Okay." I smile but I know it doesn't reach my eyes. I'm just praying that she doesn't say anything else. I really don't want to cry.

"Talk to Asher about it if it's bothering you."

"I will," I promise her, knowing that it's time we talk about his ex-wife and the reason he got divorced. It's completely irrational that it bothers me. I know he loves me, but part of me wishes he didn't have a past. Well, at least one that he was married in. Stupid, I know since I was engaged, but I love him more than I ever thought possible. And now that I feel this kind of love, I realize that I didn't actually love my ex. He was a crutch. I wanted him so I could start a life on my own, one where my mother didn't have any control. I'm glad it didn't work out. I'm not glad that he slept with my mom, but our relationship wouldn't have been fair to him in the long run.

"Hey, baby girl." I turn and see my dad walking into the kitchen with my grandma following close behind him.

"Daddy." I take two steps and his arms are around me. He tilts my face back with his hands on my cheeks.

"Are you okay? You look sad."

"I'm fine. Just helping Susan." I smile. I don't want him to worry about me. His eyes narrow, but before he can question me, Asher walks into the kitchen.

"Mike." He pats my dad on the back. He looks at me and his eyes narrow. "What's wrong?"

"Nothing. I'm just happy." I roll my eyes.

"You don't look fucking happy. You look sad."

"Geez, did either of you stop to think that I haven't had this before, and I'm just sad that I missed out on it for so long?"

"Shit," Asher mumbles, rubbing his hands down his face. My dad's eyes turn angry. Once again, I put my foot in my mouth.

"What did you do on holidays?" Dad asks. Crap, crap, crap. Me and my damn foot. When will I learn to keep it out of my mouth?

"I went to a friend's. Can we please not talk about this and just enjoy tonight?" I ask softly.

My dad takes a deep breath while pulling my head to his chest and kissing my hair. I lift my head and smile at him. My grandma and Susan are watching me closely.

"I'm going to help Susan finish these platters," I say, pulling away from my dad and stepping in front of the platter I was making.

"Okay, baby girl. I'm going to go get a drink. We can visit when you're done," Crisis averted. Yay!

Smiling, I look over at him. "I'll find you."

My dad smiles then saunters out of the kitchen. If I had one wish, it would be for my dad to find a good woman to love. He deserves happiness more than anyone I know. Plus, my dad is good-looking. It shocks me that he hasn't had a relationship since my mom.

"You sure you're okay, baby?" Asher asks, pulling my back to his front.

"I'm fine," I say, leaning against him.

"I'm gonna finish talking to Kenton. I got worried that someone else was trying to steal you away when you didn't come back to me."

"Go talk to him. I'm okay in here. When we're done, I'll find you," I say, but I want to ask right then why he divorced Joan and why Kenton would ask if he needed to talk about her. But we'll have plenty of time later to talk about her, and it is Christmas Eve. I really don't want him to be upset.

"Okay, love you," he says against my ear and goose bumps spread across my skin. He squeezes me then I feel his presence leave the kitchen before I can tell him that I love him too.

"Nice save," Susan says, making me jump.

"Um," I mumble and she starts laughing.

"Just promise that you will talk to him about Joan. I know his history with her is bothering you."

"Promise," I say, smiling.

"Who's Joan?" Crap! Of course, I forgot that my grandmother is here. She's like a damn ninja. She's constantly sneaking up on you when you least expect it, or she is so quiet that you forget she's there and say crap that isn't meant to be heard by her.

"Asher's ex-wife," Susan shares, and I watch my grandma's eyes pop out of her head.

"Well, shit. That's not what I thought you were going to say."

"Grandma," I scold her. She has the mouth of a sailor.

"Don't take that tone with me. I've heard you pull up in that car of yours with that music you listen to, talking about bitches this and bitches that. And I know your man cusses more in one sentence than I do in a day."

Well, she had me there. Rap music did tend to use the word bitch a little too often, and Asher could curse even when there was nothing to curse about.

"Point taken," I mumble.

"Why would you be upset that he had a life before you? I hate to remind you, but you were engaged."

"You were engaged?" Susan gasps. Geez, this day started out so perfectly, and now every time I turn around, someone is talking about something I don't want to talk about.

"I was, and then I found out that the guy was a total jerk and broke it off." I look over at my grandma. "I'm not upset. I just want to understand why they split up." Grandma nods her head in understanding.

"What did he do? I mean, why did you call off your engagement?" Susan asks.

"He cheated," I say and hear my grandmother inhale. I never told my father why I called off the engagement so he was never able to tell her. Since I've been home, she's never asked.

Besides, the idea of telling them that he cheated on me with my mom didn't sound like a conversation I wanted to have.

"Well, I think you should talk to him about it," my grandmother says like she just solved all of my problems. I smile, shaking my head.

"I'm going to talk to him, just not on Christmas Eve. We should be having a good time visiting with friends and family."

"Such a smart girl," she says, pinching my cheek like I'm five.

"Thanks." I smile.

"Okay, let me and your grandma finish these and you go visit with everyone," Susan says, taking the knife and cheese away from me.

"Do you like it?" Asher whispers into my ear. It is Christmas morning and both of our families are over and most are still wearing pajamas. Somehow, everyone decided while they were drunk that we should all have breakfast and open gifts at Asher's house.

Making early morning plans while drinking is not smart. I made the coffee extra strong and put out aspirin as an appetizer before breakfast. The first person showed up at eight. Asher kissed me and got out of bed. I hid under the covers, hoping everyone would forget I was even in the house. That only lasted about five minutes. Asher came back into the room and dragged me across the bed then tried to stand me up, but I was playing dead and slumped into him, not even opening my eyes.

"Baby, we gotta make breakfast," he laughed.

"No, all I want for Christmas is to sleep," I said, trying to cuddle into his chest.

"You can sleep later," he said while rubbing my back, but that was making me sleepier.

"I'll be your bestest friend ever if you let me sleep." He started laughing harder.

"As much as I want you to be my best friend, I need help making breakfast for everyone. I'm pretty sure that last night you were jumping up and down while clapping and saying how much fun if was going to be to open gifts with everyone this morning."

Crap, I did do that, but that was also after having four cups of eggnog, so I can't be held accountable for my actions.

"I was drunk. It doesn't count."

"Hmm, so all the dirty things you said you wanted me to do to you last night don't count," he said, and I shoved my face deeper into his chest, hoping to block him out. I do not want to even think about what a drunk me would say to Asher.

"Don't worry, baby. Tonight I'll—"

I cut him off. I didn't want to know what drunk me said. "I'm awake," I blurted out. I ran to the bathroom and slammed the door before he could say anything else.

I made baked French toast and bacon. Asher made scrambled eggs that I swear could win awards. He uses whole cream and cheddar cheese. They melt in your mouth and each bite is like heaven. After we all ate, everyone was gathered around the tree. Asher pulled me into his lap so we could open gifts.

I had a hard time finding him something for Christmas, but since he was always on his phone at the job site either going through emails or putting together orders, I decided to get him an iPad mini. That way, he could have a bigger screen and wouldn't go blind from looking at the small screen on his phone. Plus, I got him a case that has a built in keyboard, hoping that it will make his life easier when sending email and placing orders. I also got him a few shirts and a New York Yankees baseball hat. He isn't actually a Yankees fan but I love him in hats and I'm a New Yorker, so it was necessary.

After everyone finished opening gifts, it took me a minute to realize that Asher didn't get me anything. I tried not to let this hurt my feelings but it did. He loved the iPad and was still playing with it as people started leaving the living room.

"I'm going to go clean up breakfast," I mumbled to myself. Asher hadn't taken his eyes off his new toy since he opened it. I pulled myself up from where I was sitting between his spread legs.

"Can you throw that shit in the closet for me, baby?" he asked, not looking up from the stupid iPad. I was starting to wonder if it was water resistant.

"Sure," I grumbled. I picked up the stuff I got him, along with the gifts I got from our families. I set my stuff on the bed then carried his crap to the closet. I debated just throwing it in there, but I didn't want to mess it up.

After about two weeks of me being at Asher's house, I'd cleaned out his closet, put all of his laundry away, folded his T-shirts, and hung anything that needed to be hung. I also organized all of his shoes. I loved his closet. I turned on the light without even thinking and set his new shirts on his shelf when I noticed my metal framed mannequin in the corner. I did a double take then saw a huge dressing table in the middle of the room with all my odds and ends on it, including a cool jewelry stand and a tall mirror with swirly legs that looked awesome.

Looking around, I noticed all my clothes and shoes were in his closet and there was a very cool chaise lounge chair in the corner with a small gift box sitting on top of it. My hands started shaking as I looked around, realizing that this was my Christmas gift. It was the most awesome gift that he could have ever given me.

"Do you like it?" I hear him whisper as his arms circle my waist, pulling me back against him.

I can't talk. All I can do is nod my head. I am speechless. When I find my voice, I ask him, "When did you do this? How did you do this?"

"My guys got here a few minutes after we left yesterday. They put up the new shelves, brought in the dressing island and the chair. Your dad and grandma brought over all your stuff and set it up before heading to Ma's for the party last night."

"I love it," I whisper. It was perfect. A dream closet. "Did you pick out the jewelry stand and mirror?"

I felt his silent laughter against my back. "Liz picked them out for you. When I told her what I was doing, she talked my ear off about closets the whole time I was in her store. I tell you, I don't know what it is with women and closets, but if the stomach is the way to a man's heart, a closet is the way to a woman's."

I smile and melt deeper into him. Liz has become a great friend and is slowly becoming more open with us. Except when Trevor is around, but I think that's because he's always growling at her. When she ignores him, it pisses him off. When she talks to him, it pisses him off, but when another guy tries to talk to her, that pisses him off even more. He normally ends up storming off, leaving Liz looking completely baffled and me laughing to myself.

With the way he looks at her, I know he is seriously into her. It's like watching a romance in the making, just waiting to see who is going to break first.

"I love this closet. I loved this closet before I even really.

He laughs, turning me in his arms. "Now you love me."

"Maybe, or maybe I'm using you for your closet. Did you ever think of that?" I ask, smirking up at him. He picks me up suddenly, making me squeal. Then I am on the chaise lounge with him lying on top of me. "What are you doing?" I exhale as his hand finds my breast and the other goes to the back of my thigh.

"I'm going to prove that you're not using me for the closet," he says, his fingers tracing the back of my thigh and around the front of my sleep shorts, slipping underneath the edge. He slowly traces my seam with his finger. My hips lift automatically, trying to get more contact.

"People are here." I moan.

"Then you better be quiet, baby," he whispers into my ear, his fingers running over my clit, circling twice then dipping down and filling me. I bite down on his shoulder, one hand going under his shirt to his back and the other to his bicep, holding on. "You're so wet. Jesus, I wish I could taste you right now."

"Please," I beg, my face coming out of his neck. I love his mouth. I want his mouth on me.

"My greedy girl. You know I love your pussy, baby, but I can't. The minute I get my mouth on you, I'm going to want to fuck you and I can't do that knowing your dad's in the next room."

I whimper. His words are turning me on even more. His fingers slide slowly in and out, then his thumb moves over my clit and I feel myself begin to fall apart, his mouth catching my moan. I pull him closer, wrapping myself tighter around him. My eyes are squeezed shut and I can still feel myself spasming around his fingers.

"Oh my God," I whisper, opening my eyes. I watch in fascination as Asher brings his fingers to his mouth and licks them clean. This causes another spasm. Then his mouth is on mine, kissing me deep and wet. When he pulls his mouth away, we are both trying to catch our breath. "Maybe I'm using you for amazing orgasms," I say quietly.

"Yeah, maybe," he chuckles and kisses my nose. I feel my face go soft.

"No, I'm definitely in love with you." I whisper my confession. It still amazes me that this guy, who seems so rough around the edges, is always soft with me.

"I love you, baby."

"I love you too." Tears sting my nose and I take a deep breath.

Asher picks up the wrapped box off the floor where it had fallen and hands it to me. "What's this?" I ask.

"Your other gift." He smiles his cocky grin and I can't help but to roll my eyes. I slowly unwrap the silver paper and lift the lid on the small jewelry box. My heart feels like it is going to jump out of my chest with the anticipation.

"Wow," I whisper, staring down at the most beautiful necklace I have ever seen. Two silver hearts intertwined, becoming one, similar to an eternity symbol. I take it out of the box and hold it in my hand, not sure if he even knows the significance of the design. "It's beautiful," I say, still whispering. I look up and he is watching me closely.

"Will you put it on me?" I ask, handing it to him. My hair is already up so I turn my back to him and he places the necklace around my neck then clasps it. I feel his lips on the back of my neck. My hand goes to the hearts and I pull it away from my chest, looking down at it. He pulls me around to face him again.

"Beautiful," he says and I start crying. He pulls me into his lap and I shove my face into his neck, absorbing his smell. "Baby, why are you crying?" That's a good question. I have no idea why I am crying. I just feel really emotional.

"I'm sorry." I sniffle, wiping my face on his shirt.

"Did you just wipe your snot on me?"

I start giggling. "No, just tears. I promise."

"Uh huh," he mumbles and kisses the top of my head. I pull my face away from his chest and look into his beautiful eyes. I'm so lucky. "So, now that you have your stuff here, baby, you know that means you're officially moved in, right?"

I'm in complete shock. He totally tricked me into moving in. Actually, come to think of it, he tricked my dad. He got his way without having to fight with me about it. I love staying here, but I like having a backup plan.

"Oh my God. You bossed me and got your way, and I didn't even notice you were doing it."

"I didn't boss you, baby. I told you that you would want to live with me." He is right, as mad as it makes me. I want to be here as badly as he wants me to be.

"You don't think this is too soon?" I mumble, shaking my head.

"Fuck, no."

Okay. He is sure about this. Me, on the other hand, I am not so sure. "I don't want this to go bad because we're so new. I feel like this is moving so fast. I'm worried that it's just because it's new to you and you don't really know what you're asking. Like you're going to lose interest sooner or later and I'll be heartbroken, and stuck moving out of a house that I love when I knew it was too soon to move into it in the first place."

His hands move to my neck, his thumbs are under my jaw, tilting my head back so he has full eye contact. "You're pissing me off." *Eeek! He looks pissed. Crap.* "I'm a grown man. I know what I want out of life. I know who I want in my life. You're not in my head, you don't know how I feel, so stop trying to make choices for me," he says, shaking my head gently. "I'm trying to slow down for you. For me, going fast would be you wearing a ring instead of a necklace. Trust me, I'm taking it slow, as slow as I can."

For some reason, I know he is telling the truth. What he doesn't know is that if he'd asked me to marry him, I would have said yes, no questions asked. From the moment I saw him, I wanted him. Granted, I thought he was a big jerk after he spoke, but I still wanted him. When my apartment was broken into and he was there with me, taking care of me, and making sure I was safe, I knew then he was really a good man. And the way he talks to me and looks at me, well, that seals the deal.

"I love you. You're it for me. I knew from the moment I met you that I was done for. I like having you here and I don't see that changing, unless you don't feel the same as I do. Then you need to tell me that so I can convince you that you do," he says, smirking at me. I wonder if he felt the same about his ex. Did he love her?

"Did you love your ex-wife?" I blurt out, feeling his body stiffen under me. "Never mind, I'm sorry. I shouldn't have asked you that." I try to escape off his lap.

His eyes narrow and he takes a deep breath. "You can always ask me anything," he says, pulling me deeper into him and pressing my head into his warm chest. "I never loved her. I thought I was doing the right thing. We had been sleeping together for about a year and I knew that I didn't want anything serious with her. She always hinted at more, but I knew she wasn't the one. I did care about her, but I wasn't in love with her.

"I had been gone for a month and when I got back, she was waiting for me outside my apartment. She told me she was pregnant and that it was mine. I knew I had to do the right thing. I never wanted my kid to grow up in a house where I didn't have access to him or her twenty-four seven, so I did what I thought was right at the time. I told her that it would work out and we would get married. That way, she would have insurance for all the medical bills, and I would have full access to my child. I thought maybe I would grow to love her. She claimed to be around three months along.

"When I was leaving to go out with my squad, I was gone for two weeks, give or take. We had been married for a month and she moved in right away. When I came back from an assignment, a friend of mine stopped me before I could go home. He told me that she had slept with him and that he was sorry. I went home and confronted her about what she had done. She didn't deny it. She said she was trying to get me jealous to make me realize that I loved her. It didn't work. I kicked her out and told her that my lawyer would be in touch.

"A couple days later, she came by and told me that she had lost the baby. I asked for proof and she never showed me any. To this day, she tries to contact me every once in a while. I don't take her calls, but she has been known to show up out of the blue. Kenton knows about her because after she claimed to have lost the baby, he did some digging for me. He found out that she never went to the doctor for any kind of treatment during the time she claimed to be pregnant. I guess she thought I would knock her up after we got married and I would never be the wiser. She didn't count on me staying wrapped up even after she claimed to be pregnant and I had a ring on her finger. But, something in the back of my head didn't feel right. I never fucked her without protection and I'm thankful to this day that I listened to my gut."

I couldn't believe that someone would do that. Claiming to be pregnant just to manipulate someone else was disgusting. "I'm sorry she did that to you," I whisper, running my fingers along the underside of his jaw.

"I am too."

"So, what does she want when she tracks you down?"

"Don't know. I don't give a fuck and I don't take her calls. I want nothing to do with her. I have Kenton keep track of her and what she's up to. Some people are unstable and she's one of them. Plus, a few years ago, she showed up in town and started talking shit. I lost a good friend because of her." Well, I am no longer worried about how he feels about his ex. I hate her and what she did to him, and if I ever see her, I might beat the crap out of her.

"I'm sorry that you had to go through that."

"Even shit like that can teach you the best lessons."

"What lesson did you learn?"

"Let's just say the road to hell is paved with good intentions."

I smile at him. "Good lesson?" My head comes up when my phone starts ringing from the bedroom. "I should get that. It might be Tia." I kiss him and climb off his lap to answer it. Being Christmas, I know that I can expect a few phone calls from my friends in New York. When I finally get to my phone, it has stopped ringing so I flip it open to see who the call is from. It is a New York number that I don't recognize but the person left a voice mail. I put my phone to my ear to listen and have to fight the urge to throw it across the room when I hear my ex-fiancé's voice.

"Hey, I…um, just wanted to wish you a Merry Christmas. I know it's been awhile, but I wanted to tell you that I love you and miss you, November. I know I messed up." There is a long pause and I think he's hung up, then I hear a deep breath. "I hope you can forgive me. I miss you. Please call me back." My face must say it all. Next thing I know, my phone is out of my hand and Asher has it to his ear. He takes it away and looks at it, and then presses a button and puts it back to his ear. I know he is listening to the voice mail I just heard. I watch in fascination as his jaw clenches and I hear my phone cracking in his hand.

"Easy with my phone, Hulk." He looks down at me and I smile. He ignores my grin, takes the phone away from his ear and then throws it onto the bed. He uses his other hand to pull out my hair tie and throw that behind him, and then wraps my hair around his fist.

"You are not calling that piece of shit back."

"I'm not calling him back," I repeat. I never planned on it. Actually, I want to know how he got my number and why he is calling me at all. The only thing I can think of is that he called my mom and she gave him my number.

"Why the fuck is he calling you?"

"That's a good question," I say, looking over his shoulder and wondering the exact same thing. He tugs my hair and I look back at him. "I have no idea. I haven't even talked to him in two years. After I found out what he did, I changed my number and avoided him like the Ebola virus." I watch his eyes go soft and his lips twitch.

"Why didn't you avoid your mom?"

I take a breath and tell the truth. "I wanted to forgive her. I wanted a mom who loved me. I felt like if I forgave her for what she had done, maybe she could forgive me for whatever it was that I had done to make her hate me so much."

"You didn't do anything to her. She was selfish and doesn't deserve to have a daughter that is as kind and forgiving as you."

"I don't know," I whisper. "She has always hated me. I was never good enough. I don't know why she is the way she is but it doesn't mean that I don't crave her attention or love. It's not easy growing up with your only comfort provided by people who are paid to take care of you. All I wanted my whole life was to feel wanted. Until I met my dad when I turned eighteen, I never felt like I belonged to anyone."

"You belong now. Not only do you belong to your dad and his family, you belong to me and mine. And one day, you will belong to our kids."

"Kids?" I ask, I don't disguise the shock of my words.

"Kids. I told you, I'm going slowly for you. But you're going to be my wife, and as soon as we sign the marriage license, I'm working on getting you knocked up."

I roll my eyes at him. "You have this all planned, huh?"

"Fuck, yeah," he, smiles. I smile back. His happiness is contagious. "I can't wait to see you waddling around, knowing that I got you that way." My eyes narrow. He smiles. "That you are my life, and that you're carrying a life that we created inside of you." I feel faint. Even though he said I would waddle, and no woman wants to ever hear that they waddle or are going to waddle, it is still the most beautiful thing anyone has ever said to me.

"How many kids do you have in mind?" I ask softly, wrapping my arms around his neck. His hands slide to my waist and under my shirt. His thumbs rub along my sides, causing goose bumps to break out.

"Two boys and three girls. The boys need to come first so they can protect their sisters, especially if they look like you."

"What happens if we have a girl first?"

"Then I'm going to buy a few more guns."

I start giggling. "You do know how hot you are, right? I mean, if we have boys, I'm going to have to buy stock in Trojan just to make sure they are always protected. Either that, or invest my money into a medical company so they can invent men's birth control." He starts shaking his head, chuckling.

"I like that you keep saying *we*," he says softly, his eyes warm. "Now I know you see a future with me." He smiles his cocky smile and I laugh.

"You know, you're very bossy and completely cocky." His lips twitch, but what he doesn't do is disagree with me. I have to admit, it is a total turn on that he is so sure about us. It puts my mind at ease. I don't worry that I am thinking things are more serious than he thinks they are. He softly kisses my nose then my lips.

"I'm going to see if Ma needs help. I'll make sure everyone is ready to go to your dad's soon."

"Thanks." I stand on my tiptoes and kiss him quickly then walk into the bathroom and shut the door. I listen to Asher leave the bedroom. Once I know the coast is clear, I pull a towel down from the shelf, shove my face into it, and scream at the top of my lungs while jumping up and down. I can't believe I am getting everything that I have ever wanted. I have a man that loves me, a great job, and a giant family. I know that I am lucky.

I remember spending Christmas in New York, watching the Macy's parade then going to Tia's house for the day. If they weren't around, I would make dinner for myself and camp out in bed with a good book while my mom was with her friends or whatever guy she was seeing at the time. Now I have friends and family who will always be around to spend holidays with.

Chapter 8

THE DOORBELL RINGING and Beast's barking wakes me suddenly. I roll to the clock and see that it's just after ten in the morning. I can't think of anyone who would be here this early, unless it's the postman and he's dropping off a package.

I crawl out of bed and find Asher's shirt that he took off last night. I slip it over my head and find my sleep shorts lying on the floor. I pull them up quickly, noticing that they're getting a lot tighter. I'm still half asleep because I got home late yesterday.

I had been out on another all day shopping adventure with Susan. This trip was much better than the last, only because I needed to get stuff for an Easter egg hunt that I was putting on at the nursing home. Hearing kids laughing and having a good time makes me happy, so I want parents to bring their kids and let them go into the patients' rooms and get an egg and some candy.

With Asher gone on jobsites more often, I am starting to feel bored. I work for my dad and Liz, plus I took on a few other small clients in town. But even with the extra work I am doing, I still have plenty of free time.

First, I started going to the gym. I was working out so much that I had definition where I never thought I would and I was losing tons of weight. Then, one day Asher looked at me and actually complained.

"Babe, I loved your body. I loved having something to grab onto. I loved how soft you were. I know that you want to be healthy, but I miss the softness."

His voice was soft and the look in his eyes said that he loved me no matter what, but he missed the way I looked. And I don't know any woman who would not want their man to tell him that they shouldn't lose weight. I really didn't care. I wasn't working out to lose weight. I was doing it out of boredom, but I was happy to hear that he liked my body the way it was.

That night, I may have gone a wee bit overboard. I hadn't been on a diet, but I had been watching what I was eating. So, that night, I made homemade chicken Alfredo with garlic bread and asparagus. For dessert, I made apple cobbler with vanilla ice cream. There were more than three days' worth of calories in that meal, but it was so worth it. In the middle of eating, Asher started laughing at me.

"What?"

"You sound like you're really enjoying your food," he said, watching me take a bite of apple cobbler.

"It's yummy."

"Yeah," he said, leaning over to give me a very sweet vanilla apple kiss.

After dinner, I was sprawled out on top of Asher with him still inside me and his hands running along my back. Our breathing returned to normal and I broached the subject of money. "Since I'm living here now, we should talk about how we're going to divide the bills for the house."

"You're mine. I take care of you. You use your money to buy clothes or groceries for the house, unless I'm with you. Then, I'll pay. Also, you're going to need a new ride soon. That thing you call a car is not safe. There are too many deer around here. If one runs in front of you, your car will be totaled. If I'm lucky, I will just be visiting you in the hospital. If I'm not, I'll be visiting you at the cemetery. I don't want that shit, so we need to go to the dealer that I got my jeep from and we can pick out something for you."

I lifted my head from his chest, looking down at him. There were a few things that pissed me off, so I was deciding what pissed me off the most before I opened my mouth. I was sated, I had three orgasms and I was in a chill mood, so I was trying really hard not to flip out.

I watched his eyes roam over my face. "This is non-negotiable."

My eyes narrowed at his words and my temper flared. "Really? So how I spend money and what car I drive is non-negotiable?" I asked, just to make sure that we were on the same page.

"Yep, we might as well get all this shit out of the way," he said, rolling so I was under him. I felt him slide out of me and I couldn't help the mewl sound that I made at the loss of him. He kissed my nose and bit my bottom lip. The kiss started to get good when I pulled away.

"What shit?" I asked before he had a chance to put me in an Asher fog, where I unknowingly agree to everything he says.

"You don't need the money that your grandparents left you. When we have kids, you can put it in a college account for them, but I make enough money to take care of you, me, and any kids we have."

I took a deep breath, calming myself before I started to yell at the top of my lungs. "I love you, but you are not paying my way. I have taken care of myself for a long time. We need to come to an agreement that we can both live with," I said in a tone that was a lot calmer than I felt.

"We're starting a life together. If you never got that money, we would still be living the same way we do now. I'm not selling my land or building a new house somewhere else. This was my dream. I knew when I built this house that the woman who I fell in love with would live here with me, and my kids would grow up here on this property. I don't need more. I have a good car, toys in my garage, and money in the bank. I was planning for you before I even knew who you were. I never wanted to be a millionaire. Money does shit to people's heads. I like your head the way it is. We don't need it."

Well, he had a good point. Money did mess with people. We were happy and I had never even touched the money from my inheritance. But I knew the money could do some good and I wanted a swimming pool badly. I also wouldn't mind getting a new car with the money, and maybe a boat. I have always loved the water and have wanted to try skiing. The only thing with that was if I sucked at water skiing, we would be stuck with a boat we didn't use.

"I have a few requests before I put the money away for our future children," I said, shaking my head.

He gave me a crooked smile and kissed my nose again. "Go for it."

"First, I'm paying for my own car, if I decide to get a new one." He started to talk, but I covered his mouth with my hand. He narrowed his eyes, but I carried on like I didn't notice.

"Second, I would like a swimming pool, and third," I said loudly before he could cut me off or talk over me. "I would like a boat, but only if it can be returned if I end up not liking it."

"First, you're getting a new car whether you want one or not."

"If—" I started, but he cut me off with a quick kiss.

"Second, we can have a pool put in, as long as it's childproof. And when we have kids, they have to take swimming lessons. And third, I have a boat so you don't need to think about borrowing someone's boat to test it out."

I squealed, doing a happy dance. "Wow, that was easier than I thought," I said, smiling. "But I want to confirm that I'm paying for my new car when I decide to get one, and the swimming pool when it's put in."

"We'll figure it out."

"Hell no!" I said, rolling him to his back. I was looking down on him, making sure I had his full attention. "I will pay for that stuff, Asher, or I'll buy you a gift every week, and I will make sure they are extravagant and expensive. Trust me, you don't want to test me. I'm thinking along the lines of a unicorn."

"You don't get it. This is my land, my house. I pay for the pool. And I hope to God that you know unicorns aren't real."

Okay, that hurt. "So, I'm just a guest. I'm not living here with you? I'm not the woman that you plan on having a family with? If that's the case, let me know so I can pack my stuff. I don't want to be in the way when the one you plan on sharing your life with shows up. And who knows? Money is power. I'm sure I can convince someone somewhere that unicorns exist, and that they should locate one for me."

I watched as his face became hard and his jaw started to tic. "You know I don't mean it that way. You're my woman. I take care of you."

"If I'm your woman, as you put it, then you're my man. Relationships work both ways. They give and take. It's called compromise. I need to feel like I'm doing something for you. I won't be happy thinking that I live here with you for free. You take care of me, make me feel safe, give me a home and unconditional love, and I don't do anything for you? I won't live here feeling like I'm not bringing anything to the table. That's not me. I need to feel like I'm pulling my weight."

"Baby, don't you see it's the other way around?" he asked with both his hands holding my face. "All I have to offer you is stability and love. I have nothing else. If you left me tomorrow, some other guy would be there giving you the same thing I do. You're beautiful, funny, smart, kind. And the sex, fuck me, sex with you is off the charts. If you left me—Christ!" He closed his eyes, shaking his head. "If you left me, I would never be able to find another you. Someone who fills my life with the beauty that only you give me."

Okay, I couldn't help it. I started bawling like a giant baby. I laid my head on his chest, wrapping myself around him and trying to get as close as I could without crawling inside of him. I no longer cared about the pool or the car or anything else to do with money.

"I feel the same," I said through a sob. "You are an amazing man, Asher James Mayson, and you better not ever forget it."

"I love you, baby," he whispered and I felt his lips at the top of my head. His arms were around me, holding me tightly against him. I was so comfortable that I knew I could easily fall asleep that way. "I only want you to be happy."

"I am." My heart was full. There was no room in it for sadness or anger. I felt happy and loved. Even when I was arguing with him, I felt unconditional love.

It was in that moment that I decided to do something with the money my grandparents left me. I love the place that I now called home. And I wanted to do something that would benefit others. Something to share the love that I felt and hopefully give someone else a piece of that love and happiness. I knew that there were people who lived in the area that were struggling. I also knew they took donations each year for community projects and child outreach programs. I needed to find things to fill my time with. The spring and summer months were his busy seasons. The days were longer, the weather was nicer, and I knew Asher would be working extra hours. He and his team just won the bid on a new development, so they were all excited about that and the amount of money it would bring in. So I needed to keep myself occupied.

The pounding started to get louder, taking me out of my head and bringing me back to reality.

"I'm coming! I'm coming! Hold your horses!" I shout while running to the front door. I push Beast out of the way so I can get to the peep hole. When I look out, I see a young guy holding flowers. "What the heck?" I mutter to myself. I open the door and the man standing there smiles and holds out a bouquet of roses.

"Hi," I say, my eyebrows coming together in question. Asher has given me flowers in the past, but he has never given me roses. He has always brought them home to me. I've never received a delivery.

"This is a delivery for November," the guy says, looking up at me from where his head was bent down, reading the paper in his hand.

"That's me," I say, and before I can get anything else out, he shoves a clipboard into my hand.

"You need to sign where the Xs are."

I quickly sign by the two Xs. He then smiles and takes the clipboard, putting it under his arm. He hands me the flowers and then walks off. I set the flowers on the island and look for a card but can't find one. I know the flowers are from Asher because he is the only person who would send them. I walk back to the bedroom to find my phone.

Once I have my cell phone, I send Asher a quick text.

Me: *Thanks for the flowers.*

There is no reply right away, so I set the phone down and jump in the shower. I am blow drying my hair and drinking coffee with I hear my phone signal a message.

Asher: *Didn't send anything ;-(*
Me: *Oh. Maybe my dad sent them.*

"Hey, baby girl," Dad answers on the first ring.

"Hi Dad, um, I was wondering if you sent me flowers?"

"No. Why?"

"I got a delivery of roses this morning and Asher didn't send them."

"I didn't send anything."

My breathing starts to pick up and I know my dad can hear it through the phone.

"I'm sure they are from someone you know," he says quietly. I'm not as sure as he is. I feel paranoid, but after the roses that someone left me at my dad's house, there is always a nagging in the back of my head telling me that something bad is going to happen to me again.

"I can tell you're scared but don't worry so much. Nothing has happened since the break-in."

"You're right. I'm acting crazy," I tell him. Flowers are not a big deal.

"If you feel unsafe, just tell me and I will be over there."

"No, Dad. You're right. I'm fine."

"Okay, baby girl. I'm going to go to sleep. My phone is on if you need me."

"Thanks, Dad. Love you," I whisper, feeling like an idiot.

"Love you too, baby girl." He hangs up and I call everyone else I know who might have sent the flowers. No one did.

Asher: *Was it your dad???*
Me: *He said no. I called around and no one else sent them.*

Less than a second later, I get a response.

Asher: *I'm calling Dad now.*

Me: *I don't think that's necessary.*

Asher: *Dad will be there in 5. I'm on my way. Stay inside and lock the door.*

Me: *I'm fine. Stop worrying. It's making me freak.*

Asher: *Rather you be paranoid.*

I hear the car pull up and I jump off the couch from where Beast and I are cuddling, and run to the front door. I look out the peephole just as Asher's dad is getting out of the police cruiser. I open the front door and step out onto the porch, and hear the crinkle of paper under my bare foot. I bend down to pick it up. It is a plain card-size envelope. I can feel the weight of the card inside. I start to open it when it is snatched out of my hand.

I jump and let out a startled yelp. I had been so caught up in the envelope, I forgot about Asher's dad. "Crap, you scared me," I say, looking up at Mr. Mayson.

He chuckles. "I got that when you screamed."

"I didn't scream," I say in my own defense. I've become close with all of Asher's family. His parents have taken me in as one of their own. And his brothers treat me like I am the little sister they missed out on having. Now they're making up for lost time by picking on me and torturing me on a regular basis. Sometimes Asher gets annoyed with them, but most of the time, he joins in on the fun of pissing me off.

Mr. Mayson smiles like he thinks I'm being funny, then looks down at the envelope. The smile leaves his face quickly and his eyes come back to me. "I hope you made sure to look out the peep hole before you came outside." His tone is serious.

"I made sure," I mumble, hoping this is nothing serious. I don't want to start living my life looking over my shoulder.

"Let's go in and you can show me what you got and tell me about the person who dropped them off."

"Are you going to open that?" I ask, pointing at the card.

"When we get inside."

We walk into the house and I close and lock the door behind us as we turn to go into the kitchen. Mr. Mayson is standing at the kitchen island in front of the flowers. I notice that he now has on a pair of gloves. His head is bent and he is looking at the open card.

"What does it say?" I ask.

He holds it up for me to see. On the front of the card is a picture of Manhattan at night. When he opens it, I stumble back and my stomach drops. I am looking at the words written in bright red ink.

Coming events cast their shadows before
I had a vision in the summer light—
Sorrow was in it, and my inward sight
Ached with sad images. The touch of tears
Gushed down my cheeks the figured woes of years
Casting their shadows across sunny hours.
Oh, there was nothing sorrowful in flowers.

"Holy crap." I cover my mouth and run to the hall bathroom to throw up the piece of toast I had for breakfast and the coffee that I drank. I feel a cool rag on my neck and a hand rubbing my back.

"Are you okay?" he asks and I can hear the anger in his voice.

"Yeah," I say, flushing the toilet. I take the rag off my neck and wipe my mouth with it. I look up into his eyes and can tell he is pissed off. I just hope he isn't mad at me for bringing this kind of trouble to his son's front door. "I'm so sorry," I say, putting my face into my hands. I can't figure out why this is happening to me. I feel him pull me in for a hug.

"We will figure it out. We won't let anything happen to you."

"I don't understand why someone's doing this to me," I cry into his shirt. I hate it more that Asher is dealing with this too. If something happened to him because of me, I don't know what I would do. "Can you give me a minute?" I ask, pulling out of his hug and wiping my eyes.

"Sure, darling."

I shut the bathroom door, turn around to the vanity, and look at myself. My eyes are blood shot. I tie my hair up quickly and turn on the cold water then start splashing my face. I need to brush my teeth, but

I'm not ready to leave the safety of these four walls. I know that once I walk out that door, I'm going to be asked more questions that I don't have the answers to. I rinse my mouth a few times jump up on the counter and try to think of anyone who would do this to me. I can't think of anyone that I've wronged. There isn't anyone that dislikes me enough to try to kill me or stalk me to another state and harass me. Then I start to wonder where they have been during the last few months. Nothing has happened since a week before Thanksgiving. Not that I missed them, but why did they go away, and why are they back now?

"November!" Asher bellows from the front door. I hop off the counter and start to open the bathroom door when it is shoved open and hits me in the head.

"Shit!" I cry and my hands go to my forehead where the door just slammed into me.

"Jesus Christ! Baby, are you okay?" I don't know if I am alright. I know my head hurts a lot. Who the heck opens a door with that much force? "Let me see," he says, pulling my hands away from my face. "Fuck!" he shouts and I know from the look on his face that I don't want to see the damage. I now have a headache on top of all the other crap.

"I'm sorry, baby. I'm so fucking sorry." He looks really upset. Jeez, it hurt, but it wasn't bleeding. How bad could it be? I turn to the mirror and want to laugh. I have a bright red and purple mark in the center of my forehead. I look like Harry Potter. I start to giggle and Asher's eyes narrow. "This shit's not funny. I could have really hurt you."

"I know that," I snap. "What the heck are you? The Incredible Hulk or something? Seriously, who opens a door to a bathroom like that?"

"Dad pointed out that you were in here. I didn't even think. I just had to make sure you were okay."

Now I feel bad. "Sorry, it just hurts," I say softly, feeling like a total bitch. He always worries. Even when I'm safe, he worries, so now that I'm actually in danger, I might as well handcuff myself to him.

He kisses the mark. "So, why were you laughing?" he asks, wrapping me in a hug.

"I was laughing because I look like Harry Potter." His eyes come back to my face and his lips twitch. I glare at him. "Now I'm going to have to give myself bangs to hide it so I don't have to listen to your stupid brothers and the jokes they'll make about it," I say, pointing to my forehead.

"They love you." They do, I know they do. We have become great friends. I know if Asher wasn't around, I could count on any of them to help me out with whatever was wrong. And they aren't perverted, just brotherly. For that, I am thankful.

Now Sven, he is a different story. He makes me uncomfortable. I'm not sure if it's because he is handsome, or if it is just him as a person. Sometimes the way he looks at me or the words he uses makes it seem like he is coming onto me. But I've seen him in action when we all went to the bar together. I know that when he comes on to a girl, he doesn't hold anything back. He is over-the-top aggressive and women still swarm him like a bee to honey. One day, when he meets a girl he's serious about, she's going to have to be really strong in order to deal with his personality.

"I know they love me," I grumble.

"Is everything okay?" Mr. Mayson asks from outside the door. I step away from Asher and open the door. Mr. Mayson looks down at me. "What the fuck?" he asks, looking up at Asher.

"It's fine. I just need to put some ice on it and take some aspirin," I say, stepping around him.

"How did it happen?"

"It's either because your son is the Incredible Hulk or he has a thing for Harry Potter," I say over my shoulder. I laugh when I hear Asher groan.

"It's my fault," Asher says, picking me up and setting me on the counter, removing me from where I was standing in front of the fridge. "The door hit her when I shoved it open to get to her." I watch him go to the drawer and grab a baggie then back to the fridge. He fills it with ice wraps it in a kitchen towel and brings it to me and presses it to my head.

"Thanks, honey," I mumble.

"You're welcome, baby. I'm sorry your day sucks."

"Me too." He kisses my temple and then looks over to his dad, but his eyes stop on the roses that are sitting on the counter.

"Some guy delivered those?" he asks. I swallow and look at Asher's dad. He hasn't told him about the card yet. Mr. Mayson looks at me then at Asher. "What aren't you telling me?" Asher asks his dad.

"When I pulled up, November came outside and found a card."

"Where is it?" Asher asks. I can see his body expanding and his muscles bunching under his shirt. Mr. Mayson hands Asher the card that is now inside a gallon zipper bag. The card is open so we can see the inside and outside of it. Asher looks at the front for a second and sees that it's a picture of New York and then he flips the bag over. I can tell that he's using all of his control to not rip the thing in half.

"What does this mean?" Asher sounds wild and nothing like himself.

I pull my phone out and Google the words that are written in the card. "The person who wrote on my living room wall also wrote this poem," I tell Asher and his dad.

"We know the other poem is called November. What is this one called?" Asher asks.

"Anticipation," I tell them and get a shiver down my spine when I read the poem aloud.

'Coming events cast their shadow before.'
I had a vision in the summer light—
Sorrow was in it, and my inward sight
Ached with sad images. The touch of tears
Gushed down my cheeks:—the figured woes of years
casting their shadows across sunny hours.
Oh, there was nothing sorrowful in flowers

Wooing the glances of an April sun,
Or apple blossoms opening one by one
Their crimson bosoms—or the twittered words
And warbled sentences of merry birds;—
Or the small glitter and the humming wings
Of golden flies and many colored things—
Oh, these were nothing sad—nor to see Her,
Sitting beneath the comfortable stir
Of early leaves—casting the playful grace
Of moving shadows in so fair a face—
Nor in her brow serene—nor in the love
Of her mild eyes drinking the light above
With a long thirst—nor in her gentle smile—
Nor in her hand that shone blood-red the while
She raised it in the sun. All these were dear
To heart and eye—but an invisible fear
Shook in the trees and chilled upon the air,
And if one spot was laughing brightest—there
My soul most sank and darkened in despair!—
As if the shadows of a curtained room
Haunted me in the sun—as if the bloom
Of early flow'rets had no sweets for me,
Nor apple blossoms any blush to see—
As if the hour had brought too bright a day—
And little birds were all too gay!—too gay!—
As if the beauty of that Lovely One
Were all a fable.—Full before the sun
Stood Death and cast a shadow long before,
Like a dark pall enshrouding her all o'er,
Till eyes, and lips, and smiles, were all no more!

"That sounds a lot more threatening than the last poem he left," Asher says, looking at his dad. I look toward Mr. Mayson too. His face is blank. "What do we do?"

"I need November to tell me about the delivery and anything that she can remember from when she was attacked in New York. I also need to know if either of you have noticed anyone out of place or someone who made you uncomfortable."

I look from Asher dad to Asher and see that his body is still ready for attack. I lean forward on the counter and grab his shirt at the back and drag him toward me. Once he's close, I wrap my arms around his middle and lay my head on his back. I feel his hands rest on top of mine then he takes a deep breath and his body relaxes.

"I need to go out to the car and get my notebook. When I come back in, we can talk."

Asher turns to face me and pulls me closer to him. "I'm really sorry about this," I mumble into his chest, letting his smell relax me.

"Don't apologize about this. It isn't your fault."

"Maybe I should lea—"

The words are not even out of my mouth before he cuts me off. "Don't even fucking think about leaving me." His arms go super tight around me like he is expecting me to vanish into thin air. "I will track your ass down and drag you back here. I want you to listen to me." His hands hold my face, and his lips come closer to mine. "Dad is on this. I'm on this and now I'm putting Kenton on this. We will find out what's going on and who is doing this. And while we're doing that, you will be safe."

"I would die if something happened to you because of me," I whisper my biggest fear and then do a face plant into his shirt.

"Baby," he says, running his hand down my back. "The worst thing that could happen is if you left me and I had no way of knowing that you were okay. I won't let anything happen to you and I will make sure that nothing happens to me either. Do you think I would let something happen to myself, knowing that there are about six guys that I know waiting to take my place?"

"You know you're crazy, right?" I ask in all seriousness. Only he would say one of the reasons he was staying safe is so random, non-existent guys don't try to take me away.

"No, I'm selfish. I know what sleeps next to me every night. You are mine, November. Until the day you leave this earth, you are mine. And I take my responsibility very seriously." What could I say to that? Before I say anything, his dad comes in the front door carrying a notebook and a file.

"Alright, let's get started," Mr. Mayson says, setting his stuff down on the island and pulling out the stool to take a seat. Asher kisses my forehead then jumps up next to me on the counter, grabbing my hand.

I tell them about the delivery then about the attack. Then I remember the roses that had been outside the apartment door when I got home from the hospital in New York. I had never gotten flowers before, and my mom would get them all the time from whatever man she was seeing, so I assumed they were for her. I took them into the apartment and left them on the counter. I never even thought about them again until that moment.

"White roses," I whisper to myself.

"Pardon?" Mr. Mayson asks.

"White roses were left outside my apartment door after I was attacked. I thought they were for my mom but I guess maybe they weren't."

"Why do you say that?" Mr. Mayson asks, and I remember my mom's shocked face when she opened the card.

"The card said 'I'm sorry.' We both assumed they were from the guy she was seeing, the one that took me to the hospital. That he was sorry for what happened to me. But I remember she seemed shocked by the apology. Like he wouldn't write something like that, you know? That he wouldn't apologize. When I was packing my car later that evening, the same boyfriend who I thought the flowers were from stopped by to drop off Beast. He had kept him while I was in the hospital. He didn't want him to end up at the shelter. He made me pinky promise that if I was going to give Beast away, he got first dibs. I remember thinking that he was a really good guy and hoping that it would work out for him and my mom. He hugged me then got in his car and left. I figured he was just busy. I left a few minutes after he did, so I'm not sure what happened with him and my mom."

"I'm gonna need your mom's number, and the contact information for the detective in New York who was working on your case," Mr. Mayson says, and I nod my head in agreement.

"I have a friend who's been looking into things," Asher says, and I look over at him. I never knew this. We talked about what happened to me, but he never told me anything about someone looking into it.

"You do?" I ask, wondering when he had asked someone to check on it.

"Yeah." That was all he said while pulling me closer so he could kiss my forehead.

"Okay," I say slowly. "When were you going to tell me about that?"

"Right now."

"Don't you think that I should know about things like that?"

"You know now." I narrow my eyes and he brings my hand to his mouth, kissing my fingers that are wrapped around his. "Nothing has happened in the last few months. We weren't even sure if the break in had anything to do with what happened in New York."

That's a good point. We didn't know anything. I don't even know why I cared. I was grateful that he was looking into it.

"Have they come up with anything?" I ask, hoping that some detective was using his skills so I didn't have to live my days worried about my life being in danger, or worse, having Asher or either of our families in danger.

"Nothing new. They think it was an isolated incident."

"So, do they have any idea why this is happening?"

"No, baby."

"Do you think someone is stalking me?" I ask, looking at Asher then his dad.

"I'm not sure what's going on. And before I jump to any conclusions, I need to talk to the florist who delivered the flowers and ask about the person who placed the order. Then I need to contact your mother and find out what she remembers from the night of your attack. I also need to contact the officer who was handling your case and see if there are any cases similar to yours," Mr. Mayson explains.

"Asher already found that out. They said it was isolated."

"Yes, they did, but he was talking about the attack. I'm talking about the flowers and the messages," Mr. Mayson says.

"Smart." I smile at him and he shakes his head, chuckling.

"In the meantime, I want you to be extra cautious when you're out. I also need you to make a list of people that you have dated. There might be someone who wasn't ready for your relationship to be over."

"That's simple. I dated my ex-fiancé and Asher."

"I mean anyone you went out with, even if it wasn't serious."

"I know, and it was only my ex and Asher. I never dated in high school. My mother wanted me to work, and if I wasn't working, I had to be at home. I met my ex during my sophomore year of college and I dated him until I caught him with my mother. After I broke it off with him, I needed time and I was never really interested in anyone, so I didn't date. Although, before the attack happened, my boss made me sign up for a dating service, so I did that, but I haven't even checked the activity of that account."

"Do you have the account information?" Asher asks and I can see his jaw tightening.

"Yeah, it's in my phonebook."

"So, you didn't think about closing the account since we met?"

I rolled my eyes and looked at him, wanting to determine if he was being serious.

"I haven't even thought about it." His eyes narrowed. "What? You've been keeping me busy," I shout, throwing my hands in the air. "I'm sorry if I haven't thought about a dating site that I didn't even want to be a member of."

I hear Asher's dad laugh from across the kitchen and I look up at the same time as Asher. His dad puts his hands in front of him in a stay back gesture and laughs harder. I laugh, and Asher's eyes come to me.

"You think this is funny?"

"Um…no?" My answer sounds like a question and I start laughing louder.

"What did I tell you about laughing at me, baby?" he asks. I see the look in his eyes so I jump off the counter and start to run to get away from him. Sadly, his legs are longer and his speed is faster, so I don't have a chance to escape before I am lying on the floor and his big body is pinning me down, tickling me.

My head is thrashing back and forth. I am begging him to stop and then Beast comes over, not to help me, but to assist Asher in his torture. He is licking my face while Asher tickles my ribs.

"Are you going to close the account?"

He keeps up the tickling. "YES!" I screech my agreement about the dating site. "Please stop. I'm going to pee." I am finally able to say a full sentence and he stops immediately. I jump up and run to the bathroom without looking back. When I am walking back toward the kitchen, I hear Asher and his dad talking.

"I want this shit done."

"Call Kenton and ask him to make November a priority. You can always send her to him to keep safe." Hmm, that's interesting. I've been wondering what Kenton does for a living but every time I ask about it, I get the run around.

His laugh holds no humor. Then he answers, "He met November at the Christmas party and was getting ready to go in for the Kenton kill when I told him she was mine."

"He would never cross that line and you know it."

"The only thing I know is that I want this shit done," he growls. "I'm too selfish to send her away. I wouldn't be able to function knowing she was staying with Kenton." I hear him take a breath. "If things escalate, I'll take her to the cabin."

"Your cousin is a good man. He's also one of the best at what he does."

"I don't give a fuck. You were not there. You didn't see the way he looked at her. I know Kenton better than anyone. And unless something else happens, she stays here with me."

"Your jealousy could end up getting her hurt," his dad whispers and my heart starts beating double time.

"I would never let anything happen to her. I have my fucking reasons for not trusting anyone with her." I know I need to quit eavesdropping, but it is like I'm glued in place. "We don't even know what's going on. The only thing we do know is that she was attacked in New York. That may not even have anything to do with what's happening here."

"The card shows the New York City skyline. I think whoever is doing this knows her from New York. We don't know if the attack and the things happening here are connected, but since she's been in Tennessee, she has had two separate instances where someone left poetry. This thing is messy. We just need to clean it up and put the pieces together. I'm going into town to the florist. I'll call and let you know if I find out anything from them."

"In the meantime, I'm gonna talk to my friend in Jersey and tell him about what happened today." I can hear the frustration in Asher's voice.

I walk out of my hiding place in the hall just as Mr. Mayson is opening the front door. He tips his head in my direction, his eyes soft on me. "I want you to be extra careful." I can tell that his tone is not that of the sheriff, but as a man who cares about me like a daughter. "If you're out, you need to watch who's around you. If anyone makes you feel even the slightest bit of unease, you go somewhere where with a lot of people and call me or one of my boys. As I told Asher, this whole situation is a mess. I just need to see if I can dig anything up that will straighten everything out. In the meantime, stay safe."

"Thanks for everything." I walk to him and hug him around the waist. He gives me a one-armed hug, his other arm full with his notebook, his plastic bag with the card inside, and a coffee cup.

"I'm sure Susan is going to be stopping by soon and will want to see for herself that you're safe." He was not wrong. Susan was a momma bear and very protective of her cubs. Since being brought into the family, she has taken me under her care and made it known far and wide that if you messed with me, you would have to deal with her.

"Okay," I murmur. My real mother might not want me, but Susan loves me and she is better than anything I could ever ask for in a mother. Asher's brothers are always giving me a hard time, telling me I am a suck up but I don't care.

Asher hooks me around my waist, pulling my back to his front. "Talk to you soon, Dad," Asher says, shuffling us to the door as his dad closes it behind him. He locks it and turns me around, his hands framing my face. "You okay?" I can see the worry in his eyes.

"I'm fine. I just want to know who is doing this and why."

"Me too, baby," he says, laying his forehead against mine.

"Is it me, or is that poem totally creepy?" I whisper.

"It's not just you."

"What do you think it means?"

"I don't know, baby," he says quietly. I wrap my arms tighter around him and hold on. I can tell he hates this more than I do.

Chapter 9

"BYE," I CALL over my shoulder as I walked out of Temptations. "Bye, honey," Liz calls through the open door of her shop. I got up early to meet Liz for coffee and to explain to her about what happened yesterday. She knew I received flowers yesterday because I had called her, and everyone else I knew, to see who sent them. She, like everyone else, said she didn't send anything and wondered why I was asking but I couldn't explain the situation at the time. Plus with each phone call I made, I got more and more scared and was too freaked out to talk to anyone about what happened. Then Mr. Mayson showed up and we found the card. So, I knew it was more than just a nice gesture from a friend.

After Mr. Mayson left, Asher dragged me into the office, sat me at the desk, got my phone book and had me log onto the online dating site. He dragged me out of the chair, sat down, and pulled me into his lap. I poked around on the website and looked at any messages I had received from guys. I clicked on my profile and the picture I used was not my favorite. He grunted a few times while reading some of the information I posted. I was surprised by the amount of inquiries I received. Some were normal, others disturbing. The normal ones were just, *would you like to have dinner with me* questions. Others were, *would you like to meet to have sex?* Those surprised me. I never knew people used the internet for one night stand type of situations.

Once he was satisfied that no one from the website was stalking me, he canceled my account. I sat quietly in his lap the whole time, fighting the laughter that was getting ready to explode out of me while he was clicking away on the computer. When he was done and the computer was shutting down, I turned to look at him. "All mine." He grunted and

I could no longer hold it in. I started laughing.

"You're such a caveman," I said, kissing him.

"OH MY GOD. I'm so sorry," I'm apologizing to the person I just bumped into.

The woman mumbles and her body bends down to pick up a file. "You need to watch where you're going."

I know that voice. My body freezes.

"Mom?" I whisper in complete shock as her head comes up. Her hair is different, a little longer and I can see a few new wrinkles around her eyes. She probably had to cut back on her Botox treatments now that I'm not there to help her with money.

"November," she says and gives me a curt nod, but she doesn't say anything else. She is wearing her usual gear. Black, wide leg slacks, a lavender blouse that I know is real silk, and shiny, black dominatrix shoes. Well, that's what I call them. The heel looks like it can be used as a weapon. I also know that those shoes have a red bottom.

One of her ex-boyfriends bought them for her before his wife found out that he was keeping a woman on the side. She told him that if he continued on with the affair, she was going to take him to the cleaners. That was the last gift he gave my mother and the only thing she kept. All the jewelry and expensive handbags he bought for her got pawned. Well, any jewelry or handbags that anyone bought for her went to the pawn shop. She never kept anything except clothing unless it had the tags. Then, she would either get the money back or get a store credit for the item and find something else that she liked more.

"Mom, what are you doing here?" I ask, starting to freak out. I don't want my dad to see her and I really don't want my grandmother to see her. I look around to see if there is anyone out that I know, and luckily for me, the streets are quiet.

"Well, it's good to see you too," she snaps. Her tone says that it isn't good to see me.

"Sorry, I'm just surprised. I mean, I tried to call you and you haven't returned any of my phone calls."

"You abandoned me for your father. He wanted nothing to do with you, yet you still left me for him." Great, now how do I deal with this? My dad didn't abandon me. My mother kept me from him, but I really don't want to get into an argument with her in the middle of the town square. Word travels fast in this town and I don't want my family to know that she has even been in the city.

"Mom, please. I didn't abandon you. You know what happened to me. I couldn't stay in New York anymore."

I watch her roll her eyes, completely disregarding my attack. "That kind of thing happens every day in the city, November. Don't be such a drama queen."

Oh my God. I want to scream in her face. I know that bad things happen in the city. I lived there my whole life. I watched the news, and read the paper. But it didn't happen to someone else. It happened to me, her daughter, someone that she was supposed to love and look after. "Mom, I could have died. I could have been raped. You heard what the police said. And trust me, I know that bad things happen, but I didn't feel safe there anymore." I take a deep breath. "You didn't answer my question. Why are you in town? Is everything okay?"

She shakes her head and presses her lips into a flat line before answering me. "Everything is fine. I had to see the lawyer in town for something that doesn't concern you." I am kind of curious about her meeting with the lawyer, but I'm not going to ask her about it. I want her to leave before anyone sees her.

I take a breath, hoping that the answer to my next question is a big no. "Are you in town for long?"

She looks around and scrunches up her face in disgust. "No, it's a one day trip. My flight leaves in a few hours." Well, thank God for small favors.

"Okay." That was all I could say. I wasn't sad that she was leaving.

"You look like you fit in here with these people," she says, looking down her nose at me. The words "these people" was said like they were, in fact, not people at all, but a secret alien race trying to take over the world. She takes a step away from me, pulling her bag closer to her body like I'm planning on ripping it out of her hands and taking off down the street with it. I almost laugh. I look down at what I am wearing and I do fit in here. I have on a pair of dark jeans and long sleeve black shirt with a puffy pink vest over it. And on my feet, I have a pair of plain black boots. I look normal. Not New York upper west side normal, but Tennessee normal.

"Thanks." I smile.

She huffs out a breath then looks around. Obviously, I didn't give her the response she wants. "I need to go," she says and I feel tears sting my nose. Stupid, I know, but she is the only mother I have and I hate that we aren't close. For my whole life, I wished for her to act like she cared about me. It killed me each time she proved that she never would.

"Okay, have a safe fight," I mumble, realizing that I'm not a kid anymore. I don't have to explain to people why my mother was never around like all the other kids' moms. Realizing that I have family and friends here, people who love me, gives me strength. She has no part in my life. I don't need her. With that thought in my head, I walk around her, down the sidewalk to my car, get in and call Asher.

"Hey, baby. I'm in the middle of something. Can I call you back?"

"No. Uh…um…that's not necessary. I just wanted to tell you I love you."

"Are you okay? You sound freaked."

"I'm great, actually. Really, really great," I tell him truthfully. I know happiness because of him, his family, and mine.

He is quiet and I hear him take a breath. "Love you too, baby." His voice sounds gruff.

"Good," I whisper, closing my eyes.

"Good," he whispers back. He is quiet a minute then he tells me, "I'll see you at home."

"Okay," I whisper again.

"Later," he chuckles and that makes me giggle.

"Yeah, later." I hang up before I am an even bigger dork. I look in my rearview mirror and see my smile. I am going home. Home. To a home I have with Asher and Beast. I put my car in reverse and drive.

"No," I WHINE to Asher, who is behind me in bed. It's Saturday and he's been trying to get me up for the past hour. I'm ready to strangle him.

"Baby," he laughs, shoving his face in my neck.

"Asher, I'm telling you right now, if you don't leave me alone, I'm going to kill you."

"That's not very nice," he chuckles.

"I don't care. Go away. Geez, you have three brothers and a boat load of friends. Can't you find someone else to bother?"

"I'm not going to ask one of them to shower with me."

"Oh my God!" I yell. "Go away. I'm sleeping." I shove my head under my pillow, trying to block him out.

"You sound awake to me." I hear his muffled reply and I can tell he's smiling just by the tone of his voice.

"That's it." I roll over and straddle him. His face lights up and he smiles. I smile back then grab my pillow and hold it over his big, stupid face. His hands run up my sides and start tickling me. When I finally call mercy, we're both breathing heavily.

"Now, are you going to shower with me?" he asks, his eyes shining with laughter.

"You are seriously relentless, you know that, don't you?"

"I like showering with you." He shrugs.

I shake my head and start laughing. "No, you don't. You like getting off in the shower."

His face goes serious and I hold my breath. "No!" His voice is low and deep. "I like taking care of you. I can fuck you anytime. I'm not always able to take care of you."

I feel my face go soft. I swallow against the lump in my throat then lift my head, pressing my mouth to his. "Let's go shower," I whisper against his lips.

He carries me to the bathroom and takes his time taking care of me. Then, I take care of him. It's beautiful.

Standing at the kitchen counter, I watch Beast eat while I finish my coffee. Asher walks around the corner wearing his overly washed jeans that hang low on his hips, no socks, and the T-shirt he's going to put on is in his hand. My mouth goes dry. I squeeze my hand into a fist at my side to avoid reaching out and running it down his chest and abs. He shakes his head and I know he knows what I'm thinking. It is really unfair. No one should have that much power over another person.

Once he reaches me, he bends over and kisses me softly. Then, he kisses my nose and grabs a mug from behind me to make himself a cup of coffee while crowding me against the counter. His jaw has a few days of stubble that makes his face look more rugged. Something about that look makes my tummy melt. I can't help myself, so I run my hand from his hair, down the side of his face, feeling it prickle against my fingertips. I remember how it feels when it rubs between my thighs. I squeeze my legs together and drop my hand.

"You okay, baby?" I nod my head, but don't say anything. I'm happy—more than happy. Some days, I wake up and wonder how I spent the first twenty-five years of my life without him. I had no clue what real happiness was. Or maybe that was happiness and now I'm living in bliss. "You look like you're really in your head. What's going on?" he asks, taking a bite of a bagel.

"Nothing." I grin. "So, what are we doing today? Can we go riding?" I ask excitedly.

"No, someone's coming over in an hour," he says, wiping his mouth.

"O…kay," I say slowly, waiting for him to tell me who is coming over. He doesn't say anything, just smiles. "So, who is it?" I ask after he still doesn't say anything.

"You'll see." He shrugs.

"So, you're not going to tell me who it is?"

"Nope," he says, putting his cup and plate into the sink without rinsing them. He starts to walk away, so I clear my throat to get his attention. When he looks at me, I nod my head in the direction of the sink and he raises his eyebrows. So I nod my head in the direction of the sink again. "Do you have a tic, baby?" he asks, his mouth twitching.

I narrow my eyes. "I'm not your maid, Asher." He straight out smiles, giving me the dimple, then walks to the sink, takes his plate and cup out, and places them in the dishwasher without rinsing them. "You have to rinse them before you put them in the dishwasher," I tell him, feeling and sounding like a total nag.

"It's a dish*washer*," he says slowly, walking towards me.

"Ye—" Before I can get the words out, his mouth is on mine. The kiss is deep, wet, and so yummy, that when he pulls his mouth away, my hands are wrapped around his neck and my legs are around his hips. I'm in an Asher fog so deep that he could tell me it's not a dishwasher, but a microwave, and I would agree with him completely.

My eyes flutter open. He's looking down at me with a cocky smile and mumbles, "That's better." Then, he squeezes my ass in his hands, sets me on the counter and leaves the kitchen, putting on his shirt as he goes.

"Holy crap," I whisper. Beast looks at me and grunts walks to his dog bed and lays down, completely disappointed in my lack of willpower. "It's not my fault," I mumble to my dog. He lets out a breath and shuts his eyes, completely dismissing me. "It's not," I say, still mumbling. I hop off the counter, take Asher's dishes from the dishwasher, rinse off the cream cheese so it doesn't harden onto the plate, rinse out the cup then place them both back in the dishwasher. The whole time, I'm smiling.

I go to the bedroom to get dressed. I pull on a pair of leggings and choose a loose, off-the-shoulder cream shirt, and throw a black open front, oversized sweater on over it. I know Asher says he loves my body, but I need to stop eating everything that is placed in front of me before I need a whole new wardrobe.

Yesterday, I had to lie down to button my jeans, and let's just say walking around all day and having my toes tingle from lack of circulation is a hazard to myself and those around me. I flop down on the bed, exhausted from getting dressed. I'm so tired that I feel like I could sleep for the next week. I close my eyes just to give them a rest. I feel a feather light touch run down my cheek. My eyes open slowly and I see Asher's face.

"Time to get up, sleepy head. Our guest is here."

I take a deep breath and stretch. "Okay, who is it?" I grumble, thinking that this guest better be awesome enough for my sleep interruption.

"You'll see." He smiles and pulls me out of bed, tucking me under his arm and walking us out to the living room where there is a guy about Asher's age. He's wearing jeans and a black shirt with the words, *Crystal Clear Pools and Spas* written in white on the breast.

"Oh my God!" I screech and start jumping up and down. My tiredness is a long forgotten memory. The guy takes a step back and looks nervously to Asher for help.

Asher starts laughing. "Don't mind her, Jack. She does this when she gets excited." I look at him and I can see he's thinking about when he told me he was taking me four-wheeling. I bite my lip when I see his eyes turn hungry.

Jack clears his throat. "Nice to meet you, November." He sticks out his hand and I place mine in his.

"Nice to meet you, Jack," I say then take a step back. "Sorry about scaring you. I'm just so excited," I mumble, slightly embarrassed by my outburst.

Asher pulls me back into him and his arms wrap around me, his chin resting on top of my head. I feel his body shaking with silent laughter behind me. "I think he got that, baby."

"Whatever," I say quietly, wondering if it would be rude to elbow him in his ribs in front of a guest. I give Jack a big smile after I see him shaking his head.

"So, do you guys know the type of set up you want?" Jack asks, looking between us.

"Um, it has to be childproof," I say, remembering Asher's pool requirement.

Jack's eyebrows shoot up. "You havin' a baby, man?" he asks and I wonder if it's normal in Tennessee to ask a stranger that you're going to be working for such a personal question. In New York, that question would surely get you fired, maybe even shot.

Asher must feel me go still, because he starts talking. "Me and Jack have been friends since high school, baby. He used to spend every summer with my family up at the cabin. Now he owns the pool and spa company with his old man and does jobs for us when we have a client who wants a pool put in on their property."

I nod my head, thinking someone should shoot me. Asher's friend, and not some stranger, saw me jumping up and down and being a total dork.

"So, are you havin' a baby?" Jack asks again.

"Not yet," Asher says, squeezing me. I don't know if his words or the lack of oxygen is responsible for the dizziness I'm feeling.

Jack nods his head. "Alright, so the only request you have is child safety?" he asks, looking at me.

"Um…" I know nothing about pools except how to swim in one. This isn't as fun as I thought it would be.

"You want a Jacuzzi, a grotto, a deep end?" he asks, looking at me expectantly.

"Um…" I repeat, feeling like an idiot.

"You got any books or pictures of work you've done that we can look at for ideas?" Asher asks and I'm thankful that he's smart. I sag into him with relief and he kisses the top of my head.

"Yeah, of course. Let's go to the table."

"Would you like something to drink?" I ask as we make our way into the kitchen.

"Coffee would be good, if you've got it."

"Of course."

I pour him a cup of coffee and get one for me and Asher as well. I set out sugar and cream on the counter and then take a seat between Asher and Jack.

"So these are some of the pool designs we did last year." He pulls out three pictures. The first one looks like a tropical paradise. It has tons of flowers and plants around it. The pool is bright blue with sand colored cement surrounding it. The second is a plain, bean shaped pool with an area for chairs and a table. The third is large and has two areas for sunbathing. It had a Jacuzzi that you could get to from inside the pool by walking up a set of stairs or you could get to it from outside the pool. It also had a shallow end that you could lay in and the water would only be about five inches deep. If you had kids, you could stay with them in that area.

"I love this." I point to the third picture.

"I like this," Asher says, indicating the first picture.

"Well, we can incorporate what you both like into your pool."

"Awesome," I whisper.

"So, when can you start?" Asher asks, and I turn my head so fast that I'm surprised it doesn't fly across the kitchen.

"Don't you think we should discuss price?" I ask.

"You like it?"

"Uh yeah," I say in a duh tone.

"So we're getting it."

"I like the pool, babe, but I also like diamonds. I still wouldn't buy one without knowing the price," I say quietly.

"I would," Asher says with a completely straight face, causing me to do a double take.

"I guarantee the price is competitive," Jack cuts in. "And you're getting the family discount."

"Oh." It's all I can say.

"So, when can you start?" Asher asks again and I shake my head. I don't think that it's normal to make this kind of decision in less than twenty minutes. The prices of pool installations that I saw in my research online were twenty thousand or more. That seems like a lot of money to spend just by looking at three pictures.

"It should take a week or so to get the permit then. We can break ground. After we start to dig, it should take about six-to-eight weeks to finish. You guys should be swimming by the time the weather really changes."

"Wow, that's so fast," I say, smiling at Jack. He smiles and shakes his head, looking over my shoulder at Asher.

"You get it?" Jack says, looking at Asher. I look at Asher, wondering what the heck he's talking about. He pulls me close and kisses my temple.

"Alright, man. Send me the blueprints," Asher says, standing. "Let me know when you get the permit and are gonna break ground."

"I'll call you later this week," Jack says, putting all of his stuff back in his folder.

"Next weekend is Gran's birthday. Everyone will be expecting you." Asher changes the subject and reminds Jack of the upcoming celebration.

"I'm driving to Atlanta with Meg this week, but we should be back in time for the party unless her family convinces her to stick around through the weekend."

"Bring her."

"What?" Jack asks, shoving his folder under his arm and walking towards the front door.

"Bring Meg."

"Bring Meg?" Jack repeats.

"Yeah, why not?" Asher shrugs like it's no big deal.

"You hate Meg," Jack says, looking at me. I shrug. I have no idea who Meg is or what her history is.

"No, I hated that Meg was a friend and she believed the bullshit that bitch fed her about having my baby. Then, I was pissed that she confronted me in front of people in town about abandoning Joan after I knocked her up without ever asking me about it first. To top it off, she told Joan where I lived, so when I got home from a public blow out with Meg in town, I had to deal with Joan sitting on my front porch waiting for me." Wow, I didn't like Meg very much right now either. How could you claim that someone is your friend then believe a stranger over them?

"So, you're tellin' me you're over that shit?" Jack asks, looking like he understands why Asher was mad. I think *anyone* would understand why Asher was mad.

"No, I'm tellin' you that I know it's not easy to choose sides, and that I'm willing to work on my relationship with Meg so you don't have to choose."

Jack looked relieved. I could understand that. I'm sure it's not easy loving two people who don't get along. "Okay. We'll be there for the party," he says, opening the front door. "It was nice meeting you, November."

"You too," I say as the door closes behind him.

Once Asher locks the door, I yell, "We're getting a pool!" And I launch myself at him.

"No, I'm getting summers full of you in nothing but a bikini," he says, giving me the dimple.

"Ugh." I scrunch up my nose. "I have never worn a bikini."

"Well, you're not getting in the pool without one." He looks at the ceiling, smiles and looks back down at me. "I will make an exception for you if you're in your birthday suit."

"Of course, you will," I say sarcastically. "How generous of you." I shake my head. "Hey, what are you doing?" I screech from my now upside down position.

"I'm going to make sure your birthday suit still fits, baby."

"Oh." I smile as he carries me to the bedroom and shows me his birthday suit. Let's just say that his fits him perfectly. I didn't ask how mine fit, but I did note that he wasn't complaining.

Chapter 10

I COULDN'T BELIEVE it. I looked at the calendar again, thinking that something had to be seriously wrong. But every time I counted, I came up with the same thing. I was not only late, I was L-A-T-E, as in three months of no period. I knew that my pants were fitting tighter, but I had also been eating like a pig. Now I knew the reason why I had been eating like a pig and the reason for my tightening clothes. If I was correct, I was about three months pregnant.

"Holy shit," I whispered into the top of the desk where my head had landed with a loud thud, I was on the shot. I had been on the shot since I was sixteen and my mother forced me to get on birth control. She quickly found out I wasn't very responsible with taking the pill, so she made my nanny take me to the hospital where they offered several different forms of birth control. I chose the shot only because I never had to think of it after I got it. Obviously, I didn't think about anything. I didn't think about my clothes becoming tighter. I didn't think about feeling tired. I thought about nothing. If I hadn't been planning on getting my shot prescription refilled, I wouldn't have thought about the fact that I hadn't had my period. I would have ended up on that show where the girl says, "I didn't know I was pregnant until I felt the baby coming out of my vagina."

No woman wants to think that she's so out of tune with her body that she doesn't realize when another human is growing inside of it. I started to laugh, and then a sob came out.

What was Asher going to think? Seriously, we had only been together for a few months. I needed to buy a test. I needed proof. I let my head thud on the desk a few more times, hoping that it would put my brain cells back in order. I called Asher and told him that I was leaving the club, got in my car, and began the mission of getting proof.

I asked Liz to go with me to Target. Her job was to provide a distraction if we came across anyone that we knew while in the store. Lord knows, if anyone from town saw me buying a pregnancy test, they would assume that I had gotten knocked up on purpose and rumors would run rampant.

"So, you're late?" Liz asks, looking over at me.

"Late is an understatement," I tell her as we walk down the aisle of the store. It's ironic that tampons and pregnancy tests are located in the same section.

"So, what are you going to do if it's positive?" She holds up a box, reading the back.

"I don't know," I say quietly.

"Well, you know he loves you so I'm sure everything will be okay." She gives me a reassuring smile. I smile back and pick out a test. I thought about putting it in my purse until we reached check out, but I really didn't want to get arrested for shoplifting, so I just put it under my arm, trying to hide it. Going towards the front of the store, my worst fear is realized when Trevor walks around the corner.

"Hey, sis," he says, trying to give me a hug but the test is still under my arm and I don't want it to fall out, so I half pat his back. "Liz," he says, smiling, and I watch her face turn pink.

"What are you doing here?" I ask, looking around, trying to come up with a plan to abort the mission.

"I came with Cash. He's picking up a cable for his TV." He looks between me and Liz. "What are you doing here?" he asks and I look at Liz, hoping that she'll think of something since my mind has gone blank.

"Tampons," Liz blurts out and I notice a few people stop and look at us as she covers her mouth. Trevor seems taken aback for a second then he laughs, shaking his head.

"Well, I'll let you guys get back to that." He bends over and kisses my cheek and then reaches over and tugs a piece of Liz's hair. Without another look, he turns around and walks away.

"Tampons," I hear Liz whisper to herself. I start giggling. "You owe me huge for this," she says, groaning. After Trevor is out of sight, I run to check out with Liz following behind me.

"You guard the door while I take the test," I tell Liz while walking into the small stall.

"Let me know if you need me," she says from the other side.

"Holy shit," I whisper. There it is. The proof I wanted is right there in black and white. Okay, white and pink, but it is there in my face, proving that I'm an idiot. I've taken four tests, all different brands, so I know they couldn't all be wrong. When I bought the first one and it came out with a giant plus sign, I left the stall that I had been holding up in.

With Liz following behind me, we went and bought water from the coffee shop and a few more tests. Now all the tests have been taken and they all say the same thing. I had my proof. I shove the boxes and all except one of the tests into the little garbage can that hangs on the wall in the bathroom stall.

"You're pregnant!" Liz squeals with excitement. I want to be happy, but I'm afraid about Asher's reaction. "I hope it's a girl. They always have so many cute girl things. So, what now?" she asks, looking at me expectantly.

"I…um, need to make a doctor's appointment. I need to have them confirm it."

"I'm pretty sure that the four tests you've taken confirm it."

"I know. I mean, I need them to tell me that everything is okay, and that I haven't harmed the baby over the last few months."

Liz must have read the look on my face because she pulls me into a hug. "Hey, everything is going to work out," she says quietly.

We decide to wander around Target for a while. I need time to think. I need to figure out what the heck I'm going to say to Asher. There is no way I can keep this from him. I don't want to keep this from him. I want his support. I need him to tell me everything is going to be okay.

By the time we go to check out, the cart is overflowing. I know how I'm going to tell Asher that I'm pregnant. Even if we didn't plan this, I want it to be special. I also bought a few pairs of maternity pants with the stretchy material at the waist. My jeans are becoming so tight that I have to lie down to button them. I had been avoiding buying a bigger size because I didn't want to admit to gaining weight. Now I know I have to wear something bigger. It can't be healthy for the baby to be squashed inside of me like that. Liz and I walked around the baby aisles looking at clothes, bedding, and toys for a lot of the time we were there. There were so many cute things and Liz's excitement started to rub off on me.

I WAS SITTING at the island in the kitchen when I heard Asher's jeep pull up. I had been trying to read, but my mind was so busy going over all the outcomes of the news I was getting ready to announce, that I ended up reading the same page about five times already. The minute Asher walked through the door, I wanted to throw up. Normally when he walked through the door, I wanted to throw myself at him. But now, my stomach was in knots, and I was having a difficult time breathing.

"Hey, baby," he said as he walked to me, kissing my forehead. "What's wrong?" he asked. I started to tell him, but then I smelled nothing but the paint that was splattered on his clothes. I ran to the bathroom. Apparently, the baby didn't like that smell. My hair was lifted out of my face and off my neck and then a cold cloth was laid there. "Feel better?"

I nodded, even though I didn't feel better. My nerves were shot. "Come shower with me." He didn't give me a choice. He picked me up, my head laying on his shoulder and my arms going around his neck. He sat me on the vanity in our bathroom, and then started the shower. I hopped off the counter and started brushing my teeth, watching him in the mirror as he got undressed. I knew I needed to do this now before I completely chickened out or ended up in an Asher-fog where I would forget everything.

"I'll be right back," I told him and took off out of the bathroom before he could stop me. I went to the kitchen and picked up the box that I had wrapped. I shoved the test that was in my purse in the back pocket of my jeans. Once I was back in the bathroom, he only had on his boxers and was standing in front of the mirror, so I hopped back up on the vanity and handed him the box.

"What's this?" he asked, looking at the box that was wrapped in yellow paper.

"Just open it," I said with my stomach in my throat.

He unwrapped it then set it down on the counter to open the lid. I watched his eyebrows come together in confusion. Unless he remembered the conversation we had about kids, he wouldn't know why there was a box of Trojan condoms and a little kid's pink gun in the box. He stared into the box for what seemed like an eternity then his head came up and his eyes looked wet.

"Does this mean what I think it means?"

I nodded my head. He swallowed and shook his head. I leaned forward, taking the test out of my back pocket and hand it to him. His hand came up, his fingers wrapping around it. His head bent and there was no way for him to misinterpret the words *pregnant* that were on the screen of the test. "Fuck me," he whispered and I couldn't tell what he was thinking. His eyes were still locked on the test in his hand.

"I'm sorry," I whispered after he still didn't say anything. "I'm on birth control. I don't even know how this happened." I watched him drop the test into the box and close the lid. I was nervous. He didn't look at me. He hadn't said anything. He picked up the box and left the bathroom. I knew it was too soon. I knew it. I knew it. Oh God, what was I going to do? I put my head in my hands and tried to control the tears that I knew were coming. We needed to talk about this. Then, I needed to figure out what to do with myself.

Abortion was out of the question, and I couldn't live my life knowing that my child was out in the world being taken care of by someone else. It had to be okay. We had to be okay. The thought of being without him made me sick. I needed to pull up my big girl panties and talk to him about this. I pulled my head away from my hands and started to get off the counter to go track him down. I was starting to get pissed. He married someone he didn't love because she said she was pregnant with his child. He told her that it would be okay. He was supposed to love me. He needed to tell me right now that it would be okay, or I was going to walk away, regardless of how broken my heart would be.

I jumped back when Asher walked back into the bathroom. His hands went to my shirt and then it was gone. I was so surprised that I couldn't form words. Then, my jeans were coming down and I was standing in my bra and panties.

"We need to talk," I whispered, not knowing what the hell was going on with him. His face was blank; his eyes determined. Then, my panties were gone along with my bra. I was sitting back on the vanity before I even had time to think. "What the heck are you doing?" I pushed at his chest. He grabbed my hand, holding it between us.

"Seriously, you need to stop. We need to talk about this." My voice was getting louder. I tried to shove him again. He didn't move. My heart was racing, my breathing escalated. I noticed that he wasn't even looking at me. His eyes were on my hand that he was holding. I looked down and my breath caught in my throat. On my left ring finger was a beautiful diamond ring. The center stone was round and surrounded by tons of smaller diamonds that traveled down and around the band. My hand flexed in his and he finally looked at me.

His voice was gruff when he spoke. "I've wanted to see you wearing nothing but my ring since I bought it for you. Knowing that, like the ring I put on your finger, I'm the only one. The only one who will ever see you in nothing but my ring. The only one who will wake up to your beautiful face every day for the rest of my life. The only one who will make love to you. The only one who will make babies with you." I watched his eyes get wet. "I can't tell you how happy I am that you are carrying my child."

His face came closer to mine. "I know that it's fast, but this is right. We are right. You are the only one for me." He kissed me deeply. When he pulled away, he laid his forehead against mine. "Tell me that you'll marry me," he whispered against my mouth.

Tears started to fall from my eyes. I couldn't ask for a more perfect proposal. "Yes." I shoved my face into his throat, wrapping myself around him. "Yes, I'll marry you."

He picked me up, carrying me into the shower. He put me under the spray, taking his time to wash my hair. Then, he took his time washing me from head to toe, paying special attention to where his child was now growing. I helped him wash, and then we got out. He wrapped me in a towel and tied one around his waist. He picked me up again, carrying me to the bed where he sat me on the edge, my feet hanging over the side. He dropped to his knees in front of me. He opened my towel, his fingers traveling down the sides of my breast along my ribs down to my waist. His fingers resting on my sides, his thumbs moving over my lower stomach. His eyes met mine and the look of pure love that I saw shining through them made me hold my breath.

"It's amazing," he whispered, "to know that my purpose in life is sitting in front of me." His hands moved to hold my face. *Holy crap, I can't believe that he just said that.* Before I could even tell him I loved him, his lips touched mine and then traveled along my jaw and down my neck.

My hands went to his head and my head fell back. His hands were along my sides, up my thighs then down again. Heat was pooling between my thighs with every touch. I whimpered when his mouth found my nipple and he gave it a firm tug. Then he sucked deep. My back arched and I moaned loudly. His hands traveled up my inner thighs, his fingers finding my center. "Soaked." His fingers were moving through the wetness he was creating, passing over my clit. I felt the heat building but it wasn't enough.

"Asher," I whimpered. His mouth left my breast and he pulled my face to his. He sucked my bottom lip into his mouth, dragging it through his teeth. My mouth opened under his. His fingers were still slowly sliding through my wetness. Two fingers were filling me. My head flew back and my nails dug into his scalp.

"Yes." His fingers were suddenly gone. My head came up and I watched as he pulled my other nipple into his mouth, bit down, and then dragged it through his teeth the same way he did my lip. He kissed the tip of my nipple. Then, his fingers were again moving through the wetness. I knew I was drenched. He licked down my stomach around my navel. Finally, I could feel his breath against my clit. I spread my legs wider, not caring that I was becoming desperate.

"Asher." I moaned as I watched his tongue licking me from bottom to top then circling my clit. I was on the edge. I knew that once his mouth focused on that one spot, I was going to explode.

"Jesus, is it possible that you taste sweeter?" He groaned, licking me again and circling my clit. Then, he filled me again with two fingers at the same time. He latched onto my clit. My whole body came off the bed with the force of my orgasm. I could feel the walls of my pussy contracting, sucking his fingers deeper as he sucked my clit and I saw stars. My thighs tightened around his shoulders and my hands were holding onto his head. He kissed my inner thigh, above my pubic bone, along my stomach, up to each breast. His hands moved under my arms, pulling me deeper onto the bed. One of my legs was straight, the other bent, resting on the back of his thigh. My hands went to his jaw. His hand wrapped around his cock and he entered me.

"Yes!" I moaned, loving the sensation of him filling me. I opened my eyes to see his were closed tight. I circled my hips and his eyes flew open.

"Don't." His voice was firm. He grabbed my hips, stopping my movement. He kissed me softly and pulled out just an inch and slid back in. I bit my lip to keep myself still. His hands moved to my thighs spreading my legs wider. He pulled out so just the tip was still in, and slammed in so hard that my breath hitched. Then, he slid out and started a slow pace while kissing me. His hands were pinching my nipples then traveling down, pressing against my clit. My hands were traveling up his back; my mouth and tongue kissing and licking whatever I could reach. Then I felt it start. It was slow and deep, and I knew that I couldn't hold back. My mouth found his and I held his face close to mine.

I moaned against his mouth. My thighs wrapped tighter around him. "Please, don't stop." He didn't. His pace increased, his strokes deeper, and I felt him grow. I knew he was close too.

"Come with me, baby," he grunted, one hand fisting into my hair while his other was traveling between us, pinching my clit and setting me off. My whole body tightened around him, pulling him deeper inside of me. I moaned into his mouth as he groaned into mine. I could feel his strokes start to slow and turn lazy. He kissed me all over my face and down my neck. "I get this for a lifetime," he whispered into the skin below my ear.

I tightened my arms and legs around him. "Love you, babe," I whispered against his shoulder. He rolled to the side, taking me with him.

"Love you, baby," he said against my hair. Closing my eyes, I cuddled deeper into his chest and fell asleep.

My stomach growls so loud that it wakes me from my doze. I can feel Asher's silent laughter against my cheek. "Sounds like both my babies are hungry."

"Yeah," I mumble. I know I need to eat, but seeing the expanse of his chest in front of me, I can't help but want something else that has nothing to do with food.

I'm rolled to my back and Asher is hovering over me. His eyes are watching his hand travel down my throat between my breasts. "I'm excited for these to get bigger," he says, palming both my breasts.

He smiles up at me and I shake my head and giggle. Then, his hand starts to move again and he stops gently on my stomach, which has become slightly rounder over the last few months.

"I'm going to be a dad." He shakes his head in disbelief. His eyes focus on his hands as he gently rubs my belly. Then, he kisses me right below my navel. His eyes meet mine and I see nothing but the same happiness I feel reflecting back at me. The mood is completely broken when my stomach gives another loud growl. We both start laughing.

"Alright, Daddy's going to feed you," he says into my stomach. We get out of bed and I pull on one of his shirts and a pair of panties. He pulls on a pair of baggy sweats that hang low and give the most amazing view of his abs. I hear him clear his throat. I look up and he's smiling.

"I'm going to waddle and you're going to walk around looking like that?" My hand moves up and down, indicating everything that is him.

"You're carrying the life we made together inside of you. Your body growing to take care of our child is amazing. I can't wait to see you with a big belly," he says.

"I love you," I blurt out. "I mean, you already know that, but I'm glad that you're happy about this."

"Happy is not the word I would use to describe how I feel, baby."

"I know," I whisper. "This is bliss."

"Yeah," he says, walking towards me. "This is bliss." His hands frame my face and he softly kisses my nose then my lips.

I WAKE UP feeling the sun warm the skin of my back. Last night, after Asher fed me a toasted peanut butter and jelly sandwich, we lay in bed and talked about the sex of the baby. I said I wanted a girl. Asher was still stuck on having a boy first. Really, I don't care what I have as long as he or she is healthy. I smile into my pillow, thinking about the ring on my finger, the child growing inside of me, and the man who put both of them there. I pull my hand out from under my pillow and hold it up in front of my face, watching the light reflect off the gems. The diamonds are shining so bright that I could go blind by looking at them.

"You awake, baby?"

I scream and almost fall out of bed from flipping over at the sound of his voice.

"Jesus, what the fuck?"

"You scared the crap out of me," I say, holding the sheet to my chest. "I thought you were working today?" I look at the clock and see that it's ten thirty.

"Took the day off so we could go to the doctor."

"Doctor?" I ask, confused.

"You're pregnant and need to get checked out. Your appointment is at one."

"Oh…yeah, of course." Yikes, I knew I needed to go to the doctor, but hadn't even thought about calling to set up an appointment. "You just beat me to it," I say, playing it off and grabbing the shirt at the end of the bed.

"Come to the kitchen. I made you some tea."

"Tea?" I ask in disgust. I'm sure my face shows how revolted I am at the idea of tea. "I only drink tea if I'm sick," I say, shaking my head at him.

"Baby, you're pregnant."

"I know that. I took four tests yesterday to prove it," I snap. First, he offers me tea then he reminds me that I'm pregnant. Seriously?

"You can't drink coffee when you're pregnant," he says softly, and I realize that I just sounded like a total bitch. It must be the hormones.

"That's not funny, Asher."

"Baby," he starts laughing, "It's the truth. No coffee when you're pregnant."

"Is that a rule? Where did you see this?" I ask, starting to panic. This can't be true. What was I going to do if I couldn't drink coffee?

"It's in that book that you brought home yesterday."

"Did you check Google?"

"Baby," he says again, shaking his head, and I can tell he's fighting a smile. "We, can ask the doctor today and see what he says about it. But for now, come eat something so we can shower and get ready to go."

"Fine," I grumble, getting out of bed. Once I've eaten breakfast and showered, we head out to the doctor's office.

"Well, there you go," the doctor says, pointing at the screen beside my head. We had been at the doctor's office for a while. First, they ran a urine test to confirm what I already knew. Then, we had to wait for the ultrasound machine to free up. Now, I am looking and listening to our baby. Tears start to pool in my eyes from the overwhelming emotions I'm feeling. I can see little arms and legs and the heartbeat is so loud in the background, it drowns out all the other noise. Asher is squeezing my hand so hard that I'm losing the feeling in my fingers. He has a look of amazement on his face. He bends his head and kisses my nose, smiling. The doctor types some information into the computer then clicks several times on the screen.

"From the measurements, I would say you're about fifteen weeks along," he says, looking at me. I immediately feel guilty for not knowing sooner that I was pregnant.

"Is everything okay? I mean, is he healthy?" Asher asks.

"Everything looks perfect."

"I was on the shot and had no idea I was pregnant," I blurt, not wanting him to think that I'm going to be a horrible parent.

"You would be amazed at the number of times I've heard that story. It's not as uncommon as some might think."

"Really?" I am so glad I'm not the only one this has happened to.

"Really!" He chuckles.

"You're far enough along to know the sex, if you would like to find out?" he says, looking back at the screen.

"Um." I bite my lip and look at Asher. He nods his head, so I take that as a yes.

"Yes, please."

"Okay, let's have a look," the doctor says, moving the wand around a bit. "I hope you like the color pink." He smiles.

"Oh my God," I whisper, looking up at Asher's pale face. "Babe, are you okay? You look sick," I say, trying to sit up. I didn't expect this from him. He seemed so excited.

He swallows and shakes his head. "I'm having a daughter."

"Yeah," I say slowly, hoping that he isn't going to start freaking out. I need him to be together. I didn't even remember that I needed to make an appointment. I didn't know that I couldn't drink coffee until he told me. He had to be the one to hold it together.

"Look at you." His hand frames my face and his eyes roam all over me. "Jesus, God is fucking playing a joke on me."

"What?" I whisper.

"You're so beautiful. I was not a good guy before you. God is getting even."

I can't help it, I start laughing. I grab his face and look into his worried eyes. "Honey, you're going to be able to pick out the bad boys from a mile away. She will be a total daddy's girl, and you will keep her safe. I love you, okay?"

He takes a deep breath and kisses me, bringing his hand to my stomach where we know our daughter is. His eyes come back to me. "I keep thinking that this is all a joke, that no one should ever be this happy."

"I know," I laugh, shaking my head. It feels unreal.

"So, I read in that book that you should wait to tell people until you're twelve weeks. We're past that so who do we want to tell first?" he asks with a smile.

"Miss Alice," I say right away. She has been so happy since me and Asher got together. I know that she will be excited to hear that we're having a baby.

Asher smiles and I know that I chose the right person.

I AM STANDING in front of the barbecue with the lighter in my hand and I'm getting ready to set the stupid pregnancy book on fire. It's been four weeks since we went to the doctor and confirmed that I am pregnant. Everyone has been so excited. When we told Miss Alice that we were having a girl, I thought she was having a seizure. She started jumping around in her chair, clapping and mumbling incoherently. Then she told me that I needed to go to her old house and pick up all the stuff for the baby's room. I looked at Asher and he shrugged his shoulders.

After we left Miss Alice, we went to my dad's house and told him that he was going to be a grandfather. I think he almost fainted. Then he called my grandmother, uncles, and cousins, and had everyone come over so we could share the news. For Asher's mom, I sent her a dozen pink balloons and a card telling her that she was going to have a granddaughter. When she called me screaming into the phone, I knew that she was happy. She made us promise not to tell Mr. Mayson or her boys until that evening at dinner. When Asher stood up at the table and announced that he had, as he said, knocked me up, I thought I would be bruised from the amount of hugs I got from everyone. After that, the book started to make appearances like Chucky.

Two days after dinner with his family, we went to Miss Alice's house to see what she was talking about. We found a beautiful antique baby bed, dresser and changing table that she had stored up in the attic. They all needed to be refinished but even with the paint chipping and peeling, I could tell they would be beautiful. I told Asher that I wanted to repaint them but he'd read in the book that strong chemical fumes weren't good for the baby. But he promised to get his brothers to help him refinish them in time, so I agreed without a fight. A week later, when all of Asher's extended family came over for a big barbecue to celebrate our news, I had been getting ready to dig into a delicious looking tuna steak when it was taken right out from under my fork. Asher told me that I wasn't allowed to eat it due to the mercury in the meat. Again, I wasn't happy about this, but I wasn't going to risk anything happening to our baby, so I had a piece of chicken instead.

Last week, I had been outside looking around the area where they started digging for the pool, when Asher ran outside like the house was on fire. I stumbled and almost fell into the hole when he caught me and made me go back inside, saying that they had sprayed some kind of chemical in the area and I couldn't be in the backyard. Once again, I agreed, but was noticing that the list of things I couldn't do was becoming quite long.

Then, this morning, I was on the phone with the salon in town, making an appointment to get my highlights touched up and to have a manicure and pedicure, when the phone was yanked out of my hand and Asher proceeded to tell the salon that I had to wait until after I had the baby to get my hair done, but that I could get a mani pedi. Then he kissed me senseless, and left the room before I could clear the fog and yell at him. Now he is out somewhere on the property, and I am on the back porch in front of the grill with a lighter and the book that seems to be the root of all my problems. I am ready to kill him. I love him and am over the moon that he is happy about this baby but he's driving me insane. I know that he means well, but I swear, he won't be happy until the doctor puts me on bed rest for the duration of my pregnancy.

The doorbell chimes and I look down at the book and sigh while putting everything down. I plan on coming back to it as soon as I get rid of whoever is at the door.

"Stay," I tell Beast as I go into the house through the sliding door. I walk through the living room and look out the peep hole. I can't believe my eyes. How the heck did she find me? I look out the peep hole again, just to make sure that I'm not seeing things. Nope, not seeing things. My mother is standing on the other side of the door. I get off my tiptoes and take a step away from the door.

"Who's at the door, baby?" Asher asks loudly from behind me. I jump and spin around, putting a finger to my lips and using the universal symbol for 'be quiet.'

"Who is it?" he asks again. This time, his eyes are narrowed. The doorbell rings again and my mom yells through the closed door.

"I can hear you in there."

"Crap," I hiss, glaring at Asher for blowing my cover. He walks to the door and unlocks it before I have a chance to block it or tackle him to the ground.

"Can I help—" Asher starts to ask but my mom cuts him off.

"Where's November?" my mom snaps.

Crap! Crap! Crap!

"You are?" Asher asks in a low growl.

"Her mother." The air changes and I can feel the angry energy beating against my skin and it is all coming from Asher.

"What the fuck are you doing here?" he asks and I know this is going to go badly. I bend my head under Asher's arm that is holding the door open.

"Mom, what are you doing here?" I say and her eyes come to me.

"I've been calling you and you haven't answered."

"You came to Tennessee because I haven't answered my phone?" I ask in disbelief.

"No, I came here because your fiancé's in the hospital," she says and my eyes narrow.

"Her fiancé is standing right in front of you." Asher growled, taking his hand off the door and pulling me into his side.

"How did you find out where I live?" I ask, completely ignoring the fact that she said my ex was in the hospital. I hope that he isn't going to die or anything, but I'm not going to go to New York to sit at his bedside.

"The boy from the lawyer's office told me."

She looked up at Asher when his voice rumbled. "Nick?" My mom nodded. "I'm going to fucking kill him." Asher was pissed.

"I'm her mother. Why wouldn't he tell me where she lives?" she snaps, looking at Asher then back at me. "Why haven't you returned any of my calls?"

"The last time I saw you, Mom, you made it clear that you were not interested in having a relationship with me."

"You're my daughter."

"Yes, and you have never acted like my mother." What the heck is going on? I feel like I'm in the twilight zone when I see tears form in her eyes.

"I've been worried." My eyes narrow.

"What's really going on?" Just then, my cell phone rings in the kitchen. I look up at Asher in a silent plea for him to not let her in. He nods and I hope that we are on the same wave length. I walk to the kitchen and pick up my phone, seeing that it is Mr. Stevenson.

"Hello," I answer.

"November, this is Tom Stevenson."

"Hi, Mr. Stevenson. How are you?"

"Could be better, darlin'."

"Um, sorry to hear that," I mumble, looking toward the front door to make sure Asher hasn't let my mom in.

"Sorry to do this, but something just came up and I'm leaving my office in twenty minutes. If you can come now, I will put through the transfer. If not, we're going to have to reschedule for tomorrow."

"I'm sorry, but I have no idea what you're talking about," I say, confused.

"Like I explained to your mother this morning, I know that your signature is on the transfer papers but either I or a notary public has to witness you signing the documents."

"What?" I whisper.

"They have your signature, but from your tone, I take it that you didn't know."

"No," I whisper again, moving down the hall so I can talk without my mother hearing. "You said they have my signature?" I ask, making sure I understand him correctly.

"Yes." He pauses and I can hear papers shuffling in the background. "I double checked when I got them."

"Oh my God," I mumble into the phone, realizing why my mother is really here. "She's here right now," I say quietly, more to myself than to Mr. Stevenson.

"She's at your house?"

"Yes," I whisper.

"I'm calling James. Keep her there," he says, hanging up.

"Okay," I say to dead air on the phone. I look down the hall, trying to come up with a plan to keep my mom here until Asher's dad arrives. I consider going outside and slashing her tires, but figure that might be a little extreme. Then, I thought about sicking Beast on her, but if she hurt my dog, I would be really upset. So, after a few more non options pass through my head, I decide to just invite her in and ask her if she would like something to drink. I leave the hallway.

When I reach the kitchen, I can see over the island that Asher is sitting on the couch with his hands resting on top of his head. My mom is sitting on the coffee table in front of him. "I guess we weren't on the same wave length after all," I mumble to myself. Asher's eyes come to me as soon as my feet hit the tile floor in the kitchen. He shakes his head. I narrow my eyes. My mom looks at me, smiles, and I see she has a gun in her hand pointed at Asher.

"What are you doing?" I scream as I start running into the living room.

"Don't come any closer or I'll shoot him," she says and I stop at the edge of the living room. My heart is pounding as if it's going to jump out of my chest. I look at Asher. His eyes are on me and he looks worried. His eyes drop to my stomach and they close, but not before I see pain flash across them.

"As I was telling your boyfriend here—"

"Fiancé." Asher growls, glaring at my mom. I almost laugh. Only he would stop a crazy person with a gun to clarify our relationship status.

"As I was telling your fiancé," my mom says, glaring back at Asher. Then she looks to where I'm standing. "You need to come with me."

"Where?" I ask even though I know where she wants us to go. I just need to stall for time.

"You'll see," she says, standing. "Before we go though, you need to tie him up. I don't need him coming after us." She pulls some rope out of her bag. "This was for you, but it looks like we're going to use it on him instead," she says, throwing the rope at me. I catch it midair and look at Asher, trying to find a way to get out of this. "Come on, come on. We don't have all day." She motions to him with her gun. I walk slowly towards Asher. I don't want to do this. Tears start to fill my eyes. I can't tie him up.

I shake my head. "I can't." I sob, stopping a few feet from where he's sitting.

"Either you tie him up or I'll shoot him."

I start sobbing harder and my breath hitches. "Baby," Asher whispers, his hands coming toward me.

The gun goes off. "Keep your hands where I can see them," my mom yells as I scream. Asher places his hands back on his head with a look of pure rage on his face.

"Tie his hands behind his back and to his ankles. Do it now or I'll shoot him."

"I'm so sorry." I cry as Asher places his hands behind his back.

"Be strong, baby, for both of us," he whispers, and I know he's talking about our daughter.

"I will. I promise," I whisper. I don't want her to know that I'm pregnant. The day I started wearing the maternity pants I bought from Target, my baby bump showed up. Normally, I would wear something more form fitting to show it off. Thankfully, today I have on an oversized tee and leggings because we were lounging around the house. I worked on tying his arms behind his back then he lay with his chest to the couch and I tied his hands to his ankles. I am glad that he has on sweats and a long sleeve shirt so the rope doesn't rub his skin. When I finish, my mom walks over to the couch and tests the knot I tied.

"Let's go," she says, waving the gun in the direction of the door. My brain starts to panic. Asher's house is in the country. Who knows where his dad is or any of the other officers that work in the area. I have no idea how long it will take for someone to show up. I can hear Beast scratching at the back door, trying to get in and I wish that I hadn't locked him out there. "Come on. We need to go. You already held me up by not running to the car when I told you Chris was in the hospital."

"I need shoes," I tell her, hoping that will buy me some time.

"I saw flip-flops outside the front door. You can wear those."

"What are we going to be doing?"

"I'm not going to tell you again. Get in the car."

"Okay," I say calmly. I can tell that she is starting to panic. We walk outside and Beast runs around the corner of the house. He jumps through the air, landing right in the middle of my mom's chest. The gun in her hand goes off right before it flies through the air.

"Holy crap," I yell, running for the gun. My mom is yelling for Beast to get off her. I fall to the ground, landing on my hip. I feel pain shoot up my side. I've got my finger around the trigger of the gun just in time to see my mom grab a hold of Beast's mouth and start to pull his jaw apart. "Let go of my fucking dog!" I scream at the top of my lungs while trying to stand. I aim a warning shot near where she is lying on the ground. Her hands fly above her head. Beast stands above her, growling down into her face.

"November!" Asher yells from inside the house. I can hear the worry in his voice and I know that he wants me in there, but I can't leave my mom alone until Asher's dad shows up.

"I'm okay! We're okay!" I yell back, taking a shaky breath. The sound of a car coming up the drive is music to my ears. I watch Mr. Mayson pull over the hill in his police cruiser, and for the first time since my mom showed up, I can feel that knot in my stomach disappear.

"No, no, no, no," she starts chanting, her head thrashing back and forth on the ground. I can hear Asher yelling from inside the house and know that I need to go to him.

"Are you okay?" Mr. Mayson asks, running up with his gun drawn and pointed at my mom.

"Yeah," I say shakily. "Asher's inside. He's tied up. She made me tie him up." I cry harder and the gun in my hand starts shaking. It feels like it weighs a hundred pounds.

Mr. Mayson' face is soft and full of worry when he holds out his hand to me. "Give me the gun, darlin', and go untie my boy," he says quietly. I hand him the gun and start stumbling my way into the house. My hip is killing me from where I fell on it.

I open the door and see Asher on his knees. He has gotten the rope off one of his ankles. His eyes come to me and he falls backwards onto the floor.

"Fuck," he roars and I run over to him. I realize it will be easier to untie him with a knife, so I stumble into the kitchen then back to him. He rolls to his side and I cut the rope around his wrist. Before I can do anything else, his arms are around me. I don't even realize that I'm crying until he starts wiping away the tears running down my face.

"Breathe, baby," he whispers, rocking me back and forth. One hand is on the back of my head, holding me to his chest, and the other is on my stomach where our daughter is.

"I—was—s-s-so scared." I sob. "Be…Beast saved me again."

"Shhhh, it's okay. You're safe." He repeats those words over and over into my ear.

I take my face out of Asher's chest as Mr. Mayson walks in with another officer. "We have her in th—" He looks down at us and his face pales. "Call a fucking ambulance!" he shouts over his shoulder. I look down and see that Asher's sweats have blood on them.

"Oh my God!" I cry. "You're bleeding." I try to get up. Asher's face is as white as a ghost and he starts shaking his head, pulling me closer. "Let me go. We have to see where you're hurt."

"Not me, it's. It's not me." His face is etched in worry. He picks me up and I start to squirm. Then I realize I feel wet between my legs.

"No," I whisper, looking at Asher. "No," I repeat, begging him to tell me that this is not happening. That I'm not bleeding.

"I'm taking her to the hospital. It will be faster if I drive her," he says to his dad, but it feels like a dream. This cannot be happening.

"I'm driving. Get her in the cruiser," Mr. Mayson says quietly. I feel us moving but I'm numb. No tears, nothing. I don't even know if I'm breathing. All I can think about is our daughter.

I awake to the sound of beeping and my eyes flutter open. I can see the white of the hospital ceiling and everything that happened yesterday comes back to me.

When I got here my dad and grandmother arrived ten minutes later. He was ready to go down to the local jail and kill my mother. My cousins and uncle had to physically restrain him so he didn't get arrested. The police still had to come in to take our statements, but from what I understand from Asher's dad, my mom had been trying to find a way to get the money my grandparents left for a very long time.

My ex-fiancé was her boy-toy long before I met him. She said they had been sleeping together for two years when she came up with the plan that he would date me, get me to fall in love with him, ask me to marry him, then something else. She didn't say what that something was, but it would happen to me. He would get the money and they would start a life together. Unfortunately for her, that plan fell through when I found out they were sleeping together.

Apparently, my grandparents left strict instructions that, if I was to die before I had any heirs, the money was to be donated to different charitable organizations. My mother had been scheming for a long time trying to get me out of the way. I guess she was on a roll during her questioning and told the police that she set up the attack in New York with the hopes that I would be in a coma when it came time for me to receive my inheritance.

She figured that if I was in a coma, she would automatically be granted power of attorney and would have access to the money when it became available. Then she could transfer it to herself. She also admitted that she sent the flowers to me and paid the kid who dropped them off a few hundred dollars to get my signature on the transfer papers that she took to the lawyer.

I move my head to the side and look over to where Asher is sleeping. He always looks peaceful in his sleep. His mom brought him another pair of sweats yesterday when she showed up, so he could get out of the one's that were covered in my blood. His ankle is crossed over his fleece covered knee. He has on a black thermal that is so tight, I can make out every detail of his chest. His hands are intertwined and laying on his abs. His sleeves are pushed up, the tattoos on his arms on full display. His jaw is darker than normal. He never shaves over the weekend and since he worked from home yesterday, he's extra scruffy.

Over the last few weeks, his skin has turned the color of caramel from working out in the sun. I bet a lot of women drive by his job sites just to see him without his shirt on. I know he takes it off to work, at least, occasionally. His tan is everywhere. He's always beautiful, but asleep, he's stunning. I wonder if I will ever get tired of looking at him.

My hand absently moves to my stomach. When I feel a slight flutter, I say a silent prayer that my daughter is okay. They were worried yesterday when they saw how much blood I lost. After lots of tests, the doctor found out that my cervix was bleeding due to the way I fell when I went for the gun. When I continued to bleed, they decided to keep me overnight for monitoring and put me on bed rest for a few weeks.

This morning when they came to check on me, the bleeding had stopped and her heartbeat was stronger. The night doctor said that everything should be fine as long as I don't push it. He also told me that I could be released as soon as my doctor showed up to sign me out.

"You awake?" Asher asks softly and I smile.

"Yeah," I say, looking over at him. His eyes have dark circles under them from being awake most of the night, harassing anyone who came into the room with a million and one questions.

"How are you feeling?" he asks, sitting up and placing his hand over mine.

"Better. Tired, but much better."

"Good." He smiles and kisses my hand.

"Why don't you go get a coffee?" I ask him.

"Nah, I'm good."

"Babe, seriously, you look exhausted. Go get a coffee, walk around, and see if you can track down my doctor. This bed is really uncomfortable and I would like to go home."

"I don't know. We don't have that machine at the house," he says, pointing at the monitor for our daughter's heartbeat. I look over at the machine and watch as her heartbeat thumps away. Then, I look back at him and can tell that he's still worried.

"The doctor won't let me leave if he thinks it's too risky," I tell him softly.

"I know, baby," he says, bringing my hand to his mouth and holding it there after kissing my fingers. "I could have lost you both yesterday," he says so quietly that I almost don't hear him.

"You didn't. We're here and we're safe."

"When I heard that gun go off outside, I thought that my life had ended. I thought I was never going to see your face again, or be able to see our daughter take her first breath. And I knew I wouldn't be able to survive without you here with me. I would take my life in order to go wherever you were."

"Don't say that," I whisper, shaking my head. "Don't ever say that."

"It's the truth."

"No, it's selfish," I cry. "Other people love you and count on you, not just me. No matter what happens to me, promise that you will never give up on life. That you will always fight to be happy. I'm not your only happiness."

"No, you're my bliss," he says, smiling, but I can't smile back. This is too serious.

"Promise me that you will never give up on life, no matter what, Asher. Promise me right now, because we have a daughter that is going to need you no matter what happens to me." His eyes look so lost, but I won't let him say stupid things like that. I wouldn't be happy without him either, but I would still fight to live because I know he would want that for me. "Would you want me to follow you?" I ask quietly, knowing the answer.

"No."

"So don't say things like that," I beg.

"I'm sorry, baby," he says, pulling me into his arms. "I just don't know what I would do."

"You don't have to worry about it. We're here and we're safe. Just promise that no matter what, you won't leave our daughter behind if something happens to me." I start to cry uncontrollably.

"I promise," he finally says, and I curl into his side and fall asleep.

I'm sitting in my hospital bed waiting for my doctor to show up and discharge me after he decided to keep me for one more night. Asher went to the house to get me something to wear and to drop off Beast. I hear the door open and look up.

"November?" Chris is standing at the door of my hospital room.

"What are you doing here?" I ask, scooting back in the bed.

"I heard you were in the hospital. I wanted to check on you."

"Who told you I was in the hospital?" He doesn't answer, but just walks into the room, shutting the door behind him. I press the call button for the nurse.

"You were supposed to come back to me," he says, looking sad.

"You slept with my mom." I will never forget that. Seeing them together was burned into my brain forever.

"Yes, and I'm sorry about that, but once I started to fall in love with you, I left you clues so that you would catch us."

"What?"

"I wanted to have a clean start with you. I just didn't know that after you caught us, you would ignore me completely."

"I repeat: you slept with my mom. That's not something that is easy to forget."

"I know," he whispers, looking at his shoes.

"The police are looking for you," I tell him and pray that one of the nurses comes in soon.

"I didn't know about the attack in New York. I didn't know she was going to do that to you," he says quickly.

"Okay," I say. My pulse speeds up when he looks at me again.

"I've been watching her." He looks around. "She's been in town for a while now. I wanted to warn you. I tried to scare you into going back to New York, but instead you decided to stay here with that guy."

"How did you try to scare me?"

"Broke into your apartment and left you notes."

"The poetry?" I ask, just to clarify.

He nods, looking around again. "We need to leave soon."

"No, you need to leave."

"I can't leave without you."

"I think that you need help," I say as I see Kenton looking through the crack in the door.

"I love you. We were getting married."

"Please just leave. I'm happy now. Can't you be happy for me?"

"Weren't we happy?" he asks.

I shake my head. "Chris," I say softly, "we were a lie that you and my mother cooked up. You were my first everything, and it was all a lie so you both could collect money that I didn't even know I was going to receive."

His eyes close like he's in pain and his head tilts toward the ceiling. I watch out of the corner of my eye as Kenton steps into the room, gun drawn.

"I loved you though."

"Love isn't like that, Chris. I'm sorry. I hope you get help so that one day you will know what love is but that isn't love."

His eyes meet mine and I can see the sadness in them.

"I want you to put your hands on your head and turn around slowly," Kenton says. Chris's head swings in his direction.

When he registers the gun in Kenton's hand, Chris's hands go to his head. Then his gaze comes back to me.

"I'm sorry."

I nod my head and watch Kenton pull cuffs out of his pocket and attach them to Chris's wrist.

"What the fuck?" Asher's voice cracks through the room like thunder. He looks me over and takes a step towards Chris. Kenton blocks him.

"See to your girl," Kenton says quietly.

I can tell that Asher's having a hard time not beating the crap out of someone. I think anyone would do for him right now after everything that happened. I being in danger today is playing havoc with him.

"Are you okay, baby?" he asks, taking a step towards me.

"Yeah," I nod my head as he pulls me into his arms. "It's over," I whisper into his chest.

"Yeah," he agrees.

Epilogue

"**A**GAIN, AGAIN!" EMMA screams as Asher picks her up again, tossing her through the air and into the pool. He's been doing the same thing for the last ten minutes. I look around for someone to help my eight-and–a-half-month pregnant self. It's hard to get my ass out of our lounge chairs unless I roll out, get on my hands and knees then stand. There are too many people around for me to do that today without really embarrassing myself.

"Need some help?" I look up to see Kenton standing over me.

"God, yes." I moan. "I swear, this little girl is going to be a dancer," I tell him and watch as he smiles.

"The pool turned out awesome," he says once he pulls me up. I look around. He is not wrong. The pool is amazing. It has a hot tub that is connected to it, along with so many flowers and plants that you would think we were in the jungle.

"Yeah, Jack did an amazing job," I say and look over at him. "So, where is Christen or Tina or Lisa or—"

"Very funny," he says, cutting me off.

I start to giggle and feel my belly bouncing with my laughter then I feel a kick that's so hard, I stop immediately and grab Kenton's hand and pull it towards my belly.

"What?" he starts to say. Then, his eyes get big and drop to my stomach. "Holy shit!"

"Yeah, now imagine that on your bladder." I laugh.

"That's so amazing," he says and his hand starts to rub my belly.

"I know that it's obvious by the huge ring on her finger that she's taken, but if you happened to miss that, you definitely can't miss the fact that she's obviously pregnant."

I laugh and see Kenton looking at Asher with something that looks a lot like envy in his eyes. I know he doesn't want me, but I think deep down he wants his own family.

"Yeah, both those are hard to miss," he says, smiling.

"How's it going, man?" Asher asks him while pulling me into him.

"Good. Busy. I'm seeing someone and things are good."

"Just one someone?" I ask, knowing his history. Since I've been around, there has been someone different at each event.

"Yeah, just one." He smiles and shakes his head.

"That's great," I whisper, laying my head on Asher's chest. He doesn't look like someone in love though, so I wonder if he's just trying to settle down because he is lonely. "You should invite her next time we all get together."

"Baby, leave the man alone. He just said he's seeing someone, not that he is picking out a ring."

I scrunch up my nose at my husband. "Fine," I grumble. His eyes go soft and he puts his mouth to mine. The kiss is sweet and soft. "I'm going inside then. I'm going to find Miss Alice," I whisper, biting his lower lip.

Once, I'm done in the bathroom, I track down Miss Alice. She's sitting in the baby's room. It was finished yesterday with the help of Nico, Cash and Trevor. They were there most of the night, laying carpet and touching up the walls. I look around and can see all the love that went into making this room special for our daughter. I know that she's going to have more love than she will know what to do with.

"It's so beautiful," Miss Alice says and I agree. It is beautiful. The walls are a very light blue with flowers that shoot up from the base with clouds and butterflies. Meg and Liz spent a week coming over every day when they got off work to paint every flower and butterfly on the walls.

Asher and his brothers sanded down every piece of furniture that we picked up from Miss Alice and stained the wood a dark brown. The quilt has pink and white checkers. It looks like a fairytale baby room. What really means the most to me is that everyone helped to make it beautiful. "You know that I never had a girl and Asher's mama didn't have a girl either."

"I know," I say softly.

"I'm excited that this house is going to have a little girl in it. I think all those boys needed this."

"What do you mean?"

"Oh, sweet girl. They've never really been around little girls to know how precious they are. I think when this little one comes, she's going to turn their lives upside down, and they all need it. Each one of them needs to see that all women were once precious little girls."

"You're right," I agree quietly. "But I think they all know how precious women are from you and Susan. They're just waiting for the right woman to come along and show them how precious they are."

She smiles and pats my cheek. "Smart girl." I laugh.

"Well," I say, kissing her cheek, "I'm going to go find my husband."

"Are you ever going to have a real wedding?"

"I don't know." I honesty haven't thought about it. After I got out of the hospital, me and Asher went right to the court house and got a marriage license. I was wearing sweats and sneakers and so was Asher. We just wanted to be married. The wedding didn't matter to me. "Maybe, after the baby gets here, we can have a small ceremony."

"That would be nice. She can be the flower girl."

"Yeah and Beast can be the ring bearer," I say, laughing. "Maybe you and I can start planning something small. I'm sure Mama Susan would like to help."

"I know she thinks of you as a daughter and would love to help you. Shoot, if you let her, she would probably take over the whole thing for you."

"I might just let her do that." I laugh.

"Alright, go find your husband before he starts running around the house, yelling for you and scaring all the guests."

"I'll come back and check on you soon. Do you want a piece of the baby shower cake?"

"No, thanks. I'm on a diet."

"Oh, lord." I roll my eyes.

"Hey, there's a new guy that's kind of cute. I need to watch my girlish figure."

"I'm leaving," I say, laughing and walking out the door, trying to get the image of Miss Alice and a man, any man, out of my head.

"Hey, sis, you're leaking," Nico says and I look down at the water pitcher in my hand. I don't see it leaking, but I do see water running down my legs and onto the floor at my feet. I look back at the pitcher and then back at my feet, and then I realize that it's time.

"I…I'm, well, I think my water broke," I tell him and he looks like he may fall over.

"Your water broke?" He stumbles back.

"Oh crap!" I mumble.

"What's going on?" Cash asks.

"My water broke and Nico is freaking out," I tell him, waving a hand in front of Nico's face. Then I look at Cash and he looks the same as his brother. "Come on. You can't be serious?" I groan.

"Is everything okay?" Trevor asks and I don't even tell him. What's the point? He's just going to freak and I don't have time to deal with them.

"Your water broke?" Trevor says from behind me and I notice that he sounds normal, so I stop and look at him.

"Yes, and I need to find your brother. Will you help me without going comatose?"

"Sure." He shrugs like it's no big deal, and his other two brothers aren't standing four-feet away staring into space. He grabs me around the waist and slides his arm under my thigh, lifting me. I scream and hold onto his neck for dear life.

"I could have walked," I tell him, digging my nails into his back.

"This would be easier if you would retract your claws there, kitten."

"Oh, sorry," I mumble.

"What are you doing? Put her down," Asher says when he sees us come through the backdoor.

"Her water broke. I'm taking her to the car."

"Your water broke?" he asks in the same tone as Nico and Cash.

"Asher James Mayson, if you freak out, we're going to have so many problems, especially after you shoved that damn baby book down my throat every day for the last nine months. You know everything that is going to happen. You cannot be surprised by any of this."

"You tried to burn it," he reminds me of my failure. When we finally got home from the hospital and the guys came over for dinner that weekend, they decided to grill steaks and found the baby book still inside the grill, safe and sound, not even slightly damaged by the horrible rains that we had for two days before. He brought the book inside, set it at the island, and then went back out to the grill, never saying a word about it.

"That book is like the damn Chucky doll," I complain and dig my nails into Trevor's neck again when the first contraction hits.

"Holy mother of God that hurts!" I say, breathing deep and looking at Asher.

"Go get her stuff. I'll take her to the car," Trevor tells him.

"Put me down."

"I'm taking you to the car."

"Put me down right now!" I yell and he sets me on the floor.

"What's going on?" Susan asks, walking around the corner to the living room.

"My water broke and all of your sons, except Trevor, turned comatose at the mention of it. I need to get my bag and get to the hospital."

"How far apart are your contractions?"

"I just had my first one, so I don't really know. I haven't timed them."

"It was one minute and fifty-six seconds ago," Trevor says. Asher glares at him.

I walk to the couch and sit when I feel another contraction coming on.

"Well, they're less than three minutes apart. We really need to get to the hospital," Trevor says and I'm wondering what the hell is going on.

I look up at him and he shrugs. "That book has been around a lot," he says, pointing to Asher. "He carries it with him everywhere, even to jobsites. When I was bored a few times, I read it."

"Lord, save me," I say, looking up to the ceiling then back to Asher, who's still just standing there.

"Asher, unless you want your brother to take over for you, pull it together," I tell him, waddling out to the car.

Nine grueling hours later, July Heaven Mayson, came screaming into this world.

I walk into the living room and look at the couch. Asher is lying on his back with July lying in just a diaper against his bare chest. One of his big hands is holding her bottom, the other is on the back of her head. She's facing me, her hand resting against her chin. Her eyes are the same color as her father's. His eyes are closed. I walk towards them and Asher's eyes open and the smile that comes across his face is devastating. It's a look of pure bliss, the look of someone who is right where they are supposed to be in life and is so overwhelmed with happiness that it comes through every time they smile.

"Hey, baby," he says. "How was your nap?"

"Good." I smile. "Was she fussy when you tried to give her the bottle?" I ask, knowing my daughter is picky and only wants the breast.

"No." He shakes his head, smiling. "Trevor came over for lunch and he got her to drink from it."

"Wow, super Trevor saves the day again, huh?"

"Yeah, Liz came with him so I think he was showing off." He laughs and I know he's right. Liz slipped a few days after July was born and said something happened, but never said what it was. When I tried to press her about it, she closed up and turned beet red. After that, they had kind of been avoiding each other but then a few weeks ago, something else happened, and now there is no Trevor without Liz.

"I'm sure," I say, rolling my eyes. "But if your brothers are trying to use our daughter to pick up women, I will kick their asses."

"I'll kick their asses," he says, patting her bottom and he's not lying. He's one scary daddy bear. The other day, some woman came up to us and started to put her hand near July, and he freaked out about germs and hand sanitizer. The lady stood there in shock the whole time. Then he walked away, shaking his head, like she was the crazy one.

"So, should we get ready to take her to Grandma's?" I ask, excited about a date with my husband. Since July came home two months ago, we haven't had any time alone, and I was very much looking forward to it. Not that I wanted to be without my daughter, but I was ready to have mommy and daddy time.

"I already packed everything up," he says, smirking, and I laugh.

"Well, I'm going to go shower."

"Shower, huh?" he says, and his eyes turn hungry.

"Yes, shower. You have to watch our daughter so you can't join me." I bend over and kiss her head of dark hair, and then kiss my husband and whisper against his lips, "Love you."

"Love you more, baby," he replies.

"DO YOU WANT to go to Nashville and have dinner?" Asher asks from the driver's seat. We just dropped off July to his mom and dad. We're kid free for a few hours.

"Have you ever gone skinny dipping?" I blurt.

I watch as his dimple appears. "You wanna go skinny dipping, baby?"

"Maybe," I say softly. I have always wanted to try it, but since the pool was finished and July was born, there hasn't been time or the opportunity.

We pull into our driveway fifteen minutes later, and before Asher can even get his door open, I'm in the house, running across the living room and pulling my dress over my head. Then I dive into the pool in my bra and panties. I surface and watch as Asher takes off his shoes then jeans. He's going kind of slow so I decide to hurry him along. I unclasp my bra and toss it in his direction. He jumps into the pool with his boxers still on.

When he surfaces, he's right in front on me, pulling me under my arms. "If we're skinny dipping, these are kind of in the way," he says, running his hands down my waist to the top of my lacy booty panties.

"Hmm." I smile.

Then his hands fist the sides, ripping them off and tossing them out of the pool. "That's better." His mouth meets mine and his hand goes between my legs and his fingers hit the perfect spot. My legs wrap around his hips, my arms around his neck, and my head falls back from the stimulation of his fingers. His lips run along my neck, licking and biting their way down to the tops of my breast. He stops and his hand fists my hair, pulling my mouth back to him.

"You have too many clothes on," I tell him, trying to shove down his boxers. I finally get them off him, wrapping my fist around him and stroking. I bite my lip when two fingers fill me.

"Yes." I moan. My head falls forward into his shoulder then I'm out of the pool, sitting on the edge. His hands are at my inner thighs, spreading my legs wide then his mouth is attacking me. "Oh my God," I whisper, holding his head to me. Right when I know I'm going to come, he stops and pulls me back into the water, impaling me on him. "Asher!" I scream in shock. I feel myself convulse around him.

"I love your pussy, baby," he says against my ear. I whimper as he uses his hands on my ass to slam me down onto him. My hands pull his mouth to mine. The kiss is so hungry that when I feel his teeth bite into my lower lip, I lose it.

"I'm going to come," I say against his mouth, and just as I feel myself starting to fall apart, he lifts me off him and turns me around so I have to grab onto the side of the pool. He slams into me from behind, holding onto my hips using the weightlessness of the water to lift me effortlessly. His hands slide from my waist to my chest, and his fingers roll and pinch my nipples. His mouth travels from the back of my neck up to my ear.

"You're gonna make me come, baby. Your tight, wet pussy is squeezing me and going to make me come. And when I come, I want you to come with me, so I need you to touch yourself for me."

I nod my head. I don't have the strength to say anything. When my fingers roll over my clit, my head falls back on his shoulder, my mouth finds his, and then I explode. My body is tingling from head to toe. My fingers dig into the wall at the edge of the pool. My orgasm is so huge that I see stars and can't breathe. I hear Asher groan behind me and I know that he followed me with his own orgasm. "I don't know how, but I swear your pussy gets sweeter every time I fuck you," he says in a husky whisper right next to my ear.

We're out of the pool lying on one of our loungers. I'm sprawled out on top of Asher and his hand is running up and down my back.

"I want another baby," Asher says softly to the top of my head. His hands slowly move up and down.

"Already?" I ask, not that I'm surprised. He loves our daughter and is amazing with her, but she's only two months old and I want to enjoy her for a little while longer.

"I want our kids to be close like me and my brothers. And I also miss you being pregnant."

"You miss me complaining about everything, late night store runs, foot massages and my weight gain?" I ask.

"I never complained, and you already know how I felt about your belly. Something about you waddling around with my baby inside you was fucking sexy."

"You're a strange one, Asher James."

"So, what do you say?"

"Okay."

"Okay," he says, pulling me up his body. "You're going to give me another baby?"

"Yes, I'm going to give you another baby."

"Well, then," he smiles, giving me the dimple, "let's get started," he says against my mouth.

And we did get started. It took a few tries, but two months later, I found out I was pregnant. A few months after that, we found out we were having another girl. Five girls later, Asher gave up on his dream of a boy.

Seventeen years later

"YOU LISTEN TO me, young lady," I hear Asher say. "You are not going on a date. You're only sixteen."

"Daddy," I hear our daughter cry, and I know that she's giving him the puppy-dog eyes. Each of our five girls perfected the puppy-dog eyes by the time they were old enough to talk.

I shove my face into my pillow so they can't hear me laughing through the open door. I keep listening, but all I can hear now is mumbling. This lasts awhile. Then Asher walks into our room, closing the door behind him. His face is blank as he sits down on the bed, takes off his shoes, then stands, and takes his shirt off. After seventeen years, his body is still amazing. He looks at me and I see so much love in his eyes that it's hard for me to breathe. The pillow is still against my face with my eyes peeking out over the top of it.

"So, what did you say?" I ask in a muffled voice.

"She's going on a date on Friday," he grumbles and I fall back in bed, laughing so hard that tears are streaming down my face.

Yes, this is bliss, I think to myself.

Acknowledgements

First I want to thank God. Next, I need to thank my husband for being my biggest fan and supporter. Your love and encouragement means the world to me and without you this book would not have been done. To my cookie for always keeping my head in place, I love you like a sister and I'm thankful every day that God brought you into my life and I'm able to watch you grow into the beautiful woman you are becoming. A special thanks to Hot Tree editing, for taking on the task of the mess I called Until November. You're awesome and I appreciate all your hard work. I need to give a special thanks to all my family—adoptive and real—your support means so much. To my mom, you're the first one who read Until November (even with the sex) and you said I had something, love you. To mommy for telling me that I can do anything that I put my mind to. To every book blog who took a chance on an unknown author you are all amazing. To every reader out there who has been willing to give a new author a chance, thank you so very much from the bottom of my heart. Last but not least, to my Beta Readers Jessica, Carrie, Marta and Laura. Thank you so much for all your involvement in the "Until" Series.

XOXOXOXOXO

About the Author

Aurora Rose Reynolds is a navy brat whose husband served in the United States Navy. She has lived all over the country but now resides in New York City with her husband and pet fish. She's married to an alpha male that loves her as much as the men in her books love their women. He gives her over the top inspiration every day. In her free time, she reads, writes and enjoys going to the movies with her husband and cookie. She also enjoys taking mini weekend vacations to nowhere, or spends time at home with friends and family. Last but not least, she appreciates every day and admires its beauty.

For more information on books that are in the works or just to say hello, follow me on Facebook:
https://www.facebook.com/pages/Aurora-Rose-Reynolds/474845965932269

Or Goodreads
http://www.goodreads.com/author/show/7215619.Aurora_Rose_Reynolds

Or Twitter
@Auroraroser

A Note to my Readers

I hope you enjoyed Until November. Please take a moment to leave a review. The next book in the "Until" series will be Until Trevor. Enjoy the first chapter below.

Bonus Excerpt of *Until November*

YOU HAVE ALL heard from November what it was like from her point of view the night I found out that she was carrying my child and I asked her to marry me. Well, this is my side of the story.

I pulled up to the front of my house. Knowing that it was now a home I shared with November only made coming home that much sweeter. I couldn't believe how much had changed in the short amount of time since I had met her. I'd never known it was possible to have this with a woman. I'd never fully understood exactly what my dad and granddad had been talking about until the day I met November and she changed my life with one look.

The second I shut off my Jeep, Beast was at my door, his tail wagging back and forth with excitement. "What's up boy? You been good?" I rubbed his head, pushing him out of the way so I could close the door. I walked up the front porch and opened the door. November was at her normal spot in the kitchen with her Kindle in front of her. A few weeks ago, I had gotten home to find her in bed reading.

I smiled at the memory. I had walked into the bedroom, seeing November lying on her back on the bed, her face in her Kindle.

"What are you reading?" I had asked, making her jump. She'd looked so beautiful that I'd climbed onto the bed, up her body, crowding her.

"What? Nothing." Her face had turned red, making my eyebrows draw together. Really, what could have embarrassed her so much?

"Let me see." I tried to pull the Kindle out of her hand, but she had it in a death grip. So I started tickling her until she released it. Once I got it away from her, I straddled her waist, pinning her in place. Then she covered her face with her hands, making me laugh. "It can't be that bad, baby." I started reading, my mind trying to decipher what the shit said. "What the hell is a pearl? And a honeypot?" I asked her.

"Asher, get off!" she cried out, not taking her hands away from her face, her body bucking against mine.

I dropped the Kindle to the bed, pulling her hands above her head. "No I'm going to spend some time licking your pearl. Then I'm going to fuck your honeypot," I said with a straight face, watching her eyes widen.

I snapped out the memory when I realized that November hadn't said anything and that I was almost in front of her. "Hey, baby." I kissed her forehead and looked her over, noticing that she looked pale. "What's wrong?" I asked.

She jumped off the barstool and ran to the bathroom.

I looked at where she'd just run to and got worried when I heard her getting sick. I grabbed a washcloth and ran it under the cool water before crouching down next to her, lifting her hair out of her face and off her neck, putting the washcloth there.

"Feel better?" I asked. She nodded but didn't make eye contact with me, making me worry. "Come shower with me." I didn't give her a choice. I picked her up, and she wrapped her arms around my neck as I carried her into the bathroom.

I set her on the vanity and turned on the shower. I was going to get her undressed, but she jumped down and started brushing her teeth, so I proceeded to get undressed. I was down to my boxers when she looked at me in the mirror, her eyes filled with worry. I didn't know what was going on with her, but I sure as fuck didn't like the distance I felt between us all of a sudden.

"I'll be right back," she told me before quickly leaving the room.

I suddenly wanted to punch something. I tried to think of what could have happened between our morning goodbye and now, and nothing came to mind. I was standing in front of the mirror when she came back into the bathroom holding a box wrapped in yellow paper. She handed me the box before getting back up on the counter.

"What is this?" I looked at the box. It wasn't my birthday or any other special occasion.

"Just open it."

I looked at the box for a second before ripping off the paper and opening the lid. When I looked inside the box, I was confused by the contents. A small, pink kid's gun and a box of condoms were inside. My mind worked franticly, trying to understand the hidden meaning. Then I got it.

She was pregnant. Not only that, but she was pregnant with my child. I felt my heart swell with love for her, and my eyes get wet. I lifted my eyes to meet hers and couldn't believe that this beautiful woman was now carrying my child.

"Does this mean what I think it means?" I asked, hoping I was right. She nodded, pulling out a test from her back pocket and handing it to me, letting me read the word 'pregnant' on the screen. "Fuck," I whispered, my heart overflowing with love for her.

A few weeks ago, I had walked into a local jewelry store, I hadn't known what I was doing there until I had looked in the display of engagement rings and saw one that I knew would look perfect on her finger.

I heard her say something, but my mind was too busy to catch it. I dropped the test in the box before picking the box up off the counter. I carried it into the closet, putting it up on the shelf for safekeeping. Once I had it tucked away, I went to my dresser drawer, pulling the small ring out of the box and palming it.

I walked back into the bathroom. My only thought was that I wanted her naked and wearing my ring. I walked in, noticing that she looked upset. I hoped that I would change that quickly. I pulled her shirt off over her head then eased her jeans down her legs, helping her to step out of them.

"We need to talk," she whispered.

I ignore her, pulling her panties and bra off before lifting her onto the vanity. She tried pushing me away from her, but I wasn't letting that happen.

"What the heck are you doing?" she asked, shoving me again. I grabbed her hand, slipping the ring onto her finger. "Seriously, you need to stop. We need to talk about this!" she cried, but all I could do was look at my ring, which was now on her finger. The round diamond surrounded by smaller ones was perfect for her.

"I've wanted to see you wearing nothing but my ring since I bought it for you," I tell her, looking into her beautiful eyes. "Knowing that, like the ring I put on your finger, I'm the only one. The only one who will ever see you in nothing but my ring. The only one who will wake up to your beautiful face every day for the rest of my life. The only one who will make love to you. The only one who will make babies with you." I felt tears in my eyes when I spoke my last words. "I can't tell you how happy I am that you are carrying my child." I got closer to her so that we were breathing the same air. "I know that it's fast, but this is right. We are right. You are the only one for me."

I kissed her hard with everything I had. When I pulled away, I laid my forehead against hers. "Tell me that you'll marry me," I whispered against her lips.

"Yes." She shoved her face into my neck, wrapping herself around me. "Yes, I'll marry you."

I picked her up, taking her into the shower with me, taking my time to wash her body and hair. When I carried her back into the bedroom with a towel wrapped around her, I kneeled in front of where she sat on the bed. I opened her towel, moving my fingers down the sides of her breasts, along her ribs, down to her waist, my thumbs running over her lower stomach. I couldn't believe my child was growing there, that this was mine.

"It's amazing," I whispered, looking into her eyes, "to know that my purpose in life is sitting in front of me." I cupped her face, touching my lips to hers before nipping and kissing down her jaw and neck. I ran my fingers under her breasts before running them down her sides, my lips latching onto her nipple and pulling it between my lips before sucking hard. Her body arched back as she moaned. "Soaked," I told her, my fingers playing between her legs. I loved how responsive she was for me.

"Asher," she whimpered.

I lifted my head from her nipple so I could watch her. I kissed her before pulling her lip into my mouth, scraping my teeth against it. I kissed her nipples then licked down her stomach and around her navel. Before I even got her taste in my mouth, she was opening her legs wider. I smiled as her smell hit me, and I licked her from bottom to top in one long stroke.

"Jesus, is it possible that you taste sweeter?" I asked her, knowing I would never get my fill of her.

I plunged two fingers inside her, pulling her clit into my mouth. Her body started to go wild under me. I brought her down slowly before kissing up her body and dragging her up into bed. Once I had her where I wanted her, I palmed my cock, running the head through her slick heat. Her small, soft hand cupped my jaw as I entered her slowly. I closed my eyes against the sensation. Her hips circled and my eyes opened.

"Don't," I told her firmly, bending forward to kiss her.

I pulled out just an inch before sliding back in. I moved my hands, spreading her legs wide with each thrust. I pulled out until just the tip was inside her and slid home in a hard thrust. Then I slid out and started a slow pace while kissing her. My fingers pinched her nipples then traveled down, pressing against her clit. Her hands were going crazy. Her nails were digging into my skin. I knew she was going to come when she got wetter and hotter, her pussy pulling deeper.

"Please don't stop," she moaned. I couldn't have stopped if I'd wanted to. It was too much.

"Come with me, baby." I fisted her hair with one hand, my other going down her body and pinching her nipples before going farther and circling her clit. I felt her tighten just as I started to come. I caught her whimper with my mouth as I groaned. My hips bucked before my strokes slowed. I wasn't lying—I could have stayed inside her forever. "I get this for a lifetime," I whispered into the skin below her ear.

She tightened her arms and legs around me. "Love you, babe," she whispered against my shoulder.

I rolled to the side, taking her with me. "Love you, baby," I said against her hair. Her body cuddled deeper into me before she relaxed completely. I laughed when November's stomach growled loudly. "Sounds like both my babies are hungry."

"Yeah," she mumbles.

I rolled her to her back and hovered over her, watching my hand travel down her throat and between her breasts before palming one. "I'm excited for these to get bigger." I smiled at her small laugh. Then my hand traveled on its own down her body to rest on her stomach. "I'm going to be a dad." I shook my head in disbelief. I ran my hand over her stomach in amazement. Then I slide down the bed, getting closer to her stomach so I could kiss it.

When our eyes met, I could see everything I felt for her reflected back at me. I started to say some shit that would make me look like a total pussy when her stomach growled again and the moment was broken.

"All right. Daddy's going to feed you," I said to her stomach.

We got out of bed and I pulled on a pair of baggy sweats. Then I turned around and smiled when I saw that November was looking at me like she was hungry for a lot more than food.

"I'm going to waddle and you're going to walk around looking like that?" Her hands did a whole body sweep.

"You're carrying the life we made together inside of you. Your body growing to take care of our child is amazing. I can't wait to see you with a big belly," I told her. I was hard just think about her with a round stomach.

"I love you," She blurted "I mean, you already know that, but I'm glad that you're happy about this."

"Happy is not the word I would use to describe how I feel, baby," I told her softly.

"I know," she whispered. "This is bliss."

"Yeah," I said, cutting the distance between us. "This is bliss." I framed her face, kissing her nose then her lips.

Until November

Girl #4

"THIS BETTER BE a boy," Asher says, pacing back and forth in front of me.

I want to laugh, but after what happened the last time we were here, I know better. I had never seen a grown man go into shock before and never want to see it again.

"Will you please sit down? And don't yell at the doctor when he's checking me this time," I tell him, narrowing my eyes.

"I don't know why he needs to look at you down there," he says, running his hand over his face. "Can't he just tell me what he's looking for and let me look?"

"Oh god, you can't be serious!" I cry, lying down on the table, covering my face. "I'm going to stop telling you about these appointments."

"You wouldn't even have this appointment if it weren't' for me," he says, and I pull my hands away from my face and narrow my eyes at him.

"I would have made an appointment. I have been through this three times already," I remind him. Just as I'm getting ready to find something to throw at his big fat head, the door opens and Dr. Philip comes in.

"November," the doctor smiles before looking at Asher and glaring. "Asher, the nurse didn't say you were in here."

"He promised to be on his best behavior," I tell the doctor with a smile.

"I didn't," Asher mumbles, and I glare at him.

"So today all we're doing is checking to see if we can find out what you're having. Is that right?" Dr. Philip asks, looking at his paperwork.

"That is right." I smile and look at Asher, who has come to stand next to me.

"All right. Well, let's see what we can find out," Dr. Phillip says.

I have been through this so many times that I automatically lie back on the table and lift my shirt up over my small bump. Dr. Philip goes about applying the jelly to my belly and turning on the machine. The sound of a loud heartbeat fills the room, and I look at Asher, who has the look on his face that he always gets when he is with our kids—the look of love. I love that look on him. When I look back at the screen and Dr. Philip, I see that he has gone white and swallows hard.

"What's wrong?" I ask him, getting worried.

"Maybe it's too early to tell," he says, pulling the device off my belly.

"To early to tell what?" I ask.

"What's wrong?" Asher growls this time.

"What?" the doctor asks, taking a step back. "Oh god, it's nothing bad. I just mean maybe it's to early to know for sure what the sex is."

"What did you see?" I grab a towel from next to me and wipe my belly before sitting up.

"Nothing. I saw nothing," he says, looking at Asher again.

"It's a girl." I smile and cover my mouth when a laugh escapes.

"Nothing is certain," Dr. Phillip says.

"Fuck me. Another girl," Asher says, sitting down hard in one of the chairs. "I thought for sure this time we'd made a boy."

"Sorry, honey, but no boys for you." I laugh, jumping off the table. I walk to my man, bend over, and kiss him until were both breathing heavily.

"She's healthy, right?" I ask the doctor, looking over my shoulder.

"Perfectly." He smiles warmly before moving to leave the room.

"Love you, babe," Asher says, rubbing my tummy. "You sure we can't try once more?" he asks, looking at my bump. We agreed that this was going to be our last, but the look on his face makes me want to give him whatever he wants.

"That would be five," I say, scrunching up my nose.

He smiles. "I could handle that."

"All right. One more after this." I smile back.

Bonus Until Trevor...

Trevor

"**Y**OU'RE REALLY FUCKING *tight!*" *I say, sliding through her wetness, feeling her wrap tightly around one finger. "How long has it been?" I ask her while biting down on her earlobe. Damn, I love the sound she makes.*

"Never," she whimpers, raising her hips up to meet my hand.

Jolting awake, I look at the time and see that it's just after two in the morning. "This shit is getting ridiculous," I say, scrubbing my hands down my face. Ever since the night that I had my hand down Liz's pants, this shit has been plaguing me.

The second the word "never" came out of her gorgeous mouth, everything stopped. I couldn't fuck a virgin. Especially one that was as sweet as Liz.

"You're awake?" Anna or Amber, maybe its Angie, says from the other side of the bed.

"Yeah, time for you to go, sugar," I say, sitting up and wondering why the fuck I keep doing this to myself.

Fucking these other women is like walking with a bottle of saltwater through a desert. You know it might look the same but it still won't fulfill the need you have.

"Can't I stay?" she whines, running her fingers down my back.

"Nope," I say standing and pulling up a pair of grey AE sweats.

"So you're just going to kick me out?"

"Nope, I'm telling you it's time for you to go. Kicking you out would be bad manners."

"When can we meet up again?" she asks, putting on her tight blue dress. The way it resists, I'm wondering how the hell she slipped out of it so damn fast last night.

"I'll call you. Just leave your number," I say walking into the bathroom. I know that by the time I get out, she will be nothing but a memory.

"Yo, T!" Cash says, sliding in the booth across from me. I smirk. He uses that word at least a hundred times a day. "What are you doing here?"

I raise an eyebrow and shove another piece of French toast into my mouth, answering without speaking.

"You're going to Mom and Dads' this weekend, right? Asher is finally lifting the ban on access to July so Mom's having a big party," he says, looking excited.

"Does he know that Mom's having a party?" I ask, thinking that if he doesn't know anything about this, he's going to flip the fuck out. Yep, I've only seen my niece twice and only held her once after November forced Asher to give her over.

Cash shrugs, looking over my shoulder. "Yo," he calls, waving his hand. I see Liz standing near the front door, her long, blonde hair is over one shoulder in some kind of messy braid and her strapless summer dress is fitted around her perfect breasts reaching the floor. She waves. Her cheeks turn a pretty pink then I see red when some guy pulls her in for a hug.

"And who the fuck is that?" I growl, knowing that my brothers are used to my Liz issues.

Cash shrugs again. "Don't know," he mumbles, watching them. "Yo, Liz, come here for a second," he calls her over. The guy she's with walks to a different booth and sits facing us.

"Hi, guys," she says, her voice as soft as the curves of her body. Since I know exactly what she feels like and smells like, it fucks with my head.

"You're going to Mom and Dads' for the party this weekend?" Cash asks.

She looks at me, her face closing off before she answers. "I'm umm not sure."

"Who's the guy?" I ask. She looks startled by the question for a second.

"Just a friend," she says, wringing her hands together.

"What's his name?" I ask, looking over at the guy who has his eyes pointed right at her ass. He's younger than me by a few years. His dark blond hair is a mess and he looks like a fucking bank teller in his cheap ass suit.

"Bill," she says, looking at Cash. "I'm going to go now. I might see you guys this weekend I'll, umm, let your mom know." She turns and walks towards cheap ass suit Bill who's watching each step she takes. I have to hold myself back from going over and smashing his face into the top of the wood table.

"When are you going to stop fucking around?" Cash asks.

"She's fucking innocent, man," I mumble, shoving my plate away.

"So what? Because she's not a fucking slut bag like the bitches you normally fuck, you aren't interested?" he asks. Deep down I know he's right. She was mine from the first time I laid eyes on her at my parents' house. She was sitting outside, laughing with my mom. Right then and there, I knew that she was mine. Then we became somewhat friends, one thing led to another the night my niece was born. I finally had her under me and she rocked my world with the news that she was a virgin. Ever since that day, I've tried to avoid her.

"Gotta go," I say, getting up I throw some money on the table. I look at Liz one last time. Great! The guy reaches across to put her hair behind her ear. It makes my blood boil and I know I need to get over it or step up to the plate. Either way, I need to make a move.

The guy looks over in my direction, his chin lifts in warning. "Game on, motherfucker," I say, heading out the door.

Liz

I GET TO the front door of the club and shove it open. My stomach is full of butterflies. In all the time I lived here, I've never been inside this club. I never thought I would even visit, let alone come seeking employment here. The inside was dark with the only light coming from the bar.

"Can I help you?" a very pretty older lady asks. She was standing behind the bar, wiping out a glass.

"I, um, need to see Mike," I say, taking another small step inside.

"Sure, honey, come with me," she says walking me down a long hall where she opens the last door.

"Shannon, give me a minute," Mike says without looking up from his computer. "November added some new program on this damn thing and now I can't find my e-mail," he grumbles and I smile. I walk around the desk, take the mouse from him, and click on the e-mail icon. He chuckles.

"Hey, darlin', how are you?" he asks in the fatherly tone that I've come to love. Mike and my dad were best friends until my dad passed away ten years ago. After his passing, Mike helped my mom out with me and my brother whenever she needed a hand. I used to pray that Mike and my mom would get married but they were never anything more than friends.

"Could be better," I say feeling the tears start to climb up my throat again.

"What's wrong?" Mike asks, standing from the desk and pulling me over to the couch.

"Well, I need a job."

"Okay," he says and I can tell he doesn't know what to think. "What's going on with the store?"

I can no longer control the tears.

"Tim stole all our money and I can't tell my mom," I cry, doing a face plant into his chest. I don't know what happened to the brother that I used to know, the one who would come home at night to check on me after our father passed away. We used to be close but then he moved away to school and everything changed. When I graduated from high school, I worked at a local factory for eight years before it closed down due to the economy.

Every week when I got paid, I would put money away for savings. I have always loved to shop and there were never any stores in town that carried anything I would buy so I made a plan, saved my money, and finally my dreams were realized and "Temptations" was opened.

I sat up and looked over Mike's shoulder. "Three months ago, when Tim came to visit, he asked to help me out in the store. I had been working so many hours and was exhausted so I agreed. I didn't know that the real reason he wanted to help was so that he could rob me blind. Now he's gone and so is all of the store's money and mine. I can't tell my mom what happened, and she's getting married in a few weeks and doesn't need the added stress from this situation.

"I have a private investigator looking into finding Tim and the twenty-three thousand dollars he stole but who knows how long that could take. I've already lost my apartment and had to put everything I own in storage while I stay in the back room of the store. I thought I was doing okay until I got a notice two days ago saying that I was late paying the rent for the store. I can't afford to lose my dream," I whisper, my voice hoarse from crying.

"Shhhhh, darlin', its okay. Everything will be alright. November is not using her apartment anymore so you can stay there, and I can give you the money."

I shake my head back and forth. "I can't take your money. It wouldn't feel right."

"I can't have you work for me, Liz," he says as he places his right hand on my cheek. I feel bad pulling out the big guns but I know I need money and I can't take it without earning it.

"Can you recommend another club?" I ask, pulling out my cell phone and looking like I'm going to take down whatever phone number he gives me.

"You're not going to work at another club," he says, running his hands down his face. "Jesus, I don't know what the fuck I'm thinking doing this shit." When his eyes come back to me, I can tell that he's really torn. "Look, you can serve drinks but you can't work on stage."

"Okay," I agree immediately. I never wanted to work on stage. I would if I had to, but the idea of taking off my clothes and trying to appear sexy just seemed like a lot of work.

"What's Trevor going to say about this?" Mike asks and I turn away. Trevor liked to scare away any man who showed the least bit of interest in me. I was pretty sure that I was halfway in love with him already but I knew for a fact those feelings were not mutual.

For a while, I thought of him as one of my best friends until the day July was born. We ended up at his house, celebrating over a bottle of vodka. Things ended up getting hot and heavy. He had his hand down my pants and I was so caught up in the moment that when he asked me how long it had been, I told him never. I didn't mean that I never had sex. I meant that I had never felt that kind of fire like my whole body was lit from the inside out.

As soon as I said the word 'never,' he stopped immediately. I tried to tell him that I didn't mean it like that but he completely ignored me. He handed me my shirt from the floor, and left the room. He's been avoiding me ever since. That's been a good thing because I've never been more humiliated in my life.

"Trevor has no say in what I do. We don't even talk anymore," I say, hearing the sadness in my own voice.

"Yeah, alright," Mike says, running his hand through his hair. "You can start tomorrow. Just ask Shannon to get you a uniform."

"Thanks a lot," I say quietly, looking at the hands in my lap.

"Don't thank me yet, honey."

"This means a lot to me. I know this isn't easy for you."

"Okay, darlin'." He sighs, pulling me in for another hug. "I'll see you tomorrow. Your shift starts at nine but come around eight. I'll have one of the girls show you where everything is and what you need to do."

He stands, taking a set of keys out of his pocket. "These are for the apartment. You can get in through the basement door that's around the back of the house. Just let yourself in. Tomorrow, I'll help you get your stuff from storage and get you moved in."

I swallowed hard, trying to control the emotions that are running rampant inside me. "Everything is going to be okay, Liz," Mike says again, pulling me in for another hug. "Now go get your uniform and I'll see you tomorrow."

"Okay," I whisper, taking a step away. "Thanks again, Mike. See you tomorrow." I leave the office to find Shannon back behind the bar. She gives me what is supposed to be a uniform but feels like a few pieces of silk and sends me on my way.

"Hey, girl," Beth, better known as Bambi, says, walking into the dressing room. When I first met her, I was a little intimidated. She's about five-nine, all legs, long brown hair and perfect, sun kissed skin with golden eyes. She came to Tennessee from Montana around a year ago and has been working at Teasers ever since.

She taught me to wait tables, push drinks, and smile for a decent tip, if any. I asked her why she didn't work the stage. I mean, I knew for a fact that she would make a lot of money up there. But she said she was way too clumsy and that the name Bambi wasn't given to her when she started working here but when she was little. Her parents said she could never control her legs. It was like they weren't attached to her body so they started calling her Bambi.

"Is it busy out there?" I ask, putting on light pink lip gloss.

"Not really. There's a bachelor party coming in at eleven. They booked the private room. Rex said you could help me with them. The tips should be good," she says, walking to the lockers across the room. I look in the mirror at my refection and forget who I am for a second. My light green eyes look brighter with the smokey shadow I have on. My long blonde hair cascades over my shoulders, down just below my breasts that are straining the top of the black corset that cinches in my waist, causing my hips to flare at the bottom of the fishnet stockings and black silk panties make me look like I should be going to the playboy mansion. It took me a few days of walking around in high heels to get used to them enough to feel like I wasn't going to fall on my face every time I took a step. It's been three weeks since I started working here. The tips are awesome, the hours are okay, and having a bed to sleep in at night rocks. The only down fall is that I have been tired a lot. Working two jobs is not easy, especially when one of the jobs you're working is a secret.

I met with Bill two days ago and he gave me an update on my brother. He found out Tim had been in Alabama but moved on since then. Bill has yet to track him down again. I was starting to feel like I should contact the police but the thought of my brother in jail didn't sit well with me.

"Okay, girl, I'm just going to change my shoes and we can go. Now, keep in mind that bachelor parties do tend to get a little crazy," she says, stepping into a pair of platform stilettos.

"What do you mean crazy?" I ask, feeling nervous. There had been a few times when a guy would get a little handsy but the bouncers always made sure to cut in before it could get out of control.

"Well, they tend to drink a lot more and a lot of times that makes them dumber than normal." I giggled I couldn't help it. Bambi was one hundred percent lesbian and thought all men were stupid. At first, knowing that she was attracted to women made it a little uncomfortable. Then, I realized she had a type and I was not it. She smiled and shook her head. "If you have a problem, just tell me and I'll step in."

"I'm sure they won't be that bad," I say, wondering how many people said that as their final words.

Trevor

"YEAH," I ANSWER the phone, looking at the clock and seeing it was just after twelve.

"Yo, T, you need to come to Teasers," Cash says and I sit up in bed.

"It's after fucking midnight. I'm not getting out of bed to sit with you at a fucking strip club."

"Trust me, T. See you soon," he says, hanging up before I can tell him to fuck off.

"This better be good," I grumble to the wall. Getting up, I pull on a pair of jeans and a tee and head out to my truck. When I pull up to the front of the club, I notice that even for a Wednesday night, the lot is full of cars. I spot Cash standing by the door and talking to one of the bouncers.

"Yo," he greets in his normal tone. He looks around then pulls me to the side of the building.

"What the fuck?" I ask, looking around, wondering if he's in some kind of trouble.

"When you go in, there you need to play it cool, okay?" he says and I notice he looks panicked.

"What's going on?" I ask, becoming concerned.

"When I saw her, I found Mike and asked him what the fuck was going on. He told me that she needed the money, but wouldn't take it from him and threatened to go to a different club if he didn't give her a job."

"At any point are you going to tell me who the fuck you're talking about, bro?" I ask, crossing my arms over my chest and trying not to reach out and shake him.

"Liz," he says throwing up his arms. "What other woman would I be talking about?"

"You're telling me Liz is in there stripping?" I ask through clenched teeth, thinking of her in there, on stage, half naked with men looking at her. Now I'm seeing red.

"This is your fucking fault T," Cash shouts as he pokes me in the chest.

"You tell me how's this my fault."

"When she came to Mike for the job, Mike asked her what you were going to think about this and she said that you don't get a say in what she does."

Well, that shit burned. Technically, she was right—I didn't have a say in what she did but she was mine and I wasn't sharing her with anyone.

"Look, all I'm saying is be cool when you go in there. Ed's on the door tonight and said that Liz has been working a bachelor party."

"Jesus, this shit just keeps getting better and better," I mumble, running my hands over my head.

"Alright, I'm going to talk to Ed. You go in there and pull her aside, but do not cause a scene."

Liz

OH, LORD, I think to myself. No money in the world is worth dealing with men like this. For the last three hours, I've have been blocking hands right and left. No matter how many times I tell the guys at the bachelor party, no touching, they don't get it. I swear, the next time one of them grabs my ass, I'm going to kick them.

"Can I get two more bottles, Rex?" I sigh, looking around the bar. I see Ed, the new bouncer, near the door. I squint my eyes a little trying to see who he's talking to. Damn! It looks like Cash but that would be crazy. Why would he be here? Stupid contacts. I blink a few times and still can't see clearly.

"Cash," I hear whined from behind me and my heart climbs up my throat. I look over my shoulder to see Skittles running in the direction of the door.

"Oh my God!" I whisper while ducking my head. I turn and start walking back towards the private room when my luck crumbles around me. Skittles plows me over, her giant fake boobs in my face.

"Sorry," she says in her fake whiney voice. She's lifted before I can die of suffocation. Once I'm free, I roll to my stomach and start crawling on my hands and knees towards the private room doors, hoping that Cash is not anywhere near me. I make it halfway there when I see a pair of brown work boots in front of me.

"Excuse me," I say without looking up. I start to crawl around the owner of the boots when they block my way again. I blow my hair out of my face, frustrated by the person in front of me. Can't they see I'm trying to get away? The person squats down and I see jean covered knees and then fingers are under my chin, lifting my face.

"Crap," I whisper when I see Trevor's brown eyes looking into mine.

"We need to talk," he says quietly. I can see by the look in his eyes that he's pissed.

"No, we don't need to talk," I say, trying to stand. Who knew that getting up off the ground when you're in high heels was so much work? I fall forward, my hands landing on his chest and his go to my waist to steady me.

"Thanks," I mumble. It was not the first time I wished I knew magic so I could cast a spell to stop whatever power it was that he had over me. I hated that my body craves his touch. I hated even more that I crave it even knowing that he's a big jerk. As I steady myself, I don't look at his face again before I take a step around him.

"We need to talk," he repeats. I pretend I don't hear him and continue walking towards the private room where I know kick ass Bambi the man hater is. "I'm not going to tell you again, baby," he says, coming up behind me and pulling my back to his front.

"Let me go, Trevor," I say quietly, trying not to cause a scene. He doesn't say anything, just wraps his arms around my waist, walking me down the hall towards Mike's office. I start to struggle to get away when I see the door getting closer.

I don't want to talk to him. When I had wanted to talk, he didn't want to listen. I squirm and almost make it free of him when he gets Mike's office door open, shoves me inside, and slams the door behind him. "Great. Just great," I grumble to myself. I put my hands on my hips, ready to give him some major attitude when he takes my breath away.

"Jesus, you look beautiful!" he says, walking towards me with a look of hunger in his eyes. I start walking backwards, caught off guard.

"Um… thanks," I say, looking over my shoulder and noticing that I'm heading towards the couch. I know I don't want to be near any horizontal surfaces and Trevor at the same time so I start making my way towards the desk, hoping that I can put it between us.

"Stop," I say, holding out my hand when I see how close he is to me. He stops and I roll the desk chair between us to block his way. "Okay." I breathe and he raises his eyebrows and crosses his arms over his chest. I wish he wasn't so good looking. His dark brown hair is cut low to his scalp, and his brown eyes are made more beautiful with the long lashes that frame them. His jaw is square, and like always, it looks like he needs to shave and the dark growth around his mouth makes his full lips stand out even more.

He's a lot taller than my five-five and a half. Even in the four inch heels I'm wearing now, he towers over me.

His eyes rake over me and his mouth goes into a flat line. "What are you doing, Liz?"

I look around Mike's office, avoiding his question. I notice that I'm not too far from the door and I might be able to make it there before him if I kick off my shoes.

"Try it and I'll spank you." Okay, really? I'm ignoring that comment as I slide my foot out of one heel but don't put my foot down. I don't want him to notice what I'm doing until the last possible second. "Talk to me." He growls and I glare at him.

"You're working at a fucking strip club for God's sake. What the fuck is going on?" he roars, leaning towards me.

"It's none of your business," I say, crossing my arms over my chest.

"What! None of my business?" he asks.

"Let me clarify that," I say, pausing to put my hands on my hips, trying to balance in my one shoe. "It's none of your damn business."

"I've had my hands down your pants. I know what you sound like when you're going to come."

"Well, Mister, you don't." I look towards the door again.

"Don't what?" he asks, smirking.

"Know what I sound like," I say, getting tired of this game he's playing.

"We can take care of that right now," he says and I look at him like he's crazy and shake my head.

"Um, no thanks," I say, looking toward the door wondering where the hell someone, anyone, is. Don't they realize that I'm missing? Shouldn't they be looking for me?

"Look, I'm sorry, but I just couldn't do it. You're too sweet. That's why you shouldn't be working here."

"Well, too bad. I need this job and I'm keeping it."

"You're innocent, Liz. A fucking virgin and you want to work at a strip club?" he growls.

"First of all, it's none of your business but I'm actually not a virgin. Second of all, there was not one question on my application for this place about my sexual history," I say, pissed off.

"Who the fuck have you been with since we were together?" he asks. I can see his face turning red.

"No one. Geez Louise." I wave my hand in front of me.

"How exactly do you go from you have never, to now?" he asks, looking as confused as his question sounds.

"I never said I was a virgin," I snap. "You chose to hear that, and then you walked away, completely ignoring me when I tried to explain it to you. Which, by the way, was pretty damn embarrassing." I cross my arms over my chest, feeling almost as embarrassed as I did the night we were together.

"Fuck me," he whispers, running his hands down his face.

"Look, I really need to go. I'm sure Bambi is freaking out. I left her with a bachelor party." I look towards the door again ready to run for it.

"We're leaving," he says, taking a step in my direction.

I stop and look at him. "No. I'm working, so *we're* not going anywhere."

"You just resigned. It's time for you to go home."

"Wow, you've got this whole caveman act down pat, don't you?" I say, slipping back into my shoes. There is no way I'm going to let him intimidate me.

"You come with me or I tell your mom what you're doing during your free time," he says and I feel all the color drain out of my face. My mom can be pretty cool, but if he told her I was working here, I would have to explain why I needed a second job. I can't see her being very understanding about that.

"I never thought that I could hate you but you just proved me wrong," I say quietly as tears start to fill my eyes. My shoulders slump and I start walking toward the door.

"Where are you going?" he asks as I open the door. I don't even turn around to answer him.

"Getting my stuff and going home, Trevor. Just like you wanted me to."

I see Bambi in the dressing room when I get there. She's in front of the mirror adding more lip gloss.

"Hey! Ed said you were talking to someone when I went to look for you. Is everything okay?"

"Um, not really. I'm leaving," I say, pulling my pink gym bag out and shoving everything that's mine into it while trying to avoid looking at Bambi.

"You're leaving?" she asks and I can feel her as she comes to stand next to me.

"Something came up and I need to go. I'm sorry for leaving you with those guys. I'll talk to Mike on my way out so he can send someone else to help you," I say, pulling my Vicky's hoodie on over my top and stepping out of my heels and into a pair of black high top Converse.

"I don't care about that. I'm worried about you and why you're leaving," she says, hugging me.

"Ready?" Trevor asks, sticking his head in the room. We both turn our heads in his direction at the sound of his voice.

"What the fuck, dickwad?" Bambi yells. "Get the fuck out of here. Can't you read? This is a women's' only area and unless you want me to give you a vagina, you need to shut the fucking door." She walks over, slamming the door in a stunned Trevor's face. I giggle. No matter how bad this is right now, she made it worth it. "Are you leaving with that douche?" she asks, walking back toward me.

"No. He just came to tell me something," I say, walking toward the door.

"Call me and let me know you're okay," she says and it makes me want to cry. She has made working here fun and has become a pretty good friend.

"I'll call you tomorrow," I say, opening the door and walking right past Trevor, Cash and Mike.

"You okay, darlin'?" Mike asks, putting his arm around my shoulder.

"Yeah. I'm just gonna go home. I'll see you tomorrow for breakfast and thanks for the internship."

"I'll see you then and we can talk," he says quietly, squeezing me to his side.

"Great," I mutter, walking out into the parking lot to my Charger. I open my door and throw my bag across into the passenger seat.

"Hey, we need to talk," Trevor says, turning me around with his hand on my waist.

"No, Trevor, we don't need to talk."

"We're friends, Liz. This isn't you. I just want what's best for you," he says, trying to pull me into him. I take a step back, get in my car, and slam the door, engaging the locks before he can stop me or open it. Turning on the car, I rev the engine then roll down my window an inch.

"Just so you learn a lesson from tonight, I'm going to clue you in, you know, since we're friends and all," I say sarcastically. "First, FRIENDS ask each other about their lives. Second, a FRIEND would wonder what circumstances would cause someone to work somewhere that they never would have before. And last but not fucking least, A FRIEND would never threaten another FRIEND."

With my parting words, I rev my engine and let the gravel fly behind me. My car fishtails right before I get to the stop sign. I turn up Nickelback's "Animals" on my car stereo, stick my hand out my window, and flip Trevor off.

As soon as I roll up my window, tears start sliding down my cheeks from the sadness and anger I'm feeling. I trusted Trevor at one point, and just like my brother, that trust was not earned and now I'm more stuck than I was before. I have to find a way to earn the money to save my business without getting my mom involved or my brother doing time.

Trevor

"WELL, I HAVE to say that went well, don't you think, FRIEND?" Cash asks while patting my chest before he walks off. I'm completely stunned, stuck in place, wondering what the fuck just happened.

"Yo! T, are you coming or what?" Cash shouts from across the parking lot, snapping me out of my stupor. I lean my head back and look up at the night sky. Seeing a shooting star, I make a wish. I close my eyes, let out a breath, and walk to my truck, knowing tomorrow is a different day.

Printed in Great Britain
by Amazon

35997640R00145